AT EASE WITH THE DEAD

Walter Satterthwait is the author of *Miss Lizzie, Wilde West* and *A Flower in the Desert* along with *At Ease with the Dead,* and lives in Santa Fe, New Mexico.

Acclaim for Walter Satterthwait:

WILDE WEST

'This perfect blend of mystery, satire and travelogue'
Publishers Weekly

'Immensely enjoyable and witty romp'
Mike Ripley, Daily Telegraph

A FLOWER IN THE DESERT

'A novel which says as much about America as it does about crime and punishment and which takes Satterthwait instantly and deservedly into the major league' *Literary Review*

MISS LIZZIE

'A literate, witty and utterly beguiling book which is concerned as much with the deeper mysteries of love, sex and death as with the ingenious puzzler at its centre' *Times Literary Supplement*

1

WALTER SATTERTHWAIT

At Ease With the Dead

HarperCollinsPublishers

HarperCollins*Publishers*
77–85 Fulham Palace Road,
Hammersmith, London W6 8JB

This paperback edition 1993
1 3 5 7 9 8 6 4 2

First published in Great Britain by
HarperCollins*Publishers* 1991

ISBN 0 00 647289 3

Set in Linotron Baskerville

Printed in Great Britain by
HarperCollinsManufacturing Glasgow

This book is dedicated to my friend Dick Bellow

ACKNOWLEDGMENTS

Thanks to Richard Brenner, Betsy Byrne of Computer Bazaar, Cathleen Jordan, Tasha Macklin of Murder Unlimited, Priscilla Ridgway of MWA, and Janwillem Van de Wetering. Thanks again to Jeanne W. Satterthwait and Jonathan Richards and Claudia Jessup. Special thanks to B. E. Kitsman, without whose help this would have been nothing.

For the dead
keep the promise
Time made them.
Their silence holds no
bluster, no lust or greed,
and with the dead
I am at ease.

Ragnar Sturlason, c.1250
(Author's translation)

During the storytelling sessions Geronimo would range freely over the events of his life in the characteristic Indian manner. This manner consists of telling *only that which seems to the teller important and telling it in the fashion and the order which seems to him appropriate*. I emphasize this because it is clear that certain rearrangements of the materials would make a more coherent narrative.

S. M. Barrett, editor, *Geronimo, His Own Story*

PROLOGUE

Normally a Santa Fe summer is one of the blessings of the Weather Gods. At seven thousand feet the air is mild and diamond-clear, the cloudless sky is lacquered a deep, preposterous postcard-blue. Oppressive heat isn't a factor in the equation. But that year, during those last two weeks of July, something had gone seriously amiss. The sky was still blue, the air was still clear, but the midday temperature never dipped below ninety-five degrees, and occasionally it topped one hunded.

The locals sipped frosty margaritas in the shaded bars and told themselves, as sweat streamed down their necks, that it was a dry heat, thank God, think of those poor sad bastards down in Houston. The tourists tramped sluggishly across the Plaza, fanning themselves with street maps, tugging at the collars of their Izod shirts, puffing out their cheeks as they blew elaborate sighs of discomfort and disgust.

At Rita's house, perched a thousand feet above the city of the Ski Basin road, the air was a bit cooler, but not much. And the sunlight was just as bright, tumbling down harsh and white, bouncing of the flagstone walkway, glaring off the broad picture widow.

The Greenhouse Effect. Too much carbon dioxide in the atmosphere. Soon the Eskimos would be harvesting orchids, and here in New Mexico we'd be living in tents and looking forward to the Sunday camel races.

Maria, Rita's companion, let me in at the front door and told me that Mrs Mondragon was on the patio. I crossed the living-room and stepped through the open French doors.

As usual when she was out there, Rita had rolled the wheelchair up to the balustrade at the patio's edge. Spread out below her were green piñons and junipers and, beyond them, the sprawl of brown adobe that was Santa Fe.

She looked up from the book she was reading, saw me, and smiled. 'Joshua. Hello. You're early.'

'Not much happening at the office,' I told her, and plopped down in one of the chairs at the round white metal table opposite her. 'All the bad guys are waiting for a break in the weather. What're you reading?'

She held it up to show me the cover. *Advances in Forensic Medicine*.

'Terrific book,' I said. 'I hear Spielberg's trying to nail down the movie rights.'

She smiled again. Her smile, as always, did things to the interior of my chest. 'Is it my imagination,' she said, 'or do you sound just a tad grumpy today?'

'It's not your imagination. I *am* a tad grumpy today. And a tad hot and tired.'

She smiled again, closed the book, and set it on the table. 'Goodness. And all at once, too. Do you think a beer might be a good idea?'

'A beer would be a swell idea. Two beers would be an even better idea. Do you have any of that Pacifico left?'

'I think a bottle or so.'

As she leaned forward to press the button of the intercom on the table, her long black hair swung forward and brushed against her high Indian cheekbones. She was wearing a white peasant blouse that left both shoulders bare; and they were very good shoulders indeed, brown and smooth, the flesh nicely curved over the strong bones. Her skirt was pale-yellow, the colour of jasmine, and it reached to her ankles. Ever since her spine had been smashed by a bullet, all the dresses she wore reached to her ankles.

She asked Maria to bring us two bottles of Pacifico and a pair of cold glasses, then turned to me. 'What did you find out about Mr Murchison?'

I shrugged. 'His wife's right. He's got himself a sweetie. Mrs Murchison brought in the phone bills for the past two months, and there was a lot of action on one particular Albuquerque number. I checked it against Cole's and it belongs to a Beverly James.' Cole's Directory is a kind of reversed phone book. It lists addresses and their occupants by their telephone numbers; you have a number and you look it up, Cole's tells you who owns the phone and where.

Rita nodded. 'Yes?'

'The address is a condo on Eubank. I called Leon, at the credit bureau, and he pulled her report. Twenty-seven years old, a barmaid at the Albuquerque Hilton for the last three years. Up until March all she had was a used Chevy, a rented apartment, and a Dillard's charge card.'

Maria arrived with the beer and we thanked her.

Rita filled her glass, I filled mine. She said, 'What happened in March?'

I sipped the beer. 'In March,' I said, 'Murchison got her a Visa card. With a three-thousand-dollar credit limit.'

She sipped her beer. 'What a nice man.'

'A prince. He also co-signed the note on the condo and came up with a down-payment cheque for five grand. And, presumably, he paid off what she owed on the Chevy because she cleared that out in March, too.'

Rita nodded. 'He didn't do any of this through the Murchisons' joint account?'

'Nope. Both the card and the financing on the condo went through First United. I talked to Aaron, at the bank, and he tracked it down for me. Murchison opened up an account there with a cash deposit of twenty thousand dollars.'

'In March.'

I tasted some more beer. 'Gosh, how'd you know?'

'I wonder where he got the money.'

I shrugged. 'Sold his string collection, maybe.'

She smiled. 'What else do we have on Beverly?'

'Brown hair, brown eyes, five foot eight, a hundred and ten pounds. No eyeglasses.'

'You got that from Motor Vehicles.'

I shook my head. 'It's no fun doing tricks for you, Rita. You know how they all work.'

'You've done a nice job, Joshua.'

'An hour on the telephone. A robot could've done it. If he knew the right people. And had a dirty mind.'

'We've got enough for Mrs Murchison to bring to a lawyer.'

I shook my head. 'From the way I read Mrs Murchison, she wants to keep the kids and she wants to fry up hubby's liver with bacon and onions and make him eat it.'

'She'll want photographs? Tapes?'

'Both, probably.'

'We can put Pedro on it.' Pedro was her cousin and he liked taking dirty pictures. He said it brought out the arist in him. He said this with a snigger. Sometimes it seemed impossible that Rita's and Pedro's genes had ever been swimming around in the same pool.

'Fine.' I took another sip of Pacifico, sat back, and looked away, sighing. Anyone but Rita might have thought it was a sigh of contentment.

She said, 'What's the matter, Joshua?'

I shook my head again. 'Nothing, Rita. Everything's hunky-dory.'

Eyeing me, she sipped at her beer. 'Too much dirty laundry?'

I smiled. 'Yeah, that. And the heat. And I don't know what it is, but the days seem to dag on by, one by one. And then, when I look back, it seems like they've all zoomed away. *Poof.* Faster than a blink. Last time I looked, it was just turning spring. The leaves were just coming out on the trees. Now, *zap,* we're in the middle of summer.'

She nodded sagely. 'Mood swings? Hot flashes?'

'Very droll,' I said. I drank some beer. 'Listen, why don't we get out of Dodge for a while? There's nothing going on right now that Pedro can't handle. We could jump into the Subaru and take off. Bring a tent and some sleeping bags and some fishing gear. Head for one of the lakes in Arizona.'

She smiled. 'Commune with nature?'

'Right. The murmuring pines and the hemlocks. That stuff.'

'I thought your idea of roughing it was a room at the Hilton with a black-and-white television.'

'That was the old me. This is the new me. Spurning the

hustle and bustle. Living close to the earth. Building fires.
Cleaning fish. Wrestling bears.'

'You big galoot.'

'A man's gotta do what a man's gotta do.'

'If you went this weekend, you'd miss the Tina Turner
concert on HBO.'

'I'll set the VCR to tape it.'

She laughed. 'Spoken like a true Mountain Man.'

'Let's do it, Rita.'

Still smiling, she said, 'Joshua, you know I'm not going
to go.'

'Look, Rita, it's no big deal. No one'll even see us leave.'

Her smiled faded. 'That's not the point.'

'Rita—'

Her brow furrowed above the dark brown eyes. 'How
many times have we had this conversation?'

I took a deep breath, exhaled. 'I lost track two years ago.'

She said, 'I'll leave this house when I can walk out of it.'

I nodded. 'It's been three years now.'

'Two years, ten months, and sixteen days.' She smiled
slightly, the corners of her wide mouth tight. 'But who's
counting.'

I set the glass of beer down on the table. 'Why do you
have to be so damned stubborn? Why can't you bend just
a little? I'm not asking you to go dashing through the Plaza
with me. I'm asking you to come along to the mountains.
No one knows us there. No one's even heard of the famous
Rita Mondragon.'

'Joshua, I'm not going.' Flat, unemotional, final.

'Damn it, what're you afraid of? You afraid some little
kid's going to see you and ask his mommy, What's wrong
with the pretty lady's legs? You afraid of the pity? That's
pretty chickenshit, Rita.'

With another faint smile, she said, 'I didn't know you
were licensed to practise psychology.'

'I don't have to be a psychologist to see that you're
copping out.'

'It's not your life, Joshua. It's mine.' Cool and remote,

refusing to allow herself anger, and refusing to engage mine. Whether she intended it to or not, it came off as a kind of emotional jujitsu.

'Fine,' I said, beginning to puff up with bad temper. 'It's your life. Then you live it. Meanwhile, I'm taking off for the mountains.'

She nodded calmly; an infuriating woman. 'I think that's a good idea. You deserve a vacation. And you're right. Pedro can handle anything that comes up.'

'Fine.' I stood up, bloated with ire, functioning totally in asshole mode now. 'Fine. I'll call you on Sunday when I get back.'

'You haven't finished your beer.'

'I don't want it. See you.'

I was halfway across the patio when she called out, 'Wait!'

I turned and saw her sitting there, her hair as black as ravens' wings against the blue of the sky. Smiling, she said, 'Be careful, Matt.'

I stared at her for a moment, and then I sighed. It sounded a bit like air hissing from a punctured tyre. And then, with some reluctance, I grinned. I said, 'Sometimes, Miss Kitty, you're a major pain in the ass.'

Part One

CHAPTER 1

I left the next day, Thursday, at nine in the morning.

There are two ways to reach Lake Asayi on the Navajo Reservation by car from Santa Fe. You can go the fast way, zip down I-25 south-west to Albuquerque, grab I-40 there and scoot west through Grants, then swing north at Gallup and head for Chinle. It's a drive where the scenery, for the most part, encourages coma.

Or you can go the slow way. I slipped 'River Deep, Mountain High' into the tape deck and aimed the Subaru north. Hooked a left at Espanola and cruised along the lazy brown sweep of the Chama River, past orchards and pastures and tiny farmhouses snoozing in the lavender shade beneath the cottonwoods. Glided up through the tawny bluffs at Abiqui, Georgia O'Keeffe country, and into the sun-swept green pines of Carson National Forest. Along the way, Ms Turner asked me if I ever had a puppy that always followed me around, and assured me that she'd be just as faithful as the animal in question. Ah, Tina, would that it were so.

I stopped for lunch at the Jicarilla Inn at Dulce, on the Jicarilla Reservation, which serves what is arguably the best green chili stew in northern New Mexico. My stomach pleasantly swollen, I sailed along west, through Bloomfield and Farmington, and picked up 666 at the town of Shiprock and dropped south. Shiprock itself, the immense stone galleon in the desert that had baffled the conquistadors, rose straight up to my right, towering above the parched brown plains.

Then I was running along the flanks of the Chuska

Mountains, and then I was in them, pine forest on either side of me, silent and still. I stopped at the general store in Crystal and bought some Navajo fry bread and a Navajo fishing licence, good for three days.

When I reached Asayi, at two-thirty that afternoon, I was pleased to see that it was deserted. I parked the Subaru under the ponderosas at a campsite towards the eastern end of the lake, maybe forty feet from the flat blue water. I got out, kicked brown pine needles around until they looked like they'd provide some cushioning, wrestled with shock-corded fibreglass poles until the tent looked fairly habitable, then plopped it down. Dug the fishing rod, tackle box, and insect repellent out of the station wagon, lugged everything down to lakeside, located a tree to serve as a backrest. Slapped repellent all over me, vile-smelling stuff, then popped a couple of salmon eggs onto the fish hook, cast them out there, and sat down and waited for dinner to make its appearance.

Two hours later, I was still waiting. I hadn't gotten even a nibble.

The only dinner had been provided by myself. I was sitting within a dense grey cloud of mosquitoes and kamikaze deerflies, all of whom were searching patiently for a chink in my armour of repellent.

The stuff seemed to have only a limited life span. About half an hour after I splashed it on, it began to wear off. The deerflies, nastier than the mosquitoes, buzzing like miniature chainsaws, would dive closer and closer to exposed flesh. Finally one of them, braver than others, or maybe suffering from a sinus condition, would shoot through the invisible screen and get to me. They didn't just sting, didn't just draw blood; they ripped out chunks of meat, slung them over their shoulders, and carted them home. I was supplying flank steaks to their extended families.

It was four-thirty, and I was beginning to think about quitting for the day, or for the rest of my life, when I saw the old man. He was ambling towards me along the shore to the west, right hand in the pocket of his jeans, left hand using a dark wood cane. He moved slowly, favouring his left leg as though it were wounded or rheumatic. Slender and short, his skin creased and burnt to the colour of terra-cotta, he was in his late fifties or early sixties. His shirt was a red cotton plaid, buttoned to the neck. His steel grey hair, threaded with white, was pulled back over his ears and tied in a traditional bun below the brim of his Navajo hat. A pipe jutted from the corner of his mouth, and pale blue smoke streamed from the bowl, drifted lazily up around the hat, and disappeared against the pale blue sky.

He walked as though he hadn't seen me, which I doubted. Slowly, thoughtfully, he looked this way and that, up into the trees, out across the lake.

My fishing line lay across the path; to pass me, he'd need to step over it or circle around me and my borrowed tree. I reeled in the line and examined the salmon eggs. Like all the others, they hadn't been touched. Disgusted, I tugged them off the hook and tossed them into the water.

The old man stopped about eight feet away, took the pipe from his mouth, rested both hands atop the knob of his cane, and nodded to me. Noncommittal, neither pleased nor disappointed. 'Catch anything?' he asked, without sounding especially interested. His voice was low and raspy. Zorba the Navajo.

'Nothing,' I said.

He looked off to his left and studied the lake for a moment.

A deerfly strafed my neck. I picked up the plastic bottle of goop, squirted some into my palm, slapped it on to my skin.

Still studying the lake, he asked, 'Been here long?'

'Couple hours.'

He nodded again, the same way, then bobbed his head towards the bottle of repellent. 'Bugs don't like that stuff?'

'No. I'm not real fond of it myself.'

He nodded again, put his pipe back in his mouth, his hand back into his pocket, and started walking again along the path, the cane swinging slowly, lightly, before it tapped softly against the packed brown earth. Just as he was about to pass me, he turned. His smile was so faint, a tiny upward movement of the thin lips against the pipe stem, that maybe I imagined it. He said, 'Fish like it, you think?' and then he walked on.

For a few minutes I watched his back grow smaller. Then I clambered back up the slope to the campsite. I burrowed through the gear in the back of the Subaru until I found the water bottle and the soap. I washed my hands like Dr Kildare prepping for a triple bypass, rinsed them, dried them, climbed back down to the fishing rod. Opened the jar of salmon eggs, scooped out two, impaled them on the hook, cast them out into the lake.

Within three minutes I had a strike. I lost the fish, whatever it was, but I baited the line again, and within two minutes I had myself a rainbow. A keeper, about twelve inches long.

A half an hour later, when I had two more, both bigger than the first, I saw the old man again. On the far side of the lake, a hundred and fifty yards away. Walking along, slowly, thoughtfully.

I held up the fish to show him, and maybe he saw it, maybe he didn't. Once again, it could've been my imagination—hard to tell at that distance—but I thought he nodded.

I heard the gunshots at seven o'clock.

I had cleaned and cooked the fish, scarfed them down with the fry bread, washed up everything, and returned to the lakeside to watch the sun set. Now that I wasn't worried about contaminating the bait, I splattered repellent all over me like a sophomore laying on cologne before the prom. The deerflies had retired for the night, but the mosquitoes were ravenous.

The light was fading as it slanted through the pine trees. The lake was as flat as a mirror. Here and there along the surface small clouds of midges whirled and twirled. The swallows came at them from the sky, skimmed along the water, snapped them up, soared away. The occasional trout came at them from the lake, leaping up in a muscular metallic roll, snatching at them, splashing back to leave slow concentric silver ripples. It's not easy, being a midge.

Then I heard the shots. Abrupt and peremptory, from off to my left, beyond the bend on the lake shore. Even before the sound of the blasts began to roll out across the lake, the swallows had vanished: a flutter of wings, a sudden upward swoop, and they were gone.

It might have been only someone plinking at tin cans— although it'd sounded like at least a .38, and that meant fairly expensive plinking.

In any event, it was none of my business.

But the shots had come from the same direction that the old man had gone.

And I was used to sticking my nose into things that were none of my business. That is, after all, exactly what my business is.

My own gun was back in Santa Fe, in a shoebox on the floor of my closet. Which made a frontal approach a fairly dumb idea. I scrambled up the bank into the ponderosas and, keeping low, scooted along between the tree trunks.

About fifty yards in, the trees began to thin and I was peering through the lacing of branches down a gentle slope at a wide grassy knoll by lakeside. To the right, an old pale blue Ford pickup with a battered camper shell was parked a few feet from the water. The old man stood about ten feet away, leaning on his cane, his face impassive. He might have been alone, calmly studying the movement of light and shade.

But he wasn't. To the left, closer to me and just off the dirt road that led to the lake, stood a run-down Winnebago, its white sides grimy with grease and dust. Two men leaned against it. One was short, thin, balding, and wore a white T-shirt above his faded jeans. The other was big, as tall as I was, and thick. He was wearing a cut-off Dallas Cowboys sweatshirt, and his pale meaty arms were folded above a loose roll of belly. Both men held cans of beer and both seemed enormously entertained.

The third man, his back to me, was the one doing the entertaining. He was the one with the gun.

Tall and lanky, his blue denim shirt draped outside his jeans, he laughed once now, a whoop, hard and nasal, as he aimed the pistol at the old man. 'C'mon, Chief. Do us a rain dance.'

There's something about a forest that can bring out the worst in people. Maybe it's the unlimited freedom, the absolute lack of restraints. No litter bags, no stop signs, no cops. Or maybe it's merely the indifference of wild country, its disregard for their puny little lives. They resent it—they feel compelled to mark it with the stamp of their own individual stupidity.

Whatever the reason, people who might seem perfectly respectable, back home in Rockford or Toledo or Scarsdale become slobs and oafs and occasionally worse.

And when you've got two or three morons who've learned their social graces from Johnny Mack Brown movies, idiots who live and often die by some sorry set of cowboy clichés, then the forest can become a truly dangerous place.

The man with the pistol pulled the trigger and the gun boomed. The barrel kicked back and a spout of black dirt shot up a yard to the left of the old man's foot.

The pistol was a revolver, a big one, gun-metal blue. Probably a .357, probably a Ruger. He had fired three shots now. If he were cautious enough to keep an empty chamber beneath the hammer, he had two shots left. If he weren't, he had three shots.

Figure three shots.

I wheeled around to the right and went padding down the slope, keeping the trees between me and them. The ground was soft, blanketed with pine needles, and I was able to move without making too much noise. We mountain men can do that.

At the bottom of the hill, I found what I'd been looking for. A big stick, an old branch, approximately five feet long and a couple of inches thick. The wood seemed solid, neither rotten nor riddled with insects. If I'd had time, I could've shaved it clean and whittled myself a nifty staff, just like Jim Bridger's. I didn't have time.

The closest I could get to the man with the gun, without being seen, was about fifteen feet. Beyond that, I'd be out in the open.

He was still standing there with the pistol aimed at the old man. 'Hey, Chief. You ain't cooperatin' at *all*.'

Fifteen feet. A rush, a swing, smash away the gun, smash away the shooter, get to the gun before the other two bozos got to me.

Piece of cake.

Right.

'C'mon, now,' grinned the man with the gun. 'Just a teensy-weensy dance. You don't really got to make it rain. Jest make it cloud over a little, huh?'

Over by the Winnebago, the big man laughed.

The old man merely stood there, leaning on his cane.

The man with the gun pulled the trigger.

The gun exploded and the old man's body jerked slightly to the right. Expressionless, he looked down at his leg. The slug had ripped a hole in his jeans, just above his knee. He looked up at the shooter and gave him the same small hint of a smile he had given me earlier. 'Great White Hunter,' he said, and shook his head. 'Can't even miss right.'

The other man scowled and raised the gun.

Inhale. Exhale. *Now.*

I went at him with the club raised back over my right shoulder, a roar bellowing up from down deep in my stomach. Make a lot of noise and sometimes you confuse them.

It confused him. He turned to me, his mouth open in a big round O of surprise. For a moment he was too startled to move, and then he was bringing the gun down, the barrel lining up with my chest, but by that time it was too late because I was already swinging. The stick smashed into his wrist and something snapped and it wasn't the wood.

The gun went tumbling off to the left as I followed through on the swing, and then I braced my feet and came back with the club—no time for subtlety—and slammed it into his kidneys. He gasped and started to go down, and I saw that the big man was on his way, slow but determined, like a freight train. I dropped the club and spun to the left and scooped up the gun and came around in a crouch and thumbed back the hammer. I could've slipped a nice neat hyphen between the l's in Dallas. I almost did. I was high on fear and fury.

The big man put on the brakes and stopped a few feet short of his friend, blinking rapidly.

The other man, the short, skinny one, hadn't moved at all. He just stood there by the Winnebago, frowning, puzzled, as though he'd wandered into the wrong movie. Probably he'd need the other two to explain it to him later. Slowly.

'Pick him up,' I told the big man, and jerked the gun barrel towards the man on the ground.

Except for blinking his eyes, the big man did nothing.

I took a step towards him. Through my teeth, just the way Clint does it, I said, 'Pick him up, asshole.' The only way to deal with stalwarts like these is to convince them, from the start, that you're a lot meaner and a whole lot crazier than they are. Just at that moment, I probably was.

He looked away, convinced, and then stepped forward to help his friend up. The other man groaned and clutched at his wrist.

I said, 'Now get the hell out of here. And listen.' With my left hand I reached into my back pocket, slipped out my wallet, and held it out so he could see the badge. Hector Ramirez, a friend in the Santa Fe Police Department, had arranged it for me. It was an honorary Santa Fe County deputy sheriff's badge and it was almost as official as something you fish out of a box of Fruit Loops. But these three dipsticks didn't know that. 'Nothing would make me happier, *nothing*, than blowing your guts all over the grass. You remember that when you start thinking about coming back here.'

The big man put up a hand and said, 'Okay, okay. We're leaving.' Once again, his glance didn't meet mine.

The short, skinny man, still looking puzzled—Golly, is the fun all over?—helped him load his friend into the back of the Winnebago, then got in there himself. The big man, without glancing at me at all, went around the RV, opened the front door, and climbed up, pulling the door shut behind him. The Winnebago's engine turned over, caught. The big boxy vehicle backed away from the dirt road, lurched once, and then moved forward, turning on to the wide rutted path.

As it drove away, I looked down at the gun. It was a Ruger, a .357 Blackhawk. I flipped open the loading gate and spun the cylinder. Two cartridges left. I clicked the cylinder forward until the last empty chamber was aligned with the barrel, snapped the loading gate shut, lowered the hammer.

Now that there was no one around to admire my Dirty Harry impersonation, my hands were beginning to shake.

I took a deep breath, blew it out, and looked at the old man. His head bent forward, he was fingering the hole in his jeans thoughtfully.

'You all right?' I asked him.

He looked up at me and smiled his faint smile. 'Of course,' he said. 'I was okay even before you got here.'

I smiled. 'Yeah?'

'Sure,' he said. 'I had 'em surrounded.'

CHAPTER 2

'You're not really a cop,' the old man said.

'No,' I said. 'Private detective.'

He smiled the faint smile. 'Like Magnum PI.'

'Yeah,' I said. 'Exactly. How'd you know I wasn't a cop?'

We were sitting, the two of us, on a pair of old ragged logs set at right angles along the ground. The sun was gone, the air was grey and cool, growing greyer and cooler as the sky went from violet to black. We had introduced ourselves—he was Daniel Begay, from Gallup. After he'd built a small efficient fire, he'd pulled an old blue enamel coffeepot from inside the camper shell of the pickup. Now we were both drinking coffee out of old blue enamel mugs. It was good coffee.

He shrugged his thin shoulders. 'Cops carry guns. Even when they're off duty.'

True. I wondered if the three bozos in the Winnebago would remember this, and decide they wanted a rematch.

Daniel Begay smiled and took a sip of coffee. As though reading my mind, he said, 'They won't be back. You scared 'em pretty good.'

I nodded. I hoped so.

He sipped some more coffee. 'A private detective spends a lot of time scaring people?'

I smiled. 'Not a lot of time.'

He nodded. 'You do murder cases?'

I shook my head. 'That's police business. Cops don't like it when you stick your nose in.'

He tasted the answer for a moment, then said, 'So what does a private detective do?' He moved his head in a small polite nod. 'If it's okay to ask.'

'Look for missing people. Gather evidence for insurance companies. Or for lawyers. Or for husbands and wives who don't want to be husbands and wives any more.'

He nodded, sipped at his coffee. 'You like your work?'

'Sometimes.'

He smiled again. 'And sometimes you don't.'

I returned the smile. 'And sometimes I don't.' A log shifted in the fire, crackling, and sent a thin streamer of bright orange sparks up to meet the stars. 'Used to be,' I said, 'I liked it all the time. Liked getting to the bottom of things.'

'You don't any more?'

I shrugged. 'Too many things,' I said. 'Too many bottoms.'

'Myself,' said Daniel Begay, his eyes crinkling as he

smiled behind another sip of coffee, 'every now and then I like to see a nice round bottom.'

I grinned. 'How about you? What kind of work do you do?'

He shrugged. Lightly, dismissively. 'Some of this. Some of that. A few sheep. A little land.'

'You like your work?'

He smiled again. 'Sometimes.'

I finished my coffee. 'Are you going to be here in the morning?'

He raised his eyebrows slightly, as though surprised by the question. 'Sure. I came for the fishing.'

I stood up. 'Maybe I'll see you then. Do you have some water? I'll rinse out the cup.'

'No, no,' he said, and waved a hand. 'Don't bother.'

'No bother.'

'Please,' he said, and smiled. 'Leave it.'

I didn't know the proper etiquette here—it was his lake, his forest, his coffee cup—so I only nodded, set the cup down on the log, and told him again that I'd probably see him in the morning.

'What about the gun?' he asked me. He nodded towards the big Ruger lying atop the log I'd been using.

'You keep it,' I told him. 'I'm not hunting any bear this season.'

He thought about it for a moment, then said, 'Got a nephew wants a new pistol.'

'Now he's got one.'

I was up before dawn, and down at the shore just as grey was seeping into the east and colour was returning to the world. Off in the trees, the birds were thrilled by this development.

A stillness lay over everything else. It was one of those brand-new mornings that make you think you're somehow sharing in the creation of the universe. The grass, the earth, the lake, they were all frozen in time, waiting for the ring of the starter bell. The air seemed thicker, denser, and so did the water. It looked so solid that I felt I could walk straight across its flat silver surface.

I decided to use the path instead. Realism, as usual, beating out romance.

When I came to Daniel Begay's campsite, I saw that he was already up, and had been for a while. He had lit another fire and it had burned down to coals. Warming by the side sat a cast-iron pan holding a few biscuits. The old man was sitting on the same log he had occupied last night, the brim of his hat tipped forward as he fiddled with the reel of a fly rod. I didn't know much about fly rods, but I knew that this one was expensive. Eight or nine feet long, made of slender bamboo that had aged to the colour of old ivory, it looked as delicate and as functional as a spider's leg.

He looked up as I approached, and smiled. 'You hungry?'

'Always. But are you sure I'm not imposing?'

'Not if you're hungry.'

'Okay, then. Thanks.'

Nodding, he set aside the rod and rested it carefully against the log. Moving slowly, deliberately, he picked up his cane and walked down to the shore, then bent forward at the waist and used his right hand to grasp a length of rope that led into the water. He stood straight, pulling in the rope. Twitching at the end, the rope hooked through its gill, was a thick rainbow trout, at least two flashing pounds of fish. A bigger trout than I'd ever caught in my life.

'Nice fish,' I told him, feeling a bit like the straight man in a vaudeville act. Custer and the Indian.

He nodded, dropped his cane, and reached his right hand into his pocket, pulled something out. A knife, it looked like.

'You want any help?' I asked him.

He turned to me and smiled. 'Oh, I think I'll be okay.' A knife blade suddenly sprang, *snick*, from the front of his fist. Switchblade. He nodded towards the fire. 'Have a biscuit.'

As he squatted down to clean the fish, I strolled over to the fire. I pried a biscuit from the pan and sat down on the log. Took a bite of biscuit. Crunched at it. Crunched some more. It was a lot like eating fibreboard. But I'd be willing to bet that fibreboard has more subtle nuances of flavour.

I sat there for a while, teeth sawing away at the thing, trying to produce enough saliva to soften it. Finally Daniel Begay limped up from the shore, the fish in his left hand, the knife and the cane in his right. He looked down at me. 'Biscuit okay?'

'Good,' I said around a mouthful of gravel. 'Great.'

He nodded, his face expressionless. 'Biscuits aren't my best thing.'

'It's terrific,' I mumbled. 'You've got to give me the recipe.'

He smiled then. 'Not allowed to. Old family secret.'

I laughed and some biscuit dust shot from my mouth.

In the camper he had everything he needed to fix breakfast: oil, flour, salt and pepper, blue enamel plates. He put the remaining biscuits on a plate, poured oil into the pan, set it on the coals. Before he dredged the fish with flour, he cut off the tail and tossed it into the fire. This could have been a religious observance, or it could have been a convenient way to get rid of a fish tail. After he fried the fish, the two of us ate it, drinking more of his good coffee out of the blue metal cups. The fish, flaky and sweet, was even better than the coffee.

We didn't talk much while we ate. I'm not at my best in the morning—I'm no longer sure when I *am* at my best, or even what my best is, exactly. I suspect that Daniel Begay was quiet because that was simply the sort of man he was. But his silence was as companionable as most conversations.

At one point, I nodded to the fly rod. 'That's a nice piece of equipment. Had it long?'

'Few years. A gift.'

'You've taken good care of it.'

He nodded. 'Gifts should get good care. Like this one.' Smiling, he pointed his fork at the fish on his plate. Then he waved the fork lightly around, taking in the lake, the forest, the far-off mountains. 'And this.'

No argument there, not from me.

He wouldn't let me help him with the dishes. He rinsed them down at the lake, dried them with an old strip of terry-cloth towel, and then packed everything, including the gun and the fly rod, into the camper. Finished, he turned to me and said, 'Well. Got to go now.'

I was surprised—I had thought he'd stay for the day. And I suppose I was disappointed; I'd been enjoying his company. But mountain men don't whimper when they say *ciao*. I nodded and asked him, 'Where're you heading?'

'Tuba City. Got to see some people.'

'Long drive.'

He nodded.

I didn't offer my hand—some Navajos, I knew, aren't comfortable with the tradition—but he offered his, and I took it. 'Drive carefully,' I told him.

He nodded. 'Good fishing,' he told me. He smiled his faint smile. 'You watch out for those bottoms now.'

I smiled. 'I'll do that. You too.'

'I will,' he said, his eyes crinkling. 'I will.'

Two months later, and a week after the first snow up in the Ski Basin, I was sitting with my chair swivelled around so I could stare up at the crisp line of bright white mountain against pale blue sky. A thin banner of creamy cloud was sailing over the ridge. It was as though a big fluffy ball were unravelling behind the mountain, sending out a pale streamer that slowly feathered, dissipated, finally disappeared.

The temperature out there was in the forties. Like a lot of other people in town, I was looking back to the summer's heat wave with a certain fond regard.

Maybe I should take up skiing, I told myself. Go shussing down the slopes in a pair of tights, showing off my teeth and my crotch. Hang around the lodge afterwards, get loaded on hot buttered rum. Chatter about base and powder while I ogled trim butts and jouncing sweaters.

But I'd been raised mostly in New England, and in my

circles snow had been something you shovelled, like manure. Except at a distance, I haven't liked the stuff since.

Still, every year about this time, especially when business is slow, I go through the same interior argument.

And business was slow. Pedro had long since gotten the goods on the unfortunate Mr Murchison. Three runaway kids had been traced, two to LA, one to New York. Once case of insurance fraud had been proven, another was about to be disproven. When that was closed out, the Mondragon Agency would be clientless.

And then someone walked into the office.

For a moment I didn't recognize him. For one thing, it had been a while since Lake Asayi. For another, when I last saw him he'd been wearing jeans, a plaid western shirt, and battered cowboy boots. Now he was wearing a grey wool suit, a white shirt, and a black bolo tie. Boots now, too; but dressy ones, highly polished. With the steel grey hair knotted behind his head, he looked very dapper indeed.

Then I noticed the cane. Suddenly his features became familiar, swimming up into focus on the surface of the stranger's face. 'Daniel,' I said, and stood up and came around the desk. He held out his hand, I shook it. 'Daniel Begay. Good to see you. How goes it?'

'Pretty good,' he said, smiling that faint hint of a smile. 'And you?'

'I'm okay. Have a seat.'

There are two client chairs in the office. I directed him to one and took the other myself. 'What's up?' I asked him.

'Well,' he said, 'I'd like your help.'

I was a bit surprised. He hadn't struck me, back at Asayi, as a man who'd need anybody's help with anything. But sooner or later, I suppose, it's something we all need. 'Sure,' I said. 'If I can.'

He slipped a pipe and a leather tobacco pouch from the right-hand pocket of his suit coat. 'Okay to smoke?'

'Be my guest.'

He opened the pouch, pinched some tobacco, twisted it

into the pipe. 'How much do you charge to find someone?'

'Missing person? Depends. Sometimes all it takes is a couple of phone calls. Who's missing?'

'Relative of a woman I know.' He screwed some more tobacco into the bowl.

'Man or woman?'

'Man.' Tamping tobacco down with his thumb.

'How long's he been missing?'

He put the pipe stem between his teeth. From his left-hand coat pocket he pulled a red Bic lighter. He lighted it, held the flame to the bowl, the flame flared as he puffed. 'Since Nineteen twenty-five,' he said.

I sat back, wondering how to phrase it politely. 'Well, Daniel,' I said. 'That's a long time ago. He could be dead by now.'

The faint smile came again, a fractional movement of the lips against the pipe stem. 'Oh, he is. He was dead then too.'

CHAPTER 3

'Dead,' Rita said.

'Since Eighteen sixty-six,' I told her. 'How's your Navajo history?'

It was evening. I'd closed the office, swam my mile in the municipal pool, hammered down a quick green chili stew at the Plaza Restaurant, and then driven up to Rita's. The two of us were sipping mulled claret on the living-room sofa. The air was cosy with the scents of cinnamon and clove, and a fire snapped and flapped in the big kiva fireplace across the darkened room. Shadows slid along the Persian carpet. Outside, beyond the picture window, a blanket of starlit snow glowed between the trees. Rita was wearing a light blue skirt, a silk blouse the colour of the summertime sky, and a light blue cashmere cardigan. She looked fairly cosy herself.

She smiled and said, 'How was yours, before you talked to Daniel Begay?'

'Terrific,' I lied. 'You remember Kit Carson?'

She sipped at her mug of claret. 'Vividly.'

'Then you remember that in Eighteen sixty-four he rounded up all the Navajos in the Southwest. Most of them were hiding out in Canyon de Chelly—apparently, the Canyon was a kind of focal point for the tribe. Carson had two other guys, Pfeiffer and Carey, go through the place, burning down the hogans and the orchards. Anyway, once he had them all together, maybe six thousand of them, Carson came back to Santa Fe. Carey was put in charge of the operation. He was the one who organized the walk to Fort Sumner.'

Holding the mug in her lap with both hands, she nodded. 'The Long Walk. Three hundred miles. But not all of them made it.'

'No. But the thing is, Carson hadn't really gotten all the Navajos. Some of them managed to slip away, and after Carson left they sneaked back into the Canyon. They stayed there until the others came back in Eighteen sixty-eight.'

'And this man, the one Daniel Begay wants you to find, was one of those.'

'Right. He died in 'sixty-six, and he was buried there in the Canyon.'

'Does he have a name?'

'Ganado.'

She nodded. 'His body reappeared in Nineteen twenty-five?'

I sipped at my wine. 'Yeah. There was a guy digging in the Canyon then, an archaeologist.'

Rita nodded. 'David Bedford.'

I frowned. 'Stop me if you've heard this before, Rita.'

She smiled. 'He was famous, Joshua.' She raised her eyebrows inquisitively and asked, 'Was he the one who found the body?'

I took another sip of wine. 'I'm being mollified, right?'

She laughed. 'Was he?'

I shook my head. 'Guy named Lessing. Dennis Lessing.
A friend of Bedford's. Or a friend, anyway, until they had
their big fight. He wasn't even an archaeologist, Lessing.
Taught oil geology. At the Texas College of Mines and
Metallurgy. Which is part of the Texas university system
now, you'll be happy to know. University of Texas at El
Paso.'

'What was the big fight?'

'Right. That summer, Lessing brought a bunch of his
students to the Navajo Reservation. A field trip, looking for
oil—on-the-job training, evidently. They stayed mostly at
Piñon, to the west of Canyon de Chelly. But before they
went back to El Paso, he took them to the Canyon to meet
Bedford and do a little amateur digging.'

'Why look for oil on the Navajo Reservation?'

'Because it was there, I suppose. Daniel Begay said they'd
found some on an earlier trip.'

'Yes, but the Texas fields were coming in by then, if
memory serves. Why go all the way to Arizona in the first
place?'

'What am I? Mr Wizard?'

She smiled. 'You'll always be Mr Wizard to me, Joshua.'

'Thanks, Rita. Means a lot to me.' I swallowed some
more claret. 'Anyway, Bedford was working with another
archaeologist, guy named Randolph, in the northern branch
of the Canyon. What they call Canyon del Muerte. He was
digging around the White House ruins and he told Lessing
that he and his students could dig a little farther upriver.
And a week later, Lessing found Ganado's grave.'

'And that started the big fight.'

'Yeah. Lessing wanted to take the body back with him to
El Paso. Bedford didn't want him to. Randolph, of course,
sided with Bedford. But Lessing took the body anyway.'

'Why? Why would he want it?'

'I don't know.'

'And what happened to Ganado's body?'

'It disappeared.'

'Disappeared?'

'In September, about a month after Lessing came back from the field trip, he was killed. Murdered in his house one night. And no one's seen Ganado's body since.'

Rita sipped at her wine. 'One question does spring immediately to mind.'

I nodded. 'Where was David Bedford in September.'

'That one, yes.'

'Still in Canyon de Chelly. Plenty of witnesses, according to Daniel Begay.'

'All right. What is it, exactly, that Mr Begay wants us to do?'

'Locate the remains.'

'Why now? Why sixty-five years later?'

'Evidently this Ganado has a descendant. A woman. And lately she's been having dreams.'

Her face expressionless, Rita repeated the word: 'Dreams.'

'About Ganado. Nightmares. They've gotten so bad she can't sleep. And she won't sleep, she thinks, until the remains are located and brought back to the Reservation. She came to Begay and asked him for help. He found out what he could, and now he'd like us to do the rest.'

'Why do I suddenly feel like a character in a Tony Hillerman novel?'

'If there are any records at all, anything about Lessing and the body, they're down in El Paso, at the university.'

'Why doesn't Mr Begay go down there and find them for himself?'

'He feels that this requires the skilled hand of a professional investigator.'

'Meaning you.'

I shrugged. 'He's easily impressed.'

She sipped at her wine, looked at me over the rim of her mug. 'I think it's safe to say that the trail's fairly cold at this point, Joshua.'

'Not for a guy who can sniff out a grizzly at thirty miles.'

Sighing, she put the cup in her lap and lightly shook her head. 'Don't start.'

Grinning, I said, 'I told him that if you agreed, we'd give it a couple of days. I could run down to El Paso, snoop around, see what the possibilities are.'

'The possibilities are minimal.'

'He knows that.'

'And he's still willing to pay?'

'Well,' I said, 'I did give him kind of a deal on the rate.'

'Ah.' Smiling, she nodded. 'The male-bonding discount.'

'Take me three, four hours to drive down there. Two days, probably less, of brilliant sleuthing. Then I scoot back here and give Daniel Begay what I've got. Which is most likely nothing. And then he goes back and tells this woman that he's done everything he can.'

'Why drive down there? Why not take the plane? Never mind. I see. We're keeping expenses down for our faithful Indian companion.'

'Be a nice drive. I've never been to El Paso. And let's face it, we don't have anything else going right now.'

She was looking off, into the fire. 'Who do we know in El Paso?'

'Grober.'

She turned to me, distaste tightening her face. 'I thought he was in Albuquerque.'

'He moved.' I smiled. 'He's not so bad, Rita.'

'He's the most offensive man I've ever met.'

'Well, that gives him a certain distinction, no?'

She finished off the wine, leaned forward, and set the mug on the coffee table. 'You could call Hector Ramirez and see if he knows anyone in the police department down there.'

'I already did,' I told her. 'He gave me a name. A Sergeant Mendez.'

She smiled. 'All right, Joshua. When are you leaving?'

'Tomorrow morning. After I talk to Daniel Begay.'

Another nod. 'Meantime, I'll see if the computer can come up with anything on Lessing. Or Bedford and Randolph.'

It was her new toy, the computer. She had it hooked into one of those databases that know more than God.

'I'll call you tomorrow night,' I told her.

'Do that,' she said.

Cerillos Road is Santa Fe's commercial strip. You can find a street like it, assuming you'd want to, in every fair-sized city in the country. The big boys are all there: K-Mart, Walmart, Walgreen's, Motel 6, McDonald's, Burger King. And closer to town, shouldering each other along the corridor, are the small shadowy shops owned by people named Ray and Jim and Buzz that sell, or try to sell, office siding, fan belts, faucets, used waffle irons, knives, and guns. You might be in Peoria or Duluth except for the occasional gas station built of ersatz adobe. One of these even has a tower and a ladder, so you can zip up there and hide out when the Pueblo Indians revolt again. This tells you that you're in Santa Fe.

The Dunkin' Donuts was on Cerillos, in towards town. I was there at seven o'clock that chilly Wednesday morning. Daniel Begay was late, which provided me plenty of time to savour the coffee, the glazed donuts, and the diesel fumes that seeped around the glass door, donated by the big rigs barrelling down the road outside. Plenty of time, too, to admire the plumes of exhaust from the Ford pickups, the Chevy Blazers, the lowriders, the station wagons, the delivery vans. Everyone hustling and bustling, everyone in an enormous hurry to get somewhere where he could buy something, or sell something, or be something. If that particular universe had been created that particular morning, I wouldn't have wanted to share any of the responsibility.

No hustle and bustle for Daniel Begay. He showed up at twenty minutes after seven, parking his pickup next to my Subaru. His cane swinging down lightly against the asphalt, he approached the building in the same slow thoughtful way he'd circled Lake Asayi. He stood outside the door for a moment, eyeing it as though contemplating its doorness. Finally he pulled it open and stepped in. He looked unhurriedly around the room, found me, moved down the aisle to my booth, and, slowly, thoughtfully, he sat down.

We said hello and I told him I was on my way to El Paso, and gave him Rita's home phone number. He gave me his number in Gallup. I told him, once again, that it was unlikely I'd learn anything.

'Sure,' he said. 'I understand.' He was back in jeans again, and wearing an old coat of grey wool over his plaid wool shirt. Warming his hands against the coffee mug, he said, 'And I thank you for telling the truth. Lot of people would take the money and promise me the sky.'

I shrugged. 'I'm not in the sky business.'

He smiled his faint smile. 'But I hope you find something. I got to help this woman, if I can. She comes from a good family but one with a lot of tragedy. Her grandfather, he was the head of our Tribal Council, years ago. He committed suicide. Her father died in World War Two, at Bataan. Her brother was lost in Vietnam. Missing in action. And now these dreams.' He shook his head solemnly. 'They're bad.'

'Why'd she come to you for help?'

'I know her from when she was a little girl.'

I nodded. 'When did she start having the dreams?'

'About two years ago.'

'Has there been anything in them that might be useful?'

He looked at me, unblinking. 'You believe in dreams?'

'Some kinds.'

Truth was, it'd been Rita's idea to ask the questions. Generally I don't put much stock in dreams. Most of my own, when I can remember them, are pretty prosaic affairs: waterfalls and running faucets when the bladder's full.

Daniel Begay nodded. 'There's a smell in the dreams.'

'A smell.'

'Always, whenever she has the dreams, the same smell. The smell of flowers.'

'Flowers?'

'Yes.'

'Anything else?'

'No.' He shrugged. 'Only that his spirit is tortured, and he wants to come home.'

I nodded. 'All right. I'll do what I can.'

CHAPTER 4

After you live for a while in Santa Fe, most other American cities seem large; maybe too large. El Paso, when I first saw it from I-10 as the road curved around the broad base of a bare brown mountain, seemed huge. It spread out for miles below the haze in a yellowish brown urban sprawl.

The interstate started getting complex just about then, signs sprouting up, entrances and exits shooting off in every direction, overpasses and underpasses arching all around me. When I noticed a sign for UTEP, I slid the Subaru, gratefully, down that chute.

East of the university, I found a motel on Mesa Street. I demonstrated my fiscal responsibility at the office, then drove over to my new home-away-from-home and carted my suitcase inside. The room was the same as a million others across the country: neat and clean and so bland that it slipped from memory the moment you closed your eyes. A paper strip across the toilet seat assured me that the fixture had been sanitized for my protection. The water glasses had been blitzed by the same process.

I called up the police department and after a few minutes reached Sergeant Emiliano Mendez. Hector had spoken to him, clearing the way, and no doubt Mendez was delighted to hear from me, but he managed to contain his exuberance remarkably well. He told me, in grudging monosyllables, that all police records before 1950 had been destroyed in a fire. Learning anything about a homicide committed in 1925 was, therefore, out of the question. He suggested I try the back issues of the local newspaper, available at the public library. I thanked him. He asked me if I was carrying a weapon. I told him only the purity of my heart. 'Yeah,' he grunted. 'Ramirez said you were kind of a wiseass.' And then he hung up.

Only here ten minutes and already I had a fan.

I debated for a moment whether to call Phil Grober. Decided not to. Grober was a good PI, but I had no real need, so far, for the kind of help he could provide. As a person to socialize with, he could be moderately entertaining; but he could also be, as many people had remarked, militantly offensive. He was an acquired taste—'like kerosene,' Rita had once said—and I thought I'd wait for a while before savouring it.

I went through the suitcase and selected what I thought the well-dressed investigator might wear to a Texas university. Ever-reliable blue blazer, dark blue sweater vest, light blue oxford button-down shirt, jeans, Luchese boots.

The temperature was in the sixties and I had the Subaru's windows rolled down as I drove up Mesa. The sky was a paler blue than Santa Fe's, the air denser, heavier. Students were ambling along the sidewalks in couples and clusters, all of them looking better fed and better dessed than I remembered students being, back when I was one myself. Looking younger, too; but that could've been mere jaundice.

I turned left on University Avenue, and then waited in line with the other cars to collect a campus pass at the guard house. This was evidently a system designed to keep out the riffraff. I got in anyway.

The guard told me how to reach the anthropology department, and a few minutes later I was parking before a large rectangular red-brick building that, like all the other buildings on campus, was topped by a curiously sloped, almost Oriental roof. A plaque at the front door explained that the wife of the first president of the school had been enchanted by the Bhutanese temples she'd seen in *National Geographic*. To my eyes, the buildings looked a bit stiff and awkward against the sweep of south-west sky, like Anglican bishops at a rodeo.

But she could've done worse, I suppose. She could've been enchanted by igloos.

Inside, I talked to the secretary. In her forties, with Prince Valiant hair and Clark Kent glasses, she was short and wiry and protective, like a terrier. She told me that the only archaeologist currently in the building was Dr Lowery. I asked if I could speak with Dr Lowery. She asked me what this was about. I gave her the Bureaucrat's Special: told her I was an investigator licensed by the State of New Mexico, and that I was inquiring into a crime committed back in 1925, one that involved a university staff member.

'Dr Lowery wasn't on staff at that time,' she said, and adjusted her glasses with the satisfied air of someone who's achieved a small but important victory.

'I'm sure he wasn't,' I said. 'But I've got to start some-where.' I presented my best puckish smile.

She eyed it, and me, dubiously. But she picked up the phone, stabbed at a button, turned slightly away to speak into the receiver. After a moment she set down the phone and turned back to me, her lips pursed in disap-proval. 'Dr Lowery will see you,' she said. 'Upstairs. Room 205.'

I thanked her, then climbed up the stairs, wandered down the corridor till I found room 205, and knocked at the door.

'Come in,' called a voice from inside.

I opened the door.

It was a small room, shelves everywhere, all crammed with books and bric-à-brac. Behind the grey desk, a person stood atop the office chair with his arms outstretched above him, adjusting a black ceramic bowl on another shelf. At first glance he looked maybe twelve years old. He was about five foot three and his hair was dark black, cut in a Beaver Cleaver bang across his forehead. He wore a UTEP sweat-shirt, sleeves lopped off at the elbows, and a pair of old blue jeans, knees worn down to a band of thin white horizontal threads. 'With you in a sec,' he said, and showed me two rows of bright white amiable teeth.

A moment later, when he had the bowl arranged to his satisfaction, he bounded off the chair, landed lightly on his feet, and came bouncing round the desk. 'A gift,' he grinned, jerking his thumb at the bowl. 'Just got it. Santa Clara bowl. Nice piece.' He held out his hand and I held out mine.

He was one of those men who perceive the handshake as an Olympic event. 'Emmett Lowery,' he said, pumping my arm.

'Joshua Croft.'

He set me free and he grinned some more. 'Barb said something about a crime? Grab a seat and tell me about it.'

Closer up, I could see he was in his forties and fighting it. There was a network of lines at the corners of the bright brown enthusiastic eyes, a thickening of jowl in the square enthusiastic face.

He was fit and certainly he was vibrant. He worked out, he probably ate right, he smiled a lot with those impossibly white teeth. His soul was forever young. But gravity and time were beginning to catch up with the envelope that held it, and this was something, I suspected, that he didn't care to hear. It's something I don't particularly care to hear myself.

I sat down in what I supposed was the student's chair, and I started to tell him why I was there. He leaned back against the desk, head cocked, arms folded, legs crossed, the toe-tip of his right Reebok poised against the floor, balletically.

He didn't interrupt, and he nodded in all the right places, and from time to time he murmured 'Um-hmm' and 'Hmm' and 'Ah' to prove he was actually listening. When I finished, he uncrossed his arms and put his hands palms down on the edge of the desk, on either side of his hips.

'You really think,' he said, eyebrows raised, 'that after all this time you'll be able to learn anything?'

'I don't know. I was hoping you'd be able to answer that for me.'

He smiled, shook his head. 'Doesn't look good, my friend.'

'What can you tell me about Dennis Lessing?'

He shrugged. 'Nothing. My father knew him. Worked with him. But Lessing was way before my time.'

'Your father was a teacher here?'

A nod. 'Oil geology. Same as Lessing.'

'Can you tell me why Lessing would want to bring the remains he found in Canyon de Chelly back here, to El Paso?'

'Haven't got a clue. Maybe he was an amateur archaeologist, like my father.' He grinned. 'That's how I got into the bones business.'

'Your father's deceased?'

He nodded. 'He died in 'fifty-nine.'

'Is there anyone here in town who might have known Lessing?'

Lips puckered thoughtfully, he looked up at the ceiling as though the answer might be written there. He looked back at me. 'His daughter. Alice Wright. But I couldn't guarantee you'd get much out of Alice. A little long in the tooth these days, our Alice is.' He grinned again, perhaps to demonstrate that he didn't suffer from the same affliction himself.

'You know where she lives?'

He shrugged. 'Alumni Office'd know.'

'She was a student here?'

'Student. Professor. Professor Emeritus. One of the legends of the anthropology department.' He grinned again. 'The local Margaret Mead.'

'I'll try to locate her. Any other suggestions?'

He did the ceiling trick again, then said, 'The library? They must have some kind of records over there. Yearbooks, whatever.'

I stood up. 'Well,' I said. 'Thanks for the time and the help.'

'Hey, no sweat. Sounds like a fascinating problem you've got there. Archaeology and detective work, they're a lot alike, don't you think? Digging through the strata. Unearthing the clues, piecing them together.'

'I doubt they'll ever put me on staff here.'

He grinned again. 'Who knows? Strange things can happen in the halls of academe. You take care now.'

Grinning still, he put his hand out. I took it. He mauled my fist again, but this time I gave him a little something in return. In the right circumstance, I can be as dopey as the next guy.

The grin only widened. He released his grip, looked me up and down appreciatively, and said, 'You're in pretty good shape. You work out? Martial arts?'

'A little origami on the weekends.'

He laughed. 'Listen, keep in touch, okay? Maybe I'll think of something. Maybe I can help.'

I nodded. 'Sure,' I said.

I stopped at the Alumni Office in the Administrations Building and picked up Alice Wright's address. The woman at the desk wouldn't give me Wright's home phone number—against regulations—so I had to use shrewd detective work, and the El Paso phone book, to discover it. I dialled it from the pay phone in the foyer.

'Hello?' A woman's voice, just a hint of drawl in it. It sounded too young to be the voice of Lessing's daughter.

'Hello,' I said. 'Is Alice Wright there?'

'She can't come to the phone at the moment. May I ask who's calling?'

She didn't sound like a bureaucrat, and Alice Wright wasn't a skip and she wasn't a suspect in anything that I knew about. 'My name's Croft. I'm a private investigator and I'm trying to learn something about her father, Dennis Lessing.'

'Her father?' Curious, interested. 'Why?'

'It's a fairly long story. Do you know when I can reach her?'

'You could call again around four-thirty.'

I looked at my watch. Two-thirty. 'All right. Thanks.'

'What was the name again?'

'Joshua Croft. I'll call back.'

The library looked, from the outside, exactly like a Bhutanese temple with a lot of windows, one that happened to be half a block long and six storeys tall. Inside, at the information desk, I was told that I could find the yearbooks on the fourth floor. I took the elevator up.

Opposite the elevator doors, behind a glass wall, was a small reading room. Bookshelves, tables and chairs, a young girl in charge behind a metal desk. I told her what I wanted and she disappeared off into the stacks for a few minutes, then came back with two thick hardcover books, the bound yearbooks from 1921 to 1930. The yearbook was called 'The Flow Sheet'. Somewhere there's a guy whose job is to think up clever names for college yearbooks. He may be the same guy who invents the names for hair salons.

I sat down at a table and started leafing through the first of the volumes. The paper was frail and smelled of dust and of time long past.

In 1921, there were only three buildings on the campus of the Texas School of Mines and Metallurgy. A photograph showed them atop the barren unlandscaped rock, Bhutanese temples of learning somehow plunked down in an expanse of rubble.

Among the photographs of the teaching staff, I found one of Dennis Lessing, professor of oil geology. He was an imposing man in his forties with a thick swept-back mane of black hair and an elaborate black handlebar moustache. Dark deep-set eyes, high strong cheekbones, a wide sensual mouth. He wasn't smiling, but then none of the others were either. Maybe 1921 wasn't an amusing year. Or maybe, back then, geniality wasn't a selling point in college professors.

I looked for a photograph of Emmett Lowery's father. Didn't find one.

The 1923 yearbook held a photograph of Lessing and five of his students, just returned from the first of the oil geology field trips, August of '22. They stood in front of a Model T Ford, their bodies stiff and awkward, their smiles strained, as though none of them were really quite comfortable with this photography business. Smiling, eyes narrowed against the sun, Lessing looked less imposing and more handsome than in his formal portrait.

The trip had been to Steamboat Canyon, in Arizona. Steamboat Canyon was on the Navajo Reservation, only twenty miles or so from Piñon, the site of Lessing's final trip. I asked myself the same question I'd asked Daniel Begay, the same question Rita had asked me. Why there? Why not in Texas, where oil fields were already turning up? Arizona was three or four hundred miles away, over roads that couldn't have been very comfortable back then. Did Lessing know something?

Emmett Lowery's father, Jordan, made his first appearance in the 1924 yearbook as an associate professor of oil geology. Clean-shaven, topped with a helmet of dark dashing Byronic curls, his features as striking as the early Barrymore's, he looked young and intense and like he'd be hell on wheels with women. He wasn't smiling; but probably he didn't need to.

Lessing's 1923 field trip had been to Many Farms, less than fifty miles from Piñon. Jordan Lowery, evidently, had not gone along.

The '24 trip was to the area around Fort Defiance, perhaps sixty miles from Piñon. Once again, no Lowery.

The 1926 yearbook was dedicated to the 'Memory of Professor Dennis Lessing, Whose Untimely Death Has Diminished Us All'. The field trip photograph showed Lessing with a new batch of students. The picture had been taken in August of '25, and from Lessing's big satisfied smile it was clear he didn't expect to be dead within a month.

Few of us ever do.

During that same academic year, presumably because of Lessing's death, Jordan Lowery had been promoted from associate to full professor.

Lowery bumps off Lessing so he can take over his job?

Strange things, I've been told, can happen in the halls of academe.

But why steal the remains of a long-dead Navajo Indian?

I checked my watch. Four twenty-five. Time to call Alice Wright.

She was home. Her voice, smoky with age, had a hint of

Texas dawl, similar to the voice I'd heard earlier. She told me to come right over, and then told me which streets to take to do that.

CHAPTER 5

Alice Wright lived off Montana Avenue on a quiet street lined with large single-storey houses built mostly of block or brick, with an occasional pseudo-adobe mini-hacienda thrown in to demonstrate that we were west of the Mississippi. They were the kind of pleasant, comfortable homes you find in upper-middle-class neighbourhoods throughout Albuquerque, Phoenix, Tucson. The lawns here were a bit larger than usual, and maybe a bit greener. Certainly the trees, elms and oaks, were greener than the trees back in Santa Fe, where fall had already come and gone. The trees provided not only shade but a sense of permanence, of stability—people who plant oaks generally plan to be around for a while.

Sometimes, of course, for whatever reason, they don't make it.

More oaks and elms shaded Alice Wright's lawn. I parked the Subaru in the street, walked up the asphalt driveway, up the flagstone walk, up the cement steps, and thumbed the doorbell.

The door was opened by a young woman—mid-twenties, at a guess—wearing designer blue jeans, a pale yellow blouse, and an open black wool vest. She was slender, and in her Frye boots she stood nearly as tall as I did. But even without the height she would've been difficult to ignore.

Some women are pretty, some are attractive; this one was beautiful. Her face was oval, framed by straight black hair that reached down to the soft swell of breast. She had large almond-shaped eyes, cornflower-blue, striking against the backdrop of black hair. A nose just aquiline enough to give it character. Red lips too wide by just enough to make you wonder what they looked like when they smiled. She was the kind of woman who could make you wish you were fifteen years younger, or make you forget you weren't.

She smiled at me, and I wished I were fifteen years younger. 'Mr Croft?'

'Yes.'

'Hi. I'm Lisa Wright. Alice's granddaughter. I talked to you earlier. Come on in.'

She stood aside to let me enter, pushed shut the door, and smiled again. 'This way.'

I followed her, and it took nerves of steel to avoid watching the swing and sway of that taut trim backside. I don't have nerves of steel.

To the left, a wide archway opened on to the living-room—a glimpse of grey carpeting, white walls, tan furniture, a brightly coloured painting over the sofa—but we forged ahead, came to a hallway, and turned right. At the first door on the left, she stopped and turned, smiled once more, and gestured for me to go in. I did. 'Alice,' she said behind me, 'this is Mr Croft.'

Like her granddaughter, Alice Wright would be a difficult woman to ignore.

She sat in a wingback black leather chair in the corner of the room, arms along the arms of the chair, spine as upright as the chair's back, holding herself with the poised languid angularity of an exiled queen. I could see that she was tall, almost as tall as her granddaughter, and that very likely she'd once been as beautiful. Even now, in her seventies, she was a striking woman, proof that large grey eyes and strong cheekbones will see you through the long haul. Her white hair was swirled back and held at the back of her head, Japanese style, with a pair of ivory chopsticks angled in a V. She wore a grey silk pantsuit, a white blouse opened at the collar to show a narrow chain of gold, and a pair of low-heeled grey pumps.

On the shelves around her, standing at attention like courtiers, were her books. Two walls were lined with them, ceiling to floor, perhaps half of them bound in leather and looking older and wiser than I'll ever be. More of them stood on shelves to the left of the door, above a dark roll-top desk.

Another black wingback chair sat opposite hers, and between them a window looked out on to a rock garden, an expanse of patterned sand, small grey boulders rising from its surface like mysterious islands. Below the window stood two round teakwood tables, each holding a framed photograph. On the floor was a faded Persian carpet of rose and black; in the air, a faint fragrance of lavender.

'How do you do, Mr Croft,' said Alice Wright, and held out her hand.

I took her hand. Her grip was as firm as mine.

She nodded, smiling, to the other chair. 'Please, have a seat. Would you like some sherry? It's an Amontillado and quite good, I think. Or perhaps some tea? We've a nice Darjeeling.'

'The tea would be fine,' I said, sitting down.

She turned to her granddaughter. 'Would you mind, Lisa? I'll have the sherry. And bring something for yourself, dear, if you like. Mr Croft and I shall restrict ourselves to pleasantries until you return.' She turned to me. 'You don't mind, do you, Mr Croft, if Lisa joins us?'

I didn't, and said so; but even if I had minded, I didn't see how I could have said anything. I had been, very graciously, boxed in.

As Lisa left, Alice Wright cocked her head and said to me, 'You know, I don't think I've ever met a private detective before.'

I smiled. 'I don't run into too many anthropologists, either.'

'Just as well,' she said, smiling. 'Quite mad, all of them.' She cocked her head slightly. 'But let's cut the crap, shall we?'

Neatly done; my jaw nearly dropped.

She said, 'You're not licensed by the state of Texas. I took the liberty of calling a friend of mine, in law enforcement, and he inquired for me.'

I'd just been put on notice that there could easily be a SWAT team lurking in the garage, bazookas primed and ready.

'It's a New Mexico licence,' I told her. 'It's got a nifty picture of me. Care to see it?'

She smiled again. 'May I?'

I hauled out my wallet, opened it, handed her the ticket. As she examined it, I studied the photograph on the teakwood table. Eight by ten, once black-and-white but yellowed now, it showed a much younger and very beautiful Alice Wright standing before a grey backdrop of jungle. She wore a white flat-brimmed western hat, a khaki blouse, and khaki slacks stuffed into the tops of heavy black boots. On either side of her stood an Indian wearing a kilt-like wrapper that fell from waist to shin. Both men were squat and muscular, both carried long and lethal-looking blowguns, and both looked extremely glum—bored or homicidal or maybe both. Alice Wright was grinning with a good deal more merriment than I would've shown under the circumstances.

She handed back my ID. 'Thank you.' She smiled. 'A helpless old woman can't be too careful.'

Old, maybe; but beneath that easy aristocratic graciousness she was as helpless as a drill sergeant.

I nodded to the photograph. 'South America?'

She nodded. 'Ecuador. The Montaña. I did my fieldwork among the Jivaro.'

The woman would not stop surprising me. 'The Jivaro,' I said. 'They were the headhunters.'

She smiled. 'And still are, I expect, what's left of them.' She crossed her legs in a gesture that was at once feminine and professorial. 'An interesting people. Do you know they were never conquered? Not by the Incas, not by the Spaniards. In Fifteen ninety-nine, there was a Spanish governor nominally in charge of their province. When he demanded a tribute in gold from the Jivaro, they attacked and destroyed his town, killing everyone in it, perhaps fifteen thousand people. And mutilating most of them into the bargain, quite horribly.' She smiled. This was apparently one of the pleasantries she'd mentioned earlier.

'They captured the governor,' she said, 'trussed him up, and then they gave him his gold. They melted it, pried open his mouth, and poured it down his throat.'

I nodded. 'I guess that put kind of a damper on the tribute thing.'

She surprised me once again—startled me—by laughing. A good hearty laugh, up from the stomach, like a stevedore's. 'A damper indeed,' she said, and laughed some more. She cocked her head again. 'But you know, curiously, the Jivaro themselves found the entire incident so insignificant that it never became a part of their folklore. Their stories contain only the vaguest recollection of the conquistadors. I've always rather admired that.'

I nodded. 'And how're they doing these days?'

'Ah,' she said. 'Well. When I was with them, they had perhaps the most sophisticated pharmacopoeia in the Amazon basin. In the world, perhaps. They used literally thousands of medicinal herbs. And hundreds of psychotropic drugs.'

She frowned. 'Not too long ago I read an article written by an ethno-botanist who visited the Jivaro in Nineteen eighty-five looking for native medicines. He found one shaman whose most prized possession was a jar of Vick's VapoRub.' She pursed her lips, shook her head sadly. 'The rain forests all around them are being burned away. The oil companies are drilling nearby. The Jivaro that I knew, their culture, their way of life, they're all gone now. Forever.'

I shrugged. 'Maybe they like Vick's VapoRub.'

Another laugh. 'Oh, I'm sure they do. And I'm sure they'll like television as well. And microwave pizzas. And polyester jumpsuits.' She frowned suddenly, shook her head, and then smiled. 'Do forgive me, Mr Croft. An occupational hazard. Anthropologists tend to become proprietary about the people with whom they've done their work.' She turned towards the door. 'Ah, Lisa. Just in time. I was beginning to get silly.'

'Not you, Granny,' said Lisa Wright. 'Never silly.' She set a silver tray on the roll-top desk and lifted from it a small glass of sherry and a cup and saucer. She handed the glass to her grandmother, the cup and saucer to me. We both thanked her. She returned to the desk, slid out the swivel chair and turned it around, took the other glass of sherry from the tray and then sat down, facing us. With her right forefinger she brushed a strand of hair away from her left eye. She smiled at me. I smiled back. I was beginning to wish I were ten years younger.

Alice Wright, back now in a world of sherry and afternoon tea, said, 'So, Mr Croft. You told Lisa you wanted to learn something about my father. What exactly did you mean?'

Once again I related the story that Daniel Begay had told me. From time to time I sipped at my tea, from time to time the two of them sipped at their sherry.

'These dreams the woman is having,' said Alice Wright when I finished. 'Do they contain any details that might indicate where the remains are located?'

She had asked the question with perfect seriousness. Maybe she'd learned a thing or two from the Jivaro. I told her what Daniel Begay had said about the smell of flowers.

She nodded as though she were filing it mentally away.

I said, 'Do you remember, Dr Wright, your father bringing back the remains?'

'Please,' she said. 'Doctors are people who play with tonsils. My name is Alice. And yes, of course I remember. He brought them back for me. The body of this man— Ganado, you said? It was my birthday present. I had just turned eleven.'

I sipped at my tea. 'I see.' I didn't, of course. The guy couldn't afford a pair of roller skates? A bicycle?

Alice smiled. 'My father was an unusual man, Joshua. Do you mind if I call you Joshua?'

'Please do.'

Another smile. 'An unusual man, as I say. He encouraged me in whatever I did, in whatever I was interested. That summer, before he left for Arizona, I was interested in archaeology.'

I nodded. 'So he brought you back a body.'

She cocked her head, smiling. 'It really was rather a dreadful thing to do, wasn't it? Not from my perspective, not at the time, because naturally I was delighted. Absolutely thrilled. But from the Navajo perspective. In their eyes, of course, what he did was grave robbing.'

She sipped at her sherry. 'You have to understand something, Joshua, by way of explanation. Not excuse, but explanation. Back then, even to most professional archaeologists, the remains they disinterred were simply puzzle pieces, with no more moral or spiritual content than the nuts and bolts of an Erector Set. If you backed one of these chaps into a corner, pointed out that the bones had once been a human being, he'd likely get very huffy and start prattling about Knowledge and The Search for Truth. You can't make an omelette, he might tell you, without breaking eggs. Well, then make something else, you might say, and quite reasonably, too. But the acquisition of knowledge is invariably a destructive process. The question is, finally, what value do we assign to the knowledge acquired, and what value to the thing destroyed?'

She looked at me as though she actually expected me to provide an answer.

'Beats me,' I said.

She laughed again. 'And beats me, too. But the question itself would never have occurred to my father, for all his many merits. To him, it was self-evident that if the remains of this Indian furthered knowledge in general, and his daughter's in particular, then let's by all means cart it off to El Paso.'

She smiled. 'To be fair to the man, he didn't really plan to keep the remains. He wanted me to see them, and to understand how he'd found them. He intended to return them to David Bedford, the man in charge of the dig at Canyon de Chelly.'

'But according to Daniel Begay,' I said, 'Bedford and

your father had an argument about your father taking the remains. Why would that be, if your father planned to bring them back?'

'Well, never having met David Bedford, I wouldn't know for certain. But I suspect there's a very simple explanation. Bedford was an archaeologist, and a good one, I gather. No archaeologist wants to see his puzzle piece get hauled away, off somewhere where he can't keep an eye on it. It might be damaged. Lost. Destroyed.' She sipped at her sherry. 'And in fact the remains were lost.'

'Stolen when your father was killed.'

'Yes.'

'I know it's probably painful,' I said, 'but do you think you can remember anything about his death?'

She shook her head. 'There's no pain. Not now. Not for a long while. There was at the time, yes. It was I who found the body.'

I sipped at my tea. 'Do you remember anything about that day? What the circumstances were?'

'Of course,' she said. 'It was a Saturday morning. September the eighth, Nineteen twenty-five.' She pursed her lips slightly. 'You know, I think I'd enjoy a cigarette. Lisa?'

Lisa frowned. 'The doctor said no.'

'The doctor is forever saying no. He sounds like the virgin in a melodrama. A cigarette, dear.'

Lisa reached into the pocket of her vest, slipped out a packet of Marlboros and a Bic lighter. She crossed the room, handed them to her grandmother, then put her hands, arms akimbo, on her hips. 'You know they're no good for you in the long run.'

Alice said, 'In the long run, as Mr Keynes once pointed out, we're all dead.' She took a cigarette from the pack, put it in her mouth, snapped the lighter aflame, lighted the cigarette. She sucked in the smoke, held it for a moment, blew it slowly out. She smiled up at Lisa, then handed her the pack and the Bic.

'You're an evil old woman,' Lisa said.

'Thank you, dear.' She turned to me. 'September the eighth, Nineteen twenty-five.'

'Right.' I watched Lisa Wright walk back to her chair, and I began to wish that I were five years younger.

'I woke up at seven o'clock,' said Alice. Drily, dispassionately, taking an occasional puff from her Marlboro, she recounted the events of that day.

Coming out into the hallway, she had seen that the door to her mother's room was still closed. The door to her father's room was open—her parents slept separately—and she came downstairs thinking she'd find him at breakfast, in the kitchen.

He wasn't and the house was silent. She wandered back into his study and it was there she found him, sprawled face down across the floor, wearing the clothes he had worn the night before.

'I thought at first he was asleep,' she said, taking a final drag on the cigarette, then carefully stubbing it out in the ashtray on the teakwood table. 'At that age you've heard of death, certainly, but you don't expect actually to meet it. And your own immortality extends itself to everyone close to you. Even when I saw the blood, I didn't know, didn't understand, what it was.'

There had been, she said, quite a lot of blood, black and clotted, along the floor.

She tried to wake up her father, discovered she couldn't, then at last noticed the depression at the back of his skull. She ran upstairs to her mother's room, woke her up. Her mother had come quickly downstairs, examined the body, and telephoned the police. They arrived, a plainclothes detective and three uniformed officers, soon after.

'What did the police decide?' I asked her.

'That my father had walked in on a burglary and that the burglar had killed him.'

I frowned. 'He was still wearing the clothes he'd worn the day before, you said. And he was hit from behind.'

Smiling faintly, she nodded. 'It wasn't a theory into which a great deal of thought had been put. I've always felt that a burglar was most unlikely. But really, you know, the police had nothing else to go on. There'd been a phone call that night, around ten-thirty—both my mother and I had heard the phone ringing. It stopped after two rings, so presumably my father answered it. But whoever made the call never came forward.'

'What was the weapon? What had your father been hit with?'

'The police never determined. A blunt object, they said. Whatever it was, it was never found.'

'Could it have been part of the skeleton?' A macabre thought, but maybe possible.

She thought for a moment, considering this, and then shook her head. 'I shouldn't think so. The bones were all quite fragile.'

So someone had gone there with a weapon, or with something that could be used as one, and taken it away with him. I asked her, 'You didn't hear anything else that night?'

'No. I fell asleep while he was downstairs. And I was a sound sleeper even then.'

'Was anything taken beside the remains?'

'My father's wallet. Some pottery and some jewellery that he'd found buried with the man.'

'Would it've required much strength to carry the remains off?'

'No. I could've done it myself. The skeleton, as I say, was fragile. It didn't weigh much and some of the bones had become disjointed. They were all in a cardboard box perhaps two feet wide by three feet long. Perhaps a foot high.'

'Your father kept the box in his study?'

'Yes.'

'Was anything ever found? The pottery? Your father's wallet?'

'Nothing.'

'The police ever make an arrest?'

'No. So far as I know, the case is still technically open.'

Which, since the records were missing, meant nothing. I

asked, 'Did you ever have any suspicions, yourself, as to who might've been responsible?'

'Not initially,' she said, and sipped at her sherry. 'Later, however, I became quite certain that my mother had killed him.'

CHAPTER 6

I asked her, 'What made you think that?'

'My father was having an affair and my mother found out about it.'

'With whom was he having the affair?'

Alice Wright smiled and asked me, 'Are all private detectives so careful with their pronouns and infinitives?'

'It's part of the code,' I said. 'Like putting notches on our guns.'

She laughed and then she shook her head. 'I never knew her name. But I believe she was an Indian woman. I know that he saw her on the Navajo Reservation, whenever he went on one of the field trips with his geology students.'

If this were true, it would explain what had brought Lessing back, again and again, to the same small area in north-east Arizona. 'How do you know?' I asked her.

'I found a letter she'd written to him. Hidden in one of his books, in the study. This was a year or two after he'd died. The woman who'd written it was very nearly illiterate, but there was no mistaking the sincerity of her feelings. Nor their nature. And from what she said, their relationship had been going on for some time.'

Across the room, Lisa Wright sat impassively. If she was surprised to learn that her great-grandfather was an adulterer, and her great-grandmother a possible murderer, she didn't show it. Maybe she'd already known. Maybe they were separated from her by so much time that they were curios rather than people. Whatever her thoughts were, she kept them buried below the smooth untroubled surface of her beautiful face.

I asked Alice, 'The letter was explicit?'

She smiled. 'For a twelve-year-old girl, it was a revelation.'

'Did it have a return addess?'

'No. But the envelope had been postmarked in Gallup, New Mexico.'

'When?'

'February, Nineteen twenty-five.'

'What happened to the letter?'

'I kept it for years. It was destroyed in the 'forties, in a fire. I was out of the country at the time and didn't find out about it until I returned.'

'And the woman, whoever she was, didn't sign her name?'

'No. She signed it, "Your Heart". She smiled. 'I've always thought that was rather fine. If I'd wanted to, I suppose I could've found out who she was. But it would've seemed like prying, like intruding on something very private and personal.'

'How would you've gone about finding out?'

'My father had a Navajo guide. Raymond Yazzie. He came to El Paso once with his son, Peter, a boy about my age. A very nice boy, very clever. We got along and Peter and I began writing to each other. We corresponded for quite a while, up until the time I graduated from college. If I'd asked him about the woman, I feel sure he would've told me.'

'Would he've known about her?'

'I suspect so. He often went along when his father acted as a guide for mine.'

I nodded. 'You said your mother learned about the affair. Do you know that for a fact?'

'Yes. I heard them fighting about it, downstairs, the day he returned from that last trip. Usually they were careful not to argue in front of me, but presumably this time they thought I was asleep. Or perhaps they were both so angry they really didn't care. My mother was shrieking, howling like a madwoman. I'd never heard her scream like that before. Nor curse like that, either—the phrase "that filthy bitch" came up with a certain frequency. I knew she was talking about a woman, but I had no idea then specifically who she meant. Finally, she threw something at him, a vase or a plate. I heard it shatter. He stormed out the front door and left the house.'

'And then?'

'He came back sometime during the night—he was there at breakfast, when I came downstairs. He was very subdued, very quiet, and he remained that way all week, until just before he died.'

I nodded. 'If you're right, and your mother killed him, why would she wait a week?'

'I think that what happened, probably, was that she believed she'd won. That she'd convinced him not to see this woman again. And then, the night of the seventh, I think he told her he wanted a divorce.'

'Did you hear him say that?'

'Not actually hear him, no. But it makes sense. That day, the seventh, my father suddenly stopped sulking and became his old self again. As though he'd come to an important decision. He and my mother talked for a long time in the study before she came up to bed.'

I said, 'And you really feel your mother was capable of murder?'

She smiled. 'I think that given the proper circumstances, anyone is capable of murder. And my mother was not a terribly pleasant woman, I'm afraid. She was rigid and unyielding and physically withdrawn. The classic Ice Maiden. She hated to be touched, by me or by my father. And sex, good Lord, sex was something that only happened to animals. It was at her insistence that they slept in separate rooms.'

'Which doesn't mean she killed him.'

'No. But she also hated Indians.' She smiled. 'Along with blacks, Jews, Catholics, and Democrats, in approximately that order. I think she must have found it especially galling that my father would leave her for a physical relationship, and with an Indian woman. I think that brittle reserve of hers must've simply shattered.'

I nodded. 'And so during the night, you think, your mother went back downstairs and killed him. And took the stuff from the study to make the death look like a burglary.'

'Yes. She knew how to drive, and in the middle of the night no one would've seen her leave. She could've easily gone down to the river and tossed everything in.'

'But why take a boxful of bones?'

'Perhaps she wasn't thinking clearly. Or perhaps she just wanted to get them out of the house. I know she hated having them around.'

'But with your father dead she could've gotten rid of them any time she wanted.'

She shrugged lightly. 'As I say, perhaps she wasn't thinking clearly.'

'If she killed him, what did she use for a weapon?'

'I don't know. An old candlestick, perhaps. A hammer. The police had only her word for it that nothing of that sort was missing from the house.'

'Did you tell them any of this?'

She shook her head. 'My mother's lawyer kept them pretty much away from me.' She smiled. 'For my own sake, of course.'

'They searched the house?'

'Yes. And the grounds. And so did I. Frequently, over a long period of time. Whenever my mother was out.'

I had a sudden sad vision of a young girl, as the years passed around her, slowly searching through a silent house for bits of pottery, splinters of bone, a dead man's missing wallet: something, anything, that might prove her mother a murderer.

What would she have done had she found it?

Alice Wright misread my reverie, and smiled more softly than she had before. 'You'd rather she wasn't the one responsible, wouldn't you?'

I nodded. 'Yeah.'

'I'm sorry to say so, Joshua, both for your sake and for Mr Begay's, but I think those remains are somewhere at the bottom of the Rio Grande. I don't think you're ever going to find them.'

'Did your mother ever remarry?'

'No.'

'No boyfriends, no male companions?'

'No.' She smiled. 'She was one of those women who come into their own with widowhood.'

'Hi. This is your dreamboat speaking.'

'Wilbur?'

'Rita, Rita, Rita. Here I am, all by myself in an empty motel room, a stranger in a strange land. And all you can do is make jokes and play bumper cars with my heart.'

'Why alone? Why aren't you and Grober out hitting the *boites* of El Paso? I'm sure he knows all the elegant night spots.'

'I haven't talked to Grober yet. But I spent part of this afternoon with Alice Wright. She's Dennis Lessing's daughter.'

'I know. The computer gave me that, off the database. She was an anthropologist. Apparently a very good one. Studied with Ruth Benedict at Columbia.'

'If you've got a computer to give you all this good stuff, what do you need me for?'

'I'm not entirely sure. Banter?'

'What else did the computer have to say?'

'Why don't you tell me what you've got first.'

I told her what I'd learned from Alice Wright about her father and mother.

'She's right, Joshua,' Rita said. 'If her mother did it, you're never going to find the remains.'

'But maybe her mother didn't do it. We're talking about things that were seen through the eyes of an eleven-year-old girl and then filtered through an awful lot of time.'

'She was trained as a professional observer, Joshua.'

'Not when she was a kid.'

'You're going to assume she's wrong then.'

'Wouldn't you?'

A pause. 'For the time being, I suppose. If you assume she's right, there isn't much point in your staying down there.'

'Way I figured it.'

'So what are your plans?'

'I got a couple of names from Alice Wright. First off, there's a guy named Peter Yazzie, a Navajo. The only address she had for him was a trading post on the Reservation, and that was fifty years ago. But maybe we can locate him. I tried calling Daniel Begay, in Gallup, but there was no answer.'

'Give me the number,' she said, 'and I'll see if I can reach him tomorrow.'

I gave it to her.

'And why are we trying to find Peter Yazzie?' she asked me.

'He was the son of Lessing's Navajo guide, and he went along with Lessing and his father on those field trips. If he's still alive, he may know who this woman was, the one Lessing was seeing.'

'You're thinking that jealousy, if it actually were the motive, could work just as well from someone on her end.'

'Did I ever tell you how much I admire clever women, Rita?'

'But this woman's husband, or boyfriend, or whatever, why would he steal the remains?'

'If he was a Navajo,' I said, 'he might've known what they were. Maybe he wanted to bring them back to the Res.'

'Wouldn't someone on the Reservation have known about it if he had?'

'Maybe he didn't tell anybody. Maybe he was afraid he'd get busted for killing Lessing.'

'If the remains have been back there all this time, then that woman's dreams are meaningless.'

'Meaningless dreams happen all the time. You should see mine sometime.'

'I'll pass, thanks.'

'I'll show you mine if you show me yours.'

'You said a couple of names. Who else?'

'A man named Martin Halbert. The head of Halbert Oil. His father was the guy who sponsored Lessing's field trips, and Lessing sent him regular reports. Maybe I can pick up something there. Alice knows him, he used to be one of her students. She called him up and arranged for him to meet me tomorrow morning.' Lisa had left by then, off to some cocktail party.

'Anything else?' Rita asked.

'I'm going over to the university tomorrow to see if I can find addresses for any of Lessing's former students. The ones who went with him on the field trips.'

'Joshua, if any of them are still alive, they'll be in their eighties now.'

'I know.'

Another pause. 'And is that it?'

'Pretty much. I'm having dinner tomorrow with Alice Wright, at her house. Maybe she'll remember something else by then.'

'And maybe you'll remember to ask her a question you seem to've forgotten.'

'Which is?'

'How did her mother learn about her father's adultery?'

'Ah. Right. Good point there, Rita.'

'But none of this sounds terribly promising, does it?'

'Not really, no. I'll probably be heading back to Santa Fe on Friday morning. So, tell me. Did you get anything interesting off the computer?'

'Nothing helpful about Bedford or Randolph. And nothing about Lessing that you don't already know, evidently. But I called up Jack Hogarth at the American School of Research here in town.' The ASR was a kind of heavy-duty anthropology think-tank specializing in Native American cultures.

'Who's Jack Hogarth?'

'An archaeologist. William and I did some work for him once.' William being her late husband.

'And what did old Jack have to say?'

'He told me an interesting story about your friend Alice. Did you know that she lived for a while with the Jivaro Indians in South America?'

'Yeah. The headhunters. Nice fellas, according to her.'

'Yes, well, according to Jack, for years there's been a rumour going around that while she was with them, the family she lived with was attacked by a neighbouring tribe and that one of her friends was killed. A woman.'

'Yeah? And?'

'The story is that, afterwards, she went out with the Jivaro war party on its revenge raid. She found the man who killed her friend and she killed him. And then she took his head.'

'Uh-huh,' I said. 'And does Hogarth believe that?'

'He does, as a matter of fact. He's spoken with another anthropologist, one who did fieldwork with the Jivaro in the 'fifties. A man named Lewison. Lewison told Jack that the Jivaro were still singing songs about the tall white woman who took heads.'

'Well, look, Rita, even if that's all true, it doesn't have anything to do with what happened to her when she was eleven years old.'

'No,' she said. 'But before you have dinner with her tomorrow you might want to ask her what's on the menu.'

The thought of Alice Wright as a headhunter was a fairly diverting one. I lay there for a while, wondering about it.

I wondered, first, if it were true. Under the proper circumstances, she'd said, anyone is capable of murder. Had she been speaking from personal experience? The 'tall white woman' detail in the Jivaro songs seemed persuasive. But then, maybe the Jivaro were a bunch of zanies who thought that slandering anthropologists was a nifty thing to do.

I wondered, if it were true, how she'd felt about taking a life. I wondered if she'd ever told anyone about it.

I wondered what a Jivaro song might sound like. Did it have a good beat? Could you dance to it?

But all this mental activity wasn't enough to stop a sharp splinter of guilt from jabbing occasionally at the back of my soul. I hadn't told Rita that Lisa Wright would be there at dinner tomorrow night. I hadn't told her about Lisa Wright at all.

Later, as I was falling asleep, three different images kept tumbling over each other in my head. The first image was of the young girl prowling round and round the empty house. The second was of the same person, older now, a woman in a khaki skirt and blouse, swinging a big bright machete down through the air to hack a muscular brown neck. The third was of another woman, this one in jeans, smiling as she brushed a strand of black hair away from big bright cornflower-blue eyes.

CHAPTER 7

On Thursday morning, when I went outside to the Subaru, I discovered that all four of its tyres were flat.

Each had been slashed through the sidewall.

I repored this to the overweight woman behind the counter at the front office. She received the news with admirable aplomb: She tapped cigarette ashes into a Cinzano ashtray and told me that these things happened. It was the Mexican kids, the *pachucos*. They go out and they get stoned, sometimes they get nasty. They all carry knives, I was lucky it was only the tyres that got slashed and not my belly. She was sorry, it was a tough break, but didn't I read the sign?

She jerked her thumb over her shoulder: THE MANAGEMENT IS NOT RESPONSIBLE FOR DAMAGE TO ANY GUEST'S VEHICLE.

Yeah, she said, there was a gas station up the street, and a car rental place farther along.

None of the other tyres in the lot had been slashed, but I didn't attach much importance to that. The only people in El Paso who knew where I was staying were Alice and Lisa Wright. I could picture Alice using a machete on a human neck, but not on an automobile tyre. I couldn't picture Lisa using a machete at all. And there was no real reason for them, or for anyone else, to attack me by way of the Subaru.

Probably the woman was right. Probably it'd been done by kids, Hispanic or otherwise. Or by grownup morons. New Mexico and Texas were still bickering over Rio Grande water rights. Maybe the New Mexico tags on the station wagon had gotten someone's dander up.

It was nine o'clock. If I hurried, I could still make my ten o'clock appointment with Martin Halbert.

At the gas station, I put the price of four new tyres on the credit card and paid cash to have someone haul them over to the motel and slap them on the station wagon. At the rental agency, I signed a piece of paper only slightly less imposing than the Magna Carta and took possession of a Chevy Citation with a bad case of emphysema and an interior that smelled of Pine-Sol.

Last night, Alice Wright had told me how to reach Martin Halbert's place. I took Rim Road off Mesa and then climbed up the mountain. Before people started living here, this had been a barren place—no trees, no shrubs, no brush. Now the rocky brown slopes were notched with bright green lawns and terraced gardens. The homes were pretty, beautiful even; but they seemed out of place against the rock, gumdrops on an obelisk.

The road wound and unwound as it rose, the houses getting more and more elaborate, the view getting more and more spectacular. The air was warm and clear, the sky was blue. Below me lay El Paso, a huddle of glittering downtown towers at its centre, and then the long brown curl of river, and then Ciudad Juarez on the Mexican side, stretching out across the flat valley to the distant grey mountains in the west.

Towards the top, I found the private paved road with the small wrought-iron sign that discreetly announced HALBERT. I wheeled the Chevy on to the road, did a bit more climbing, then came around a hairpin turn, and saw the house.

Alice Wright had told me that Halbert owned a larger home in Midland. It must've been a warehouse. This one was huge. Perched above a lake of asphalt, all straight lines and sharp angles, it was a science-fiction wet dream of redwood, glass, and stone, poised to blast off the mountain-side and go soaring across the valley.

I parked the Chevy on the empty asphalt lot, walked past the double doors of a garage built directly into the mountain, then trudged up a steep stairway made of old railway ties. After an hour or two I arrived at the front door. I pressed the button. I heard nothing, but only a moment later the door opened and an Asian man in black slacks and a white houseboy's jacket stood there. Short and slight, his jet-black hair combed straight back from a round forehead, he could've been anywhere from thirty-five to fifty-five years old.

'Yes?' he said.

'Joshua Croft,' I said. 'I'm here to see Mr Halbert.'

'Please come in, Mr Croft.' He spoke without an accent.

We crossed an enormous living-room. White carpeting, massive white leather furniture, a sunken conversation pit encircling a fireplace of stone. Heavy redwood beams and clerestory windows overhead. Then we slipped through an opened pair of French doors and stepped out on to a triangular redwood deck that angled out over the valley like the bow of a ship.

'Mr Croft,' said the Asian, and turned and padded away. Heading off, probably, to finish buffing up the Green Hornet's roadster. Or maybe the Green Hornet himself.

I'm not sure what I expected Martin Halbert to look like. Probably like one of the cartoons who strut through *Dallas*, a beefy good ole boy with a beer-belly swagger. A silk snap-button shirt and a pair of ostrich skin boots. A feathered Stetson he unscrewed only when he lay down, and sometimes not even then.

Halbert looked nothing like this. Maybe fifty years old, he was tall, about my height, and he was slender and very trim. His face was narrow and ascetic, his eyes were blue. His skin was tanned and his hair was short and snowy white, a colour exactly matching the white poplin East Indian shirt and the loose-fitting white cotton pants. On his feet were a pair of white plastic flip-flop sandals. He might've stepped from an ashram in Varansi or off a yacht in Cannes.

When I arrived, he had stood up from a round table at the apex of the deck's triangle. The table was set for two: white damask tablecloth, bone china cups and saucers, sterling silver flatware, a narrow cylindrical crystal vase holding a single red rose.

Now he crossed the deck and shook my hand. He moved with the easy grace of someone who doesn't need to prove much of anything to anybody. Yoga or karate can sometimes give you that. So can money. He grinned, a good grin, one that crinkled up the corners of his eyes and knocked fifteen years off his age. 'Mr Croft. Pleased to meet you. I hope you haven't had breakfast yet, because you're just in time for the food. I was able to con Milton into doing his eggs Benedict.' There was still some Texas in his voice but you had to listen for it.

I told him I hadn't eaten yet, and thanked him, and I nodded to the French doors through which the Asian had disappeared. 'That was Milton?'

He nodded, smiled, and then gestured towards the table. 'Please. Have a seat.'

The two of us sat. He asked me if I wanted coffee or tea and I told him that coffee would be fine. He poured it from a silver pot into my cup. He didn't spill a drop, and I hadn't thought for a moment that he would.

'Now,' he said, putting down the pot, 'first of all, tell me how Alice is doing. I haven't had a chance to visit with her for a long time.'

'Fine,' I said. 'She's an impressive woman.'

'An amazing woman. Really the last of the great ladies.'

Milton came back on to the deck just then, carrying a tray that held two plates of eggs and a crystal decanter of orange juice. He served us without a word and then left again, taking the tray with him.

'Orange juice?' Halbert asked me.

'Please.'

He poured some for me, poured some for himself.

'So,' he said. 'What can I do for you? Alice said you wanted to know something about her father's connection to Halbert Oil.'

For the third or fourth time now, this time adding an edited version of what Alice Wright had told me yesterday, I went through my missing-body story.

Between chapters, I enjoyed the breakfast. Strong coffee, freshly squeezed orange juice, cold and sweet. Crisp English muffins, nicely browned Canadian bacon, perfectly poached eggs beneath a glossy lemon-yellow Hollandaise. It was the kind of meal that ultimately provides work for the surgeons who specialize in liposuction.

'Amazing,' he said when I wrapped it up. 'More coffee?'

'Please.'

He poured each of us a cup. 'An amazing story. And Alice genuinely believes that her mother was responsible for her father's death?'

I nodded.

He shook his head slightly. 'Funny, isn't it, how you think you know someone, and then suddenly you learn something like this.' He frowned thoughtfully. 'Must've been a hell of a burden for her to carry.'

'But maybe she's wrong. It all happened a long time ago.' I took a sip of coffee. 'She said that Lessing sent regular reports to your father. I was wondering if I could take a look at them.'

'Certainly. I've got them here, with the rest of my father's papers.'

'Did you ever read them?'

'A long time ago.' He smiled. 'Not the most thrilling

reading in the world. Synclinal troughs, fossilliferous lime-stones, Permian deposits. The characters are weak, the plot's rather thin.'

I smiled. 'Nothing personal in them, nothing about the woman Lessing was involved with.'

'No. Sorry.'

'Did your father ever get any personal letters from Lessing?'

'Probably, but if he did, he never kept them.'

'Aside from the woman, was there any good reason for Lessing to be looking for oil on the Navajo Reservation?'

He nodded. 'People have known about oil in that area since the late Eighteen hundreds. The first wells were sunk north of the San Juan at Goodrich, just off the Reservation, around Nineteen ten.'

'Why weren't more oil companies out there looking for it?'

'Two reasons. The quality of the Goodrich crude was high, but the quantities were low. There just wasn't enough of the stuff down there to justify additional drilling. And more importantly, the Navajos didn't want to lease out their land. To anyone, for any reason.'

'Then why would your father bankroll Lessing's trips?'

He sipped at his coffee. 'By Nineteen twenty-one, when Lessing came to him with the idea, my father had already done pretty well for himself. He could afford to speculate. How much would it've cost him to outfit the trips? A couple of hundred dollars? A thousand? If Lessing came up empty, then the loss was insignificant. And if Lessing found a promising location, then maybe my father could talk the Navajos into letting him drill.'

'And Lessing found a promising location?'

He nodded. 'A seep. A surface flow.'

'Where?'

'West of Many Farms.'

'Did your father ever get his leases?'

He nodded. 'Finally. It took him two years to convince

the Tribal Council that he wouldn't do any damage to the land.'

He took another sip of coffee and relaxed against his chair, getting comfortable with the story. 'Back then,' he said, 'most of the drilling work was an ecological disaster. Wildcatters would stomp into an area, strip away the ground cover, and drill their holes. They'd toss the mud and debris off to the side, along with their garbage. If the well came in, they'd wait too long to cap the flow, and then they'd pump it out too quickly, beyond its capacity. And if it didn't come in, or when the well dried up, they'd just move on, leaving their mess behind them.

'My father hated that. In his own way, he was probably just as ruthless as the rest of them, but he always had a love for the land. And he always had a high regard for the Navajo and their culture. He probably knew more about them than most anthropologists of the time.'

'How did the well at Many Farms do?'

'Wells. Three of them. They were producers. High quantities of good crude. And because my father did respect the land,' he said, smiling, 'and maybe, too, because he gave the Navajo a larger share of royalties than most wildcatters would've done, they granted additional leases to Halbert Oil. We still do business with them. At the moment we're negotiating some geothermal leases north of Gallup.'

I nodded. 'Getting back to Lessing. Did your father ever say anything to you about his death?'

He shook his head 'No. But remember, Lessing died a long time before I was born.' He shrugged. 'Sorry. I wish I could be more helpful.'

I'd never had the owner of an oil company apologize to me before; I doubted that many of them would do it as amiably as Martin Halbert. 'You've already been helpful,' I told him. 'And I appreciate it. Thanks.'

I had used up all my questions and Halbert had evidently used up all his answers. I looked over the railing, out across the two cities, the two countries, spread beneath us.

'What's your next step?' Halbert asked me.

I shrugged. 'Try to locate some of the students from the field trips. Maybe one of them can tell me something about this woman.'

He nodded again. 'Now there, maybe, I can help. One of our geologists, man named DeFore, Brian DeFore, he was a student of Lessing's. I don't know whether he went on any of the trips, but he might be worth talking to. He's in his eighties, retired now, but I've got his address somewhere. I can dig it up for you, if you'd like.'

'Yeah, I would. Thanks.'

He placed his napkin on the table. 'Let me see if I can find it. And I'll grab those reports for you.'

He was back within ten minutes, carrying an old cardboard file and a slip of paper. Handing both of them over, he told me I was welcome to take the file with me so long as I returned it in good condition. 'The reports don't really have any intrinsic value,' he said, 'but they belonged to my father, and I'd rather that nothing happened to them.'

I said I'd be careful, and that I'd return them tonight or tomorrow morning. Tomorrow, he told me, would be fine.

As he walked me to the front door, I thanked him for breakfast and, once again, for all his help. He said it had been his pleasure. Just as I was about to leave, another question occurred to me.

'After Lessing's death,' I said, 'did your father keep sponsoring field trips for the university?'

He nodded. 'Yes,' he said. 'He did. One of the other geology professors took them over. Jordan Lowery.'

CHAPTER 8

I stopped at the motel to make sure the Subaru was driveable, then turned the Chevy around and dropped it off at the rental place. I walked back to the motel.

In the room I glanced through the cardboard file. The paper sheets were yellow and dry, so fragile I was afraid they might crumble in my hands. Dennis Lessing's hand-writing was tiny but immaculate. I read a sentence or two at random. 'The shales throughout the Chinle formation are arenaceous and calcareous. They have a noticeable argillaceous content only in division C.'

I flipped carefully through the reports. Lessing had neglected to scrawl clues for me in the margins. I decided to put off reading the rest till later. When I could pop some corn, crack open a beer, kick back, and really enjoy that prose.

The address Halbert had given me for Brian DeFore was a retirement home. I found its number in the phone book and dialled it. A woman with a pleasant voice, very Texas, said that I could visit Mr DeFore any time before 'fahve p.m.' I asked how to get there and she told me.

I looked at my watch. Twelve o'clock. If I wanted to close this thing out today, I was going to need some help. I looked in the yellow pages, found Grober's number listed under 'Private Investigators'.

When I dialled it I reached a recording. A woman's voice, sultry and smoky, magnolias and mint juleps: 'This is the Grober Detective Agency. At the sound of the tone, please leave a message. One of our operatives will return your call as soon as possible.'

One of our operatives: a nice touch. Into the phone I said, 'Phil, this is Joshua Croft. I'm here in town for a day or two and I thought—'

A sudden whining noise knifed through the receiver, and then buttons clicked, and then Grober's voice came tumbling over the wire, bluff and hearty. 'Hey, Josh, how you doin'? Where you at?'

I gave him the name of my motel and asked him, 'When did you get the answering machine, Phil?'

'While ago. Great, huh? Hey, listen to this.'

Suddenly I was on hold and a merry Muzak version of 'Dixie', piccolos and violins, was tinkling in my ear.

Grober came back on the line, chuckling. 'Great, huh? Redneck assholes around here, they love that shit.'

'Great,' I said. 'Listen, Phil, you working on anything right now?'

'Uh-uh. Was. Runaway. Fourteen-year-old. Found him too, but when I bring him home, kid's father decides he doesn't want him back.' He chuckled. 'Had to muscle the guy to get the rest of my cash. Whatty ya got?'

'I need some records checked.'

'What records?'

I told him about the UTEP yearbooks, the photographs of the geology field trips.

'Shit,' he said. 'Nineteen twenties? They're all snuffed by now, probably.'

'Maybe,' I said. 'But if they're not, the Alumni Office may have their addresses.'

'That's what you want? The addresses?'

'If you find the addresses, and you've got the time today, you could talk to some of them.'

'What about?'

I told him I was trying to locate the woman with whom Dennis Lessing, the field trip leader, had been having an affair.

'Jesus,' he said. 'Guy gets a hard-on in Nineteen twenty-three, and someone wants to know about it *now*?'

'It's a long story, Phil.'

'I'll bet. 'Kay, anything else you want from these guys? I mean, assuming they can talk.'

'Ask them if they know anything about Lessing's death.'

'When'd he die?'

'Nineteen twenty-five.'

'Jesus. Hold on. I'm writing this all down. 'Kay. That it?'

'Yeah. If the name Brian DeFore comes up, don't worry about it. I'm covering him myself. We can get together later and see what we've got.'

''Kay. What kind of rates we talking here?'

'Phil, you owe me one. As a matter of fact, you owe me a couple.'

'Hey. I know that. I *know* that. Just checking. What time you wanna meet?'

I was due at Alice Wright's at seven. 'Let's say five-thirty. Someplace near the motel.'

'There's a bar up the street.' He gave me the name. 'Catch you then.'

'All right. Phil?'

'Yeah?'

'Who's the woman? The voice on the answering machine?'

'Edie. Cleaning lady here. Great voice, huh? I got guys calling just to get their rocks off. You should see what she looks like. Face like a bucket of worms. But what a voice, huh?'

'A great voice, Phil.'

'Okay. See ya.'

Off to my right, about seventy yards away across the swath of emerald lawn, three men were performing a strange ritual in the shade of a big cottonwood. Two of them stood to the side and watched the third. This one stared ahead at something invisible. And then, smoothly, as though it were a movement in a minuet, he bent forward at the waist, drawing back his right leg and his right arm. He paused for a moment, then brought up his arm in a quick, strong, graceful sweep. He remained frozen, arm poised upright, as a tiny black object sailed from his hand in a long slow arc and swooped to the ground, all in utter silence. He stood straight and bobbed his head as his two friends clapped his back. A moment later I heard the sweet faraway clang of metal and the muffled music of their laughter.

Horseshoes.

There were more men, and women too, out here in the sunshine. Some sat on the wooden benches, swaddled in blankets, throwing bread crumbs to the pigeons – and, in the case of one muttering red-haired woman, at them. Others travelled the cement sidewalks, a few pacing upright, most shuffling along below bent backs on unsteady legs.

All those lives, each a separate universe of experience – wishes, hopes, and dreams; foods tasted, flowers scented, lovers kissed, friends embraced, children raised, battles won and lost, jobs left done and undone. All of them moving now with a wound-down slowness while they waited to slip, gentle or not, into that good night.

I started wondering – as I had before, more than once – which would be the better way to go. Hard and fast – an automobile, a bullet, a burst vessel at the back of the brain. Or long and slow – watching the skin turn to parchment, feeling the strength ebb from the fingers; becoming dull, slow, worn; fading, fading, till the flame flickered finally out.

Getting morbid. I was spending too much time lately in the Dead Letter Office of the past. Too much time rooting through the brittle brown memorabilia of other people's cluttered lives. Too much time listening to stories of the dead.

I found Brian DeFore where the nurse had told me I would. Under another cottonwood, sitting in a wheelchair on a rise of ground at the end of the cement walkway. From here he could see over the white picket fence, twenty yards away, that marked the boundary of the property. Beyond was a suburban neighbourhood much like Alice Wright's— single-storey homes, paved streets, clipped square hedges, tidy lawns.

Facing his wheelchair was an empty wooden bench. I sat down on it and said, 'Mr DeFore?'

He wheeled the chair around to look at me. A plaid blanket circling thin shoulders. Sunken cheeks, a toothless mouth, sallow papery skin. Permanent bruises beneath the cloudy brown eyes, wattles beneath the narrow jaw. Just a few wisps of yellowish white hair, swaying slightly in the breeze atop the freckled pink scalp.

He buried his hands back in the blanket and peered at me, screwing up his face. 'I know you?' A heavy Texas accent. *Ah know yew?*

'No,' I said. 'My name is Joshua Croft. I'm a private detective.'

He sucked his gums. 'I got that memory thing. What you call it?'

'Alzheimer's?' I said.

'Uh-huh,' he said. 'Memory's all fucked up.' He screwed up his face again. 'Private detective?'

'Yeah. I wanted to ask you some questions about Professor Dennis Lessing.'

He frowned. 'I watch that show with the two brothers. Rick and A.J. In San Diego. I been to San Diego.' He grinned at me suddenly, showing pale pink gums, a grey tongue. 'You get as much pussy as Rick and A.J., son?'

'I doubt it. Do you remember Dennis Lessing? He taught oil geology at the School of Mines.'

'I did,' he said, and cackled. 'More, probably. Women ever'where, son. El Paso. Dallas. Houston. Used to be, I was hip deep in pussy.' He closed his eyes, savouring the image.

'Mr DeFore?'

His eyes snapped open. 'Not one of them worth a damn. Bitches, ever' one. They want your money or they want your balls. Stick with the ones want your money. Safer. My Daddy used to say, you want you some talk, get a bartender. You want you some company, get a dog. You want you some cooze, get a hoor.' He nodded firmly, having made his point, then sucked again at his gums.

'Mr DeFore, do you remember Dennis Lessing at the School of Mines?'

He frowned. 'Course I do. Good man. Knew his geology.'

'He used to make field trips to the Navajo Reservation.'

'He surely did. Didn't I go on two of 'em myself? 'Twenty-two and 'twenty-three. I was there when he found a seep for ole man Halbert. 'Twenty-three that was. I mean, shit, there we were, out in the middle of the fuckin' desert. Hotter'n shit, son. And dryer'n a nun's twat. S'posed to be looking for awl, right? We got no magnetometer, we got no torsion balance, but goddammit, we're lookin' for *awl*. And goddammit, we *find* it.' He cackled, shook his head. 'Didn't we though.'

'You know anything about a woman Lessing was seeing at the time?'

'Sweet stuff,' he said. 'Paraffin base. Comin' out so high in gas hydocarbons—your pentane, your hexane, your octane—you coulda pumped it straight into your car. Fucker woulda run.'

'Lessing,' I said, 'was seeing some woman on the Reservation.'

'Elaine,' he said. He shook his head, looked off. 'No. Spic name. Elena?' He nodded. '*Elena*. Wasn't a spic, though. White woman.'

'Not an Indian woman?'

'Shit, what'd he want with a fuckin' Indian? Little blonde quim she was. Blue eyes. Cute as a bug. Cute ones, son, they're the ones fuck you over worst.'

'You saw her?'

'Came by in a Ford one day. This was at Many Farms. Cute as a bug. Nice pair of bouncers.'

'Do you know where she lived?'

'S'pose to be a big ole secret, Doc Lessing's got himself some strange.' He cackled. 'Shit. Ever'body knew 'bout it. Didn't he sneak out most ever' night and go drill himself some of that sweet blonde pussy?'

'Do you know where she lived, Mr DeFore?'

'Piñon. Round Piñon. What ever'one said.'

'Why would an Anglo woman be living on the Reservation?'

His eyes narrowed suddenly and he said, 'How come you're askin' all these questions?'

'I'm trying to find out what happened to Dennis Lessing.'

'He died, is what happened. Someone bashed his brains in.'

'The question is who.'

'You payin' me for this? Cash money?'

'Maybe.'

'Rick and A.J., sometimes they pay twenny dollars.'

'Rick and A.J. don't have my overhead.'

'Gimme ten then.'

I took out my wallet, slipped a ten from it, put back the wallet. Held the ten.

DeFore eyed it.

'Why would an Anglo woman be living on the Reservation?' I asked him.

He looked up at me and scowled. 'How the fuck I know? Had some buck for a husband, I reckon.'

'Did you know Jordan Lowery?'

He blinked, confused. 'Who?'

'Taught oil geology at the school. Took over Lessing's job.'

He grinned, nodded. 'The pussy hound. Met him, is all. Never knew him.'

'How'd he get along with Lessing?'

'Fine, far as I know.' He cackled. 'Expect he wanted to jump Lessing's wife.'

'He ever get past wanting?' It seemed unlikely after what Alice Wright had told me about her mother.

He shrugged. 'Who knows?'

'Were you in El Paso when Lessing was killed?'

He shook his head. 'Pennsylvania.'

'But you heard about it?'

He looked down at the ten, looked back up at me, narrowed his eyes and smiled. 'Maybe I did, maybe I didn't.'

I took out my wallet, started to slide the ten back inside.

'I heard,' he said, 'I heard.'

'You have any idea who might've killed him?'

'Gimme the ten first.'

I held out the ten. A yellow claw reached out from beneath the blanket, snatched away the bill, disappeared.

'Figured it was the buck,' he said.

'The woman's husband?'

'Who else?'

'Someone suggested recently that it might've been Lessing's wife.'

He cackled. 'Fuckin' crazy.'

'Did you know Mrs Lessing?'

Another cackle. 'Drilled her, didn't I?'

CHAPTER 9

Surprise, or disbelief, must've shown on my face, because DeFore said, 'You think it's bullshit? I'm here to tell you, son, I drilled that bitch. Drilled her good. And I wasn't the only one, either, not by a long shot.'

'When was this?' I asked him.

'Bertie Prentice, he had her too. And Bobby Dekker, he's the one tole me about it.'

'When was this, Mr DeFore?'

He sucked at his gums. 'You look at her, you think butter wouldn't melt between those legs. Came from back east. Massachusetts, Connecticut. Looked down her nose at ever 'body out here. But when Doc Lessing was outta town for the summer, she used to take ole Bobby Dekker up to her room and let 'im put it to her. She liked her fuckin', son. Liked it down and dirty.'

'And you say you slept with her too?'

He snorted. 'Slept with her, shit. Drilled her. Bobby tole me how she was. So I figured I'd get me some too. Why not? Good-lookin' quim she was, nice big bouncers, I figured why should Bobby be the only one? So I go over there one afternoon and I tell her Bobby couldn't come, he sent me instead.' He cackled. 'You get it? Couldn't *come?*'

'Bobby was one of Lessing's students?'

He nodded. 'Bertie, too.'

For the first time in years, I wished that I still smoked cigarettes. 'And when was this?' I asked him again.

This time he answered. 'Summer before I went to Philadelphia. 'Twenty-five. So anyway, I'm standin' there in her doorway and she's just lookin' down her nose at me, the bitch. *I'm sorry, Brian, but I don't know what you're talking about.*'

It was a cruel impersonation: head back, voice nasal, the words precisely enunciated, sharp as razor blades.

'So I tell her, see, I tell her Bobby tole me the whole story, and if she don't want the Doc to know, well then, she better get down off her high horse right quick. I tell her not to worry, she's gonna like it just fine. She just stands there for a minute, thinkin', and then she says, *Come along*. Bold as brass.'

The clouds had passed from his eyes; they were bright, shining with an interior light. Between his lips, the grey tongue flicked quickly, once, twice.

'So we go upstairs to her room. She closes the door and turns to me and just stands there again. Queen of the May. So I reach out and I tear open the front of her dress. Buttons go flyin' ever'where. *Lie down*, I tell her, and she does. And I pull down my pants and I get on to the bed and I give it to her. I mean to tell you, son, once she got wound up, she was an animal. An *animal*. And I made her beg for it. *You like this?* I say. *You want this?* I say.' He cackled, shook his head. 'I made that bitch sing for her supper. Didn't I though.'

I suddenly found myself wanting, very badly, to ram a fist into the weathered old face.

He was frowning now. 'But then I get off her,' he said, 'and pull up my pants, and the bitch goes and spoils it all. I look down at her and goddammit if she ain't *cryin'*. I say, What's the matter with you? You got what *you* wanted. She pushes down her dress, covers herself up, and she just keeps cryin'. Real quiet-like, with her hand over her eyes. She says to me, *Would you please go now*. So I go. Who needs that whiny shit? But first I tell her that maybe I'll be back, drill me some more of that nice sweet cooze.'

'Did you?'

'Fuck no. Like I say, don't need the whiny shit.' He shook his head sadly. 'They get you ever' time. One way or the other.'

'So this was this summer of Nineteen twenty-five?'

He was looking off, towards the neat suburban homes. 'I tole Bertie about it, though, and he tole me later he had some of it himself.'

I needed to take a shower. Preferably with lye. 'This was the summer of Nineteen twenty-five?' I asked him.

He nodded without looking at me. 'Summer of 'twenty-five.'

I asked him, 'Did you know anything about some remains that Lessing brought back from his last field trip?'

Still looking thoughtfully off at the houses, he said, 'I've had me a good life, son. Good food, good drink, heaps of good pussy. I don't owe shit to nobody, man or woman. I got no one to worry about but myself, and I got no regrets a-tall.' He turned to me. 'No regrets a-tall. I've had me a damn good life.'

'Do you know anything about the remains Lessing brought back that summer? The body of an Indian?'

Blinking, he frowned. 'What? Indian? How the fuck I know about an Indian? I was in Philadelphia.'

He looked off again at the houses.

The local elementary school had just ended its day. A few tiny forms were walking down the sidewalk, arms swinging earnestly; others ran across green lawns with the jerky unself-conscious zeal of childhood. I could hear the thin distant sound of their cries and shouts and laughter.

Brian DeFore sucked silently at his gums and watched them.

I left him there.

It was a place that had seen better days, but couldn't remember exactly when. Even at five-thirty, prime time in the alcohol business, it was nearly empty. To the right, there were padded stools along a dark wooden bar that was still, despite years of neglect, a handsome piece of carpentry. To the left, tables, chairs, a jukebox playing Tammy Wynette. Behind the bar, a wide cloudy mirror in a chipped antique cherrywood frame. Below this, on cherrywood shelves, liquor bottles lit with that soft amber glow that gives them, in the dimness, the glitter and shine of bright new unsullied hopes.

By the door, two middle-aged men in grey uniforms, Jerry

and Steve by the oval nametags embroidered on their shirts, sat explaining the universe to each other over bottles of Budweiser. Farther down, an old woman in widow's black sat staring into a highball glass as though it were a photo album. At the far end, Grober sat nursing something in a rocks glass and talking to the bartender, a big, round-bellied, sandy-haired guy wearing a red waiter's jacket two sizes too small.

Grinning, Grober got off his stool to shake my hand. 'Hey, Josh. How's it goin'?'

I told him it was going fine. He introduced me to the bartender, whose name was Jim, then asked me if I were still drinking Jack Daniels. I told him I was, on the rocks, and Jim poured one for me and another scotch for Grober.

'So how's Rita?' Grober asked me as the two of us sat down.

'She's fine.'

'She still in the chair?'

'Yeah.'

Grober took a sip from his dink, then shook his head. 'A real shame, man.'

I nodded.

Grober was in his mid-forties. About five feet ten, he was stocky and seemed soft and sloppy, but I've seen him take a punch to the gut, one that would turn a weightlifter green, and merely grin. He grew his greying hair long on the left and combed it over the bald spot at the top, something I've always hoped, if my time ever comes, that I'll have the courage not to do. His face was square, his nose had been broken at least once. He wore a plaid sportscoat, a white shirt, grey Sansabelt slacks, white socks, and spiffy white loafers with leather tassels. He looked like an overnourished, underemployed golf pro.

He said, 'Whatever happened to the guy who shot her? Martinez?'

'Still doing time.'

'He get out soon?'

'Five more years.'

He drank from his glass. 'I heard you nearly offed him when you ran him down.'

I shook my head. 'No.'

He nodded, smiling. 'Yeah, right.'

I changed the subject. 'So how do you like El Paso?'

'Hey. Great little city, man. Things happen here. You got half a million people this side of the river, a lot of 'em with cash. You got two million on the other side, none of 'em with cash. Coming this way, you got drugs, illegal aliens, smugglers, scammers. Going that way, you got guys making weapons drops, or picking up a pound of weed, or maybe getting their asses hauled in the cathouses.' He grinned. 'Some great cathouses in Juarez, we can check 'em out, you got the time.'

'What do the cops say about all this?'

Grober grinned. 'Which cops? The DEA? FBI? Customs? Immigration? The MPs outta Fort Bliss? The locals? Five or six different flavours here, and they're all pissed off at each other. Steal each other's snitches, fuck up each other's busts.'

'What about the locals?'

'I read somewhere, some guy said the El Paso cops couldn't find the bend in a pretzel. Half the money in town, *half* of it, easy, comes from one scam or another. Grass, coke, smack, women. Whatever.' He grinned happily. 'Great little town.'

'How're you making out?'

'Great, great. I got the PI work and I do a little security consulting. Alarm systems. Got a kickback deal with a guy who makes 'em. Big thing here in town, alarms. People who got the cash don't wanna share it with people who don't.'

'The American way.'

'Hey. I'll drink to that.' He raised his scotch in salute, took a gulp. 'So what's the deal with all these stiffs you got me tracking down? You gonna open up a cemetery?'

'They're all dead, all the students that went on the field trips?'

'All but two. And the other guy, that you said. Whatsis. DeFore.'

'Who was alive?'

'Guy named Brewster. Lamont Brewster. Lives in Michigan somewhere. You wanna call him, I got the phone number. Wasn't there when I called. And another guy, here in town. David Passmore. Him, I talked to.'

'Did he remember Dennis Lessing?'

'This guy remembers everything ever happened in his whole entire life. Twice, he remembers it. Also, he's a holy roller, one of those born-again bible-bangers got a personal direct line to God. Lotta stuff about God's plans for the sinners. Brimstone and fire, good shit like that. I'll take all of it, every second, over another five minutes with a jerk like him.'

'This was on the phone?'

'Yeah.'

'He give you anything useful?'

'Hernia of the ear, he gave me.'

'Anything about Lessing, anything about the woman on the Reservation?'

'A first name. Elena. That help?'

'Yeah, maybe. Anything else?'

'She was married, but he doesn't know who to.'

'Description?'

'He only saw her once. Says she was a blonde Jezebel. A blonde daughter of Satan. Means he probably wanted to pork her himself.'

Grober, I realized, would've had a better afternoon if he'd been the one talking to Brian DeFore. I said, 'No address for her?'

'Somewhere near Piñon, he says.'

'Did he know anything about Lessing's death?'

Grober shook his head. 'He was outta town. But he thinks it was God punished Lessing. For humping the blonde Jezebel, see. Musta been a slow day, no earthquakes, no floods, God was killing some time.' He sipped at his drink. 'So listen, Josh, what's the skinny? What're you into?'

I went through the story again.

Grober shook his head. 'Forget it, man. Sixty years ago, you're not gonna find diddly now. I'd milk it for a couple more days and then fold.'

I swallowed some bourbon and nodded. 'I'll probably pack it in tomorrow.'

'Listen,' he said, 'while you're down here, why don't we hook it over to Juarez, check out the action?'

'Can't,' I said. 'I'm supposed to meet some people for dinner.'

'Well lookit, let's get together afterwards. I got a new squeeze, Connie, she can call a friend. The four of us can go out, do the town.'

'I don't think so, Phil. I'm beat.'

He grinned. 'You still got a thing for Rita, right? What're you guys, Mr and Mrs North?'

I smiled. 'Really, Phil, I'm tired.'

'Josh, you got to break loose now and then. I mean, hey, it's a crummy thing happened to Rita, a tragedy and all, I feel terrible about it personally, but you got to remember that life goes on. You got to go for the gusto. World's gonna pass you by.'

I sipped at my bourbon. 'Thanks, Phil. I'll bear that in mind.'

Smiling, he shook his head. 'Jesus, Josh, you probably still help little old ladies cross the street.'

'Whether they want to go or not,' I said. 'Kicking and screaming, some of them.'

He laughed, picked up his glass, saw that it was empty. He turned to me. 'One more?'

I shrugged, smiled. 'You've got to go for the gusto.'

CHAPTER 10

Plump roast duckling in a brandied orange sauce. Wild rice. Buttery baby peas. Spinach salad tossed with a tart vinaigrette and sprinkled with crisp bacon bits. Icy white wine as dry as the desert air. All of it arranged on china and crystal atop a table spread with glossy white linen, beneath a crystal chandelier.

I was living well lately. Too well. If I wanted to work off all these carbohydrates, I'd have to swim the Rio Grande back to Santa Fe.

This evening I was sporting a tie, something I usually do only at funerals, but I still felt underdressed. Alice Wright wore a black velvet shift, simple and elegant, and a single strand of pearls. Lisa wore an Oriental-looking pantsuit of red brocaded silk. I had determined, early on, that the round breasts beneath the material were loose and free. The uncanny eye of the trained detective.

Lisa, it transpired, was an artist. The painting that hung over the sofa in the living-room was one of hers, a view through a pair of ruddy sandstone buttes towards an elaborate sunset. So was the painting here in the dining-room, a night scene looking up the length of a deep gorge. Moonlight draped the dark rocks, glazed the pale white sand and the black ribbon of river. The area looked vaguely familiar, and I said so.

'It's the east gorge of the Grand Canyon,' she said from across the table, and sipped at her wine. 'I spent a few weeks there two years ago. Do you like it?'

The chandelier was wired to a dimmer switch, and Alice had adjusted it to a level just above candlelight. In its pale yellow glow, Lisa's long black hair had the same liquid sheen as the river in the picture.

'The painting?' I said. 'Sure. But I'm the wrong person to ask about paintings. What I know about art would fit in a Dixie cup.'

Alice Wright, who sat on my left at the table's head, smiled and said, 'Now, Joshua. You oughtn't give a compliment with one hand and take it away with the other.'

Lisa laughed. 'Oh, let him be, Alice.' She turned to me and said, 'I'm sure Joshua's able to use both hands at once.' She was smiling, and those extraordinary blue eyes of hers seemed to be glowing.

If this was a come-on, and to the base of my belly it sounded like one, I wasn't sure how to react while Alice Wright was there. And I wasn't sure how I'd react if she hadn't been.

Alice herself solved the problem, temporarily, by taking up the conversational slack. 'Lisa had a show just last month. Very successful too, wasn't it, dear?'

Lisa looked at her with mock severity and said, 'Cool it, Granny.'

Alice smiled. 'Ignore her, Joshua. She's one of those artists who refuses to toot her own horn. She has galleries all over the south-west begging for her work. Even one in Santa Fe.'

I nodded to Lisa, acknowledging the achievement. 'Santa Fe's a tough market to crack.'

She smiled, and her young face actually flushed. 'I haven't actually cracked it yet. I'm supposed to fly up there next month and see some people.'

Despite myself, the machinery of my mind started clanking. Lisa Wright in Santa Fe: an interesting prospect.

Holding her wine glass lightly with the fingertips of both hands, Lisa said, 'How do you like living there?'

'It's okay,' I said. All the thing needed was a casual suggestion. *Why not give me a jingle when you get into town? We'll do lunch.*

Lisa raised an eyebrow. 'Only okay? Most of the people I've talked to are crazy about it.'

I shrugged. 'Most of them probably see only one side of it. The galleries and the glitz.' *Rita, this is Lisa Wright. From El Paso? Remember I told you about her?* Except I hadn't told Rita about her.

'I've been there a few times,' Alice said, 'and I must say I wasn't very taken by the place. It's lovely, of course, all those adobes, the mountains in the background, but it seemed terribly rich and terribly incestuous. Like high school, with money.'

I smiled. Not a bad description.

Lisa took a sip of wine. 'When are you going back?'

'Tomorrow.'

Alice said, 'Have you given up, then, on finding the remains?'

Till now, we hadn't spoken about my reason for being in their city. I nodded. 'As far as El Paso is concerned. I'll see if I can locate your friend Peter Yazzie on the Reservation. But that's a long shot. And even if I find him, he probably won't be able to help.'

'Did you get any help from Martin Halbert?'

'Some.' I had decided before I arrived here that I wouldn't tell her about Brian DeFore and her mother. 'He seems a pretty nice guy.'

Alice smiled. 'He is.' She turned to her granddaughter. 'Isn't he, Lisa?'

'Very nice,' Lisa said. She turned to me. 'Sad, I think, but very nice. He and I dated for a while. A few years ago.'

'Why sad?' I asked her, telling myself that I was asking only because the answer might somehow bear upon the case. Ignoring the flicker of—what? irritation? jealousy?— that said Lisa was far too young for him. Ignoring, too, the urge to linger over the observation that she dated older men.

Lisa shrugged lightly. 'He wants children, and he can't have them.'

'He can't adopt one?' I said.

'It wouldn't be the same,' she said. She smiled wryly. 'It wouldn't fulfil the same dynastic urges.'

Alice said, almost defensively, 'Martin's very proud of his father, and very proud of his father's company. He's given up the day-to-day running of the business to write a book about it.'

Lisa said, 'The book's become a sort of substitute for the child he can't have.'

Alice thought about that for a moment. 'Perhaps. Men like to leave something behind. Monuments to posterity. But he's still a very nice man, and very bright. One of my best students. And one of the few oilmen in Texas—in the country, for that matter—who's demonstrated a concern for the environment.'

Lisa leaned slightly towards me, cupped a slender hand around her smiling mouth, and said in a stage whisper: 'Don't get her started on the oil companies.'

Alice turned to her, eyebrows arched, and grandly said, 'One day you'll be a feeble and senile old woman yourself. I only hope that *you* find yourself saddled with wretched, thankless grandchilden who sit there and mock you.'

Lisa laughed. 'Granny, I'll be feeble and senile before you are.'

Alice smiled and turned to me. 'It's not merely the oil companies, although certainly they share the blame.' She shrugged her angular shoulders. 'Finally, of course, it's the human race.'

Lisa smiled at me. 'Alice thinks we're a rogue species.'

Alice said seriously, 'I do, yes. If you see the world as an organism, a single entity, which of course it is, then you can't help but see the human race as a kind of virus on its surface, actively engaged in killing off the host.'

I took a sip of wine. 'That sounds like a pretty bleak way to look at it.'

She smiled. 'Well, at least we're doing it more swiftly these days. That's something, I suppose. We're putting her out of her misery more quickly. We can dig hydrocarbons out of the soil, where they've lain dead and buried for millennia, burn them at an absolutely staggering rate, and destroy the entire atmosphere. We can bulldoze and dynamite and torch the tree forests, thousands of acres of them a day, and deplete the major source of oxygen for the planet. We can spill millions of tons of industrial waste into the seas, and kill off the plankton that provide the ultimate basis for all aquatic life.'

'Yeah,' I said, and smiled. 'Pretty bleak.'

Another smile from Alice. 'The irony is that from another perspective, equally valid, the human race is quite simply the pinnacle of evolution. Really quite a remarkable thing, isn't it: Matter become conscious of itself.' She shrugged again, her smile became rueful. 'Not conscious enough, alas.'

I said, 'You don't think there's any hope?'

She shook her head. 'Not for us, at any rate. Not for the human race. We're doomed, thank goodness. But I like to think that life of some kind will survive. Cockroaches, perhaps. Sharks. Some kind of new, mutated bacteria that thrives on radiation. Who knows? Life, after all, doesn't care who lives it.'

'And what do we do in the meantime?'

Another shrug of her square thin shoulders. 'If we're inclined towards morality, I suppose we try to contribute as little as possible to the destruction. And I suppose that, collectively and individually, we take a kind of comfort from the fact that no matter how bad things are at the moment, they're the very best they'll ever be, from now on.'

'And,' said Lisa Wright, smiling, 'we take coffee and brandy in the living-room.'

The end of the world notwithstanding, there were a couple of questions I had to ask Alice Wright. In the living-room, over the coffee and cognac, I did.

'Alice,' I said, 'you told me that your mother found out about the woman your father was seeing. Do you know how?'

She and Lisa were on the sofa. Alice sat upright as though doing afternoon tea at Buckingham Palace, both feet squarely on the carpet, cup and saucer squarely in her lap. Lisa sat with her long legs tucked beneath herself, one long feline arm stretched out along the sofa's back, the silk of her sleeve a line of flame against the cream-coloured fabric. I sat across the room in one of the two upholstered chairs that matched the sofa. A piano piece— something by Eric Satie, I think—was playing softly on the stereo.

At the question, Alice frowned slightly. 'Learned about the woman, you mean?'

'Yeah.'

She cocked her head thoughtfully. 'You know, I don't, really.' She smiled. 'Isn't that curious. I assumed at the time that my father had told her. But that can't've been the case. Why would he?'

Lisa said, 'Because he wanted a divorce?'

Alice shook her head. 'No. If he'd asked her for a divorce then, I would've known about it. I don't think he mentioned divorce until that last day.'

I said, 'But even then, you never actually heard him ask for one.'

'No. No, but I'm convinced he did.'

I nodded. 'Do you remember a man named Jordan Lowery? He was a professor of oil geology at the school.'

She smiled. 'Jordan. Of course. For the longest time I had a terrible crush on him. Physically he was probably the most beautiful man I've ever seen. Absolutely stunning.' Another smile as she inclined her head confidentially. 'But a terrible rogue. What they used to call a cad. He cut quite a swath through the female half of El Paso. There were stories, I remember, about him leaping out of windows to avoid outraged husbands.' She smiled once more and sipped at her coffee. 'His son, Emmett, teaches at the university now.'

'I met him the other day,' I said.

'Poor Emmett. There are all sorts of ways the sins of the fathers can be visited upon the sons. In Emmett's case, they simply replicated themselves. He became a womanizer like his father.'

She took a sip of coffee. 'Jordan didn't marry till he was in his late forties. He really didn't have any interest in children, didn't quite know what to do with them. Emmett was an only child, and he spent most of his life trying to get his father's attention and approval. And I suppose he's still trying, although Jordan's been dead for thirty years now.'

Fathers and sons, mothers and daughters—somehow I'd gotten tangled in a web of family relationships stretching back to the 'twenties, a snarl of bygone lusts and longings, bygone loves and hates. I sipped at my brandy and asked her, 'How did Jordan get along with your father?'

'Well enough, I suppose. Jordan was always pleasant and deferential.' Another smile. 'But he was also ambitious, so I've no way of knowing how genuine that was.'

'How'd your father get along with him?'

'I think my father rather envied Jordan his freedom. His roguery.' A smile. 'With a wife like the one he had, one can hardly blame him.'

'How'd your mother feel about him?'

She frowned. 'The subject never really came up. Not in front of me, at any rate. Disapproving, I should think, given her feelings about sex.'

I nodded. This wasn't the time—the time might never come—to tell her that her mother's feelings about sex had probably been a good deal more complicated than she believed.

I said, 'Do you think it's possible that Jordan might've been involved in your father's death?'

She blinked, surprised. 'Why would he be? He was ambitious, as I say, and he liked the things money could buy, but why kill my father? To obtain his position? The salary wasn't that much larger. And why on earth steal the remains of a Navajo Indian?

A good question, one I'd asked myself. I still didn't have an answer for it.

I stayed there at the Wrights' for another half an hour, finishing up the coffee and brandy. As I was leaving, both Alice and Lisa insisted that I come see them the next time I visited El Paso.

When I thanked them for the dinner and said goodbye, I was careful not to look down at the breasts sliding comfortably beneath the red silk of Lisa's blouse. And I was careful not to invite either of them—I couldn't invite Alice without inviting Lisa—to get in touch with me if they ever came to Santa Fe. Outside their house, walking to the Subaru, proud of myself, I slapped an invisible merit badge on my back. After only a moment, it felt like a sack of potatoes.

*

I parked the station wagon in the motel lot and walked down the sidewalk. My room was set back down a kind of alleyway, an alcove in the building. The alleyway was lit by two spotlights, one bolted high up on to each wall.

I'd reached the door, snagged the keys from my blazer pocket, when I heard the scuff of shoe leather against cement. I turned.

There were three of them, moving towards me without any hurry. They were all big, and they all wore stocking masks.

CHAPTER 11

For an instant, absurdly, I thought they were the three men from Lake Asayi. Somehow they'd tracked me down, spent months doing it, and now finally they were going to take their revenge.

But these three were larger and they were considerably more menacing.

There's something obscene and horrific about a stocking mask. The taut translucent fabric distorts the face, reminding you of the malleability of flesh, its fragility, its transience. It transforms the eyes and mouth to evil slits, the nose to a grotesque blob, turns them all into a vision, dreadful, repellent, vaguely remembered from ancient sweat-soaked dreams.

The man in the middle, probably the leader, was the biggest of the three. He wore jeans and a zippered red windbreaker. I think the two outriders were wearing jeans too, but by this time I had stopped paying attention to anyone's attire.

The instinctive reaction was terror. *Run*. Scream and gibber if you must, but *run*.

But the wall was at my back. Nowhere to run to, nowhere to hide.

Forget the door. They'd be on top of me by the time I

unlocked it, and then we'd all be inside the room. Where they could kick me to pieces in privacy and comfort.

There was a foot of space between the two outriders and the wall and another foot between each of them and the leader.

They were about three yards away now, still moving towards me, slowly, relentlessly. No one had said a word.

When you can't retreat and when surrender seems most likely fatal, you attack. It was the only choice I had. The only option that gave me the possibility of leaving that alley without being very badly hurt, or very badly dead.

I sucked in a deep lungful of air. Then, raising my arms in front of me like a tackle, bellowing the way I had at Lake Asayi, I ran at them.

For a moment, startled, they stopped their advance. The man in the centre put his hands to grapple with mine, and I kicked him in the crotch as hard as I could. He doubled over, hissing, and I rammed him towards the outrider on my left.

The motel key was still in my hand and I held it like a dagger. As I swerved around the big man in the centre, I stabbed out towards the outrider on the right, clawing it across his face. I felt the nylon stocking rip and the flesh beneath it split apart.

He shrieked, and then I was past him, on my way to the alley's entrance.

And then I wasn't. The man on the left had untangled himself from the leader and dived for me. His hand snared my ankle and I went down.

I hit the cement skidding on my knees and the palms of my hands. Cloth and skin shredded beneath me. I tumbled over in a roll, more momentum than strategy, and then I was up again, stumbling, but stumbling in the right direction. I was at the entrance when a diesel cab slammed into my back.

Suddenly I was moving more quickly than my legs wanted to. I shot towards the Subaru, and I would've shattered my shins against the bumper if I hadn't slammed my wounded hands against the hood. I went spinning over the fender and came down on hands and knees in the space between the station wagon and the next car.

I pushed myself up, but by then one of them was at me, slamming a fist into my kidney. I gasped and swung around and struck out wildly, backhanded. My knuckles crashed into his face and he jerked back, and then the other man was there and a fist was coming in for my throat. I dodged away but it smashed against my shoulder, and then the first guy was back, pummelling me. Fists happened for a while, and kicks and gouges, a flurry of hands and elbows and knees, and then finally they had me, arms and legs pinioned, and everyone was breathing heavily, and the third man, the leader, was limping towards us from the entrance to the alleyway with a knife in his hand.

Fifty yards away, cars cruised serenely by. Just another Thursday night in El Paso.

Walking with a slight stoop, the leader limped closer. For the first time I noticed, under the taut nylon, beneath the deformed nose, a smudge of grey.

A moustache. Have to remember that.

Why? So I could put it on the résumé?

'*Hijo de puta*,' the leader said calmly. Son of a whore. They were the first words anyone had spoken since I stepped out of the Subaru.

He was about five feet away when suddenly he was lit up, brilliantly, as though by flood lights. And suddenly a car horn was exploding behind me, honking frantically, off and on. I felt the two men at my sides wrench themselves around to look, and then the leader was shouting '*Vamanos*,' over the blare of the horn. And then they were gone and I was leaning, head lowered, against the Subaru.

I heard a car door slam, heard a quick clicking of heels against pavement. I felt a hand on my back, and Lisa Wright was saying, 'Joshua? *Joshua?*'

'Joshua, you're being ridiculous,' Lisa Wright called out from the bedroom, beyond the thin wooden door.

'Probably,' I called out over my shoulder.

'You should see a doctor.'

'Uh-huh.' This was the third or fourth time she'd told me.

In socks and shorts I bent forward and studied my face in the mirror. A small triangular gouge at the curve of my cheek—one of the men in the alley must've been wearing a ring. The wound had stopped bleeding and started throbbing.

Lisa called out: 'Why do grown men sometimes act like idiots?'

'Beats me.'

She had helped me get the first-aid kit from the glove compartment of the Subaru—my hands had a hard time with the car door. I'd made her wait in the chair while I did my repairs in the bathroom. It had taken me a while, because I couldn't begin until I caught my breath and stopped shaking.

But finally I'd been able to clean myself off, smear Neosporin on my palms, wrap them with gauze, and tape them.

Now, assessing the damage in the mirror, I decided I was lucky. I still had all my teeth. My lip was split, but that had stopped bleeding too. By tomorrow morning, probably, it would be the size of a flounder. By then, too, I'd have a nice bruise highlighting that gouge, and two or three more down along my ribcage. But no ribs were cracked, no bones were broken. The worst visible injury was to the knees of my pants, which'd been vapourized, and to my palms, which'd been scraped raw.

So had my pride. The three men had frightened me, and badly. Even now, safe in the bathroom, I still could see those smooth bullet-shaped heads coming towards me.

Fortunately for all of us, wounded pride doesn't show.

Outwardly, I seemed almost presentable, and if it weren't for every muscle in my body feeling as though it'd been hacksawed into pieces, and for my hands feeling as though I'd been juggling hot waffle irons, I was absolutely tip-top.

The pain would be worse later, when I stopped moving. Thing to do now was keep moving.

I opened the door a crack and asked Lisa to get me a clean shirt and a clean pair of jeans from my suitcase. A few moments later she was there in her red Oriental outfit, handing them over.

'Let me drive you to the emergency room,' she said.

'No thanks,' I told her.

I was holding the door open by only five inches. Lisa suddenly smiled. The blue eyes looked down the length of the door, looked back at my face, and she said, 'It's not as though you've got something I haven't seen before, you know.'

I smiled back. 'Then you're not missing anything now. Thanks for the clothes. See you in a minute.'

I closed the door and leaned against it. My virtue, such as it was, still intact.

But the rest of me feeling a bit foolish. I'd be blushing next and fluttering my eyelashes.

Gingerly, using only my fingertips, I eased into the khaki shirt and buttoned it. Gingerly I pulled on the jeans and zippered them. No problem at all, except for Lisa's presence fifteen feet away. If she hadn't been there, I could've whimpered and screamed all I wanted.

I fished my wallet out of the ruined jeans and levered it into my back pocket. Then I opened the door and stepped out into the room.

Lisa sat silently in the chair, watching me. She'd hung her coat—a black, full-length wool job, like a London bobby's uniform coat—on the rack by the door.

I crossed the room to my suitcase, which lay open on the chair by the television. I dug out my flashy sky-blue running shoes—$14.95 at Payless—and brought them over to the bed. Sat down, slipped them on, laced them up.

'Okay,' I said, and stood up. Gingerly. 'Let's go get a drink.'

She looked at me for a moment, frowning. At last she said, 'You should be in bed, Joshua.'

'Later. I think an anaesthetic is in order.' There were codeine tablets in the first-aid kit, but I wanted to ask her some questions, and I didn't want to ask them here. Even as banged-up as I was, I thought that the bright blue eyes and the round firm breasts made the room suddenly too small.

'So,' I said, setting the drinks on the wooden table, 'what's a nice girl like you doing in a neighbourhood like mine?' I swung around, gingerly, and sat down in the chair opposite hers.

We'd come in her car, with her driving, to the bar where I'd met Grober. It wasn't chic, certainly, but it had the advantage of being nearby. Jim was still behind the counter, but the afternoon customers had been replaced by the evening shift. The place was a little busier than it had been, but not much. It was a lot more quiet, no Tammy Wynette on the jukebox. These were serious drinkers, professionals, and they didn't want any distractions.

Lisa smiled. The blue eyes looked at me in a level stare. 'I came to your room to see if you wanted to sleep with me.'

'Ah,' I said. Pretty soon I actually would be blushing. 'And what did you tell Alice?'

'I told her,' still smiling, 'that I was going to your motel room to see if you wanted to sleep with me.'

'Ah,' I said. When you find a word you like, stick with it. 'What did Alice say to that?'

'She said she thought you were married. I told her I didn't think so. You're not wearing a ring.'

'Lot of married men don't wear rings.'

She nodded. 'But you would, I think.'

I shrugged, took a sip of my bourbon.

'Wouldn't you,' she said.

'Probably.'

She raised her drink, a margarita, and sipped at it. 'So you're not.'

'No.'

'But you've got a woman.' With a pointed pink tongue-tip, she licked some salt from her upper lip.

I smiled. '*Got* in what sense?'

She frowned as though mildly irritated. 'Do we have to play games, Joshua? You're in love with some woman. A simple question. Yes or no.'

'Yes,' I told her.

She nodded. 'And you don't play around.'

'No.'

She nodded again, raised the margarita, sipped at it. 'Not even,' she said, and licked away some more salt, 'not even when you're hundreds of miles away and she'd never know.'

'Right. It'd make things complicated.'

She nodded again, looked down at her drink, then back up at me. 'I turn you on, though, don't I?'

She'd said it so seriously that I had to smile. 'Lisa—'

Holding up her right hand like a traffic cop, she said, 'A simple question. Yes or no.'

'Yes,' I said.

She nodded. 'Okay. Good.' She smiled. 'If she weren't around, you'd want me. Yes?'

'Yes.'

'Good.' A single nod, final, definitive. 'I'll settle for that.' She smiled again. 'For the time being.'

I said, 'Can I ask you a question?'

'What?' Eyebrows raised. Beautiful face open and unguarded. She still lived in a world, I suddenly realized, where people told the truth and betrayals were a surprise.

'Did you or Alice tell anyone where I was staying? The name of the motel?'

She shook her head. 'I didn't. I don't think she did, either.' She frowned. 'Those three men? You think they were after you?'

'I know they were after me. I'd like to find out if there was anything personal in it.'

'I didn't tell anyone,' she repeated. 'And why would they be after you? In particular, I mean.'

'I don't know.'

'We get our share of muggings here. Like any big city.'

I nodded. Got their share of tyre-slashings too, probably. But a mugging and a tyre-slashing both, the same person on the same day?

'I'll ask Alice,' she said again. She smiled. 'She really likes you, you know.'

'I like her.'

The smile widened. 'She's wonderful, isn't she? She's taken care of me since my parents died. She and Edgar, my grandfather. He died about five years ago.'

Seemed like a lot of death for one young life.

'When did your parents die?' I asked her. I sat back against my chair. My hands were throbbing badly now and my muscles were beginning to tighten.

'When I was twelve. An automobile accident.' Her eyes narrowed and she canted her head slightly to the side. 'Are you sure you don't want to see a doctor?'

I nodded. 'Yeah. But maybe you'd better get me back to the room.'

Concern came over her face. 'What if they come back? Those three men.'

'They won't. For all they know, I've been in touch with the police. They won't come anywhere near the motel.'

'But what if they do?'

'They won't.'

'You could stay with us. We've got a spare room.' She smiled. 'I won't try to seduce you. I promise.'

I smiled. 'No. Thanks, but no.'

She pouted theatrically. 'You're really a pain in the ass. Did you know that?'

'Yeah,' I said. 'I hear it all the time.'

When she parked the car in the motel lot she turned to me. Her face very serious, she said, 'You're sure, now, that you don't want someone to tuck you in?'

'I'm sure, Lisa. Thanks.'

She smiled. 'Last chance.'

I smiled back. 'I'll probably regret it. And I thank you for the offer. I'm flattered. But it's not a good idea.'

She sighed elaborately. 'You're doing wonders for my ego.'

'I think your ego will survive.'

'Ummm,' she said, noncommittally. She leaned towards me and I could smell the faint scent of her perfume. 'If you change your mind later, maybe I could give you one more last chance.'

'I won't be changing my mind.'

'Call me if you do.'

'Yeah.' My throat was constricted. Damage from the fight, no doubt.

'Am I making you uncomfortable?'

'Yeah.'

She laughed. 'Good.' She came still closer and kissed me lightly on the cheek. She sat back, smiling. 'Think about it,' she said.

After she drove away, I went to the front desk and changed rooms. Not because I was worried about her returning for my maidenhead, although the thought did occur to me, but in case the three men came back. As I'd told her, I didn't think they would. But no harm in a few simple precautions.

The new room was only two doors down from the office, which made it, by my lights, a decided improvement. It took me a while, with two battered paws, to get my stuff moved over there, but finally I was set. I popped a couple codeine tabs, crawled carefully into bed, and waited for the pain to fall away. After a half an hour it did, and then the stocking masks stopped advancing towards me, and then I fell asleep.

The cops came for me the next morning at ten o'clock.

CHAPTER 12

When I woke up and tried to move, I felt as though I were constructed of old two-by-fours and rusty hinges. I forced myself out of the bed, across the carpet, into the bathroom. Forced myself to take a hot shower. The bandages and the wounds made it a piece of slapstick. Afterward, even more gingerly than I had last night, I dressed myself. I had just finished changing my bandages when the pounding began at the door.

Too loud to be Lisa Wright. And not likely, in broad daylight, to be three men in stocking masks. I walked to the door and called out, 'Who is it?'

'Police,' came a male voice from the other side.

I opened the door. There were two of them, uniformed cops, both about my height, both looking bulky in their dark blue satin jackets, and both with their guns drawn.

The one in front—older, in his thirties—had bushy red sideburns below his uniform cap, and a sprinkling of reddish-brown freckles across his broad pale white face. The other was a young Hispanic—olive skin, a wispy Zapata moustache.

'Hands in the air,' snapped the redhead. 'Back up.'

Never argue with a man holding a gun. I raised my hands and stepped backward, into the middle of the room.

The redhead came in first, crouching low, the butt of his service revolver in both hands as he glanced quickly around the room. The Hispanic followed him, blinking, dark eyes darting nervously. The hammer of his revolver was un-cocked. I was grateful. Twitchy as he was, if the gun had been cocked I could've been dead in an instant.

The redhead turned to me. 'You Croft?'

'Yeah,' I said. 'Can you tell me what this is about?' Cops like an asshole to treat them politely. An asshole is anybody they're pointing a gun at. Right now, for whatever reason, I was an asshole.

'Watch him,' he said to the Hispanic, then crossed over to the bathroom and disappeared inside. I heard the shower curtain hiss as he yanked it back.

The Hispanic licked his lips nervously, his glance sliding between me and the bathroom. So far, he was the one who bothered me most. If the redhead shot me, it wouldn't be by accident.

A moment later the redhead returned to the room, holding the pistol with its barrel pointed towards the floor. 'Took ourselves a shower, didn' we, boy?' A redneck Texas drawl.

He looked down at the waste basket. He reached down and, using the tips of his thumb and index finger, lifted out one of the gauze bandages I'd thrown there fifteen minutes ago.

He held it up for the Hispanic to see. 'Got us some blood here,' he said flatly.

The Hispanic nodded, licking his lips again.

I said to the redhead, 'I scraped my hands yesterday.' I nodded upward, indicating the new bandages.

'Uh-huh,' he said. He laid the bandage carefully on the dresser, then came across the room. He eyed the gouge on my cheek, centred now atop a lavender bruise. 'Got ourselves bung-up too,' he said. He reached out his left hand and jabbed his thumb, twisting it, into the wound. 'Didn' we?'

I jerked my head away. Involuntarily I clenched my fists. Pain from the injured palms shot down my arm.

The redhead saw me wince, and he grinned. The irises of his eyes were pale grey, the pupils large and black. 'Take the position, boy,' he said. 'Up against the wall.'

I moved to the wall and leaned forward. Cautiously, I put my weight on the fingertips; even so, the pressure tore at my flayed skin.

'Spread 'em,' he said, tapping me with the gun barrel, not very lightly, on the hip.

I moved my legs apart. Quickly, competently, the redhead frisked me.

'Right arm,' said the redhead.

I eased away from the wall and brought my right arm down. He grabbed my hand and, deliberately, he squeezed it between thick fingers and dug his thumb into its centre. The flash of pain was so intense my knees nearly buckled. He clicked on the cuffs, tightly, then said, 'Left arm.'

I inhaled and lowered my left arm. He did the same thing again. My breathing was beginning to get a little ragged.

He turned me around so that my back was to the bed. Holstering his pistol, he smiled at me. 'You sweatin', boy.'

'Warm in here,' I said.

'Uh-huh.' He turned to the Hispanic. 'Warm in here, Jimmy.'

Still standing by the doorway, the Hispanic nodded and licked his lips some more. 'Right, Lee.' His pistol, I was pleased to see, was back in its holster. He stood with his thumbs hooked over the buckle of his belt, but the posture didn't quite come off. He was still new enough for it to seem like a pose.

The redhead poked his forefinger in my chest. He didn't need much force—with my hands manacled behind me, my centre of gravity was off. I stumbled backward a step.

'Why'd you kill her, boy?' he asked me.

I think I'd known since they arrived that it was a killing. Their guns, their hard-ass entrance, their interest in the bloody bandage.

Lisa? Had someone gotten to Lisa?

'Who's dead?' I said.

'Who's dead,' he repeated. He turned to the Hispanic, smiling. 'He wants to know who's dead, Jimmy.'

'Right,' Jimmy said, and smiled. Like the posture, the smile didn't entirely succeed.

The redhead poked me in the chest again, harder this time. I stumbled backward till my legs were against the bed.

I'd been thumped around a lot lately. Stupidly, I said, 'Why don't you take off the cuffs and try that again?'

He grinned widely. 'Tough boy.' Over his shoulder, to the Hispanic: 'We got us a tough boy here, Jimmy.'

'Look,' I said, already regretting the mistake. 'I'm a licensed private detective. My credentials are in the wallet in my back pocket. I'll be happy to answer any questions you've got.'

The redhead found this all very engaging. He didn't once stop grinning. 'Oh, I know you will, boy. I know that.' He unclipped the portable radio from his belt, fiddled with it, frowned heavily, then turned to the Hispanic.

'Radio's broke,' he told him. 'Go out to the car and tell 'em we got him. Wait out there for me.'

If they were playing this to the standard script, right now would be a good time for Jimmy to reveal himself as the Good Cop.

The Hispanic blinked uncertainly and licked his lips once more. 'I dunno, Lee.'

'Go on ahead, Jimmy.' The redhead grinned. 'This boy resists arrest, I'll just subdue him some.'

The Hispanic's glance shifted between me and the other cop. 'Jeeze, Lee . . .' His voice was beginning to shift up the register.

The older cop shook his head. 'Just do it, Jimmy. Now.'

Jimmy looked at me again, caught his lower lip between his teeth, then turned and left the room. His shoulders seemed hunched together as he pulled the door shut behind him.

I would've preferred the standard script. I wasn't very happy with this one.

The redhead grinned at me as though reading my mind. He reached into his jacket pocket, and when his hand came out it was holding a small black device about the size of a transistor radio. Two shiny silver-coloured electrodes, each an inch long, protruded from one end.

A stun gun.

The redhead said seriously, 'Amazing, ain't it? Fifty thousand volts. All in this one tiny little package. Don't leave no marks neither. No scars, nothin'. You ever tried one, boy?' He pressed a button on the thing and a bolt of bright blue light sizzled between the electrodes.

'Cute,' I said.

He grinned again. 'Tough boy.'

He jabbed it at me, hitting me in the chest. What I felt was beyond pain. Every cell in my body exploded. My heart stopped, my breath stopped, the universe stopped. Something collapsed to the bed and I realized after a moment that it was me. My feet were hanging off the mattress and I was lying on my wounded hands.

Somehow I rolled on to my side.

My ears were still roaring when I felt him put his knee on the bed. He grabbed at my hair and he said softly, almost crooning, 'They say it don't do no permanent damage, but they mean when you use it only the one time. Who knows what happens you use it twenny times? Thirty times? Fifty thousand volts, boy. Got to put some hard duty on the old ticker, don't you figure? So you just tell me, boy. Why'd you kill her?'

I took a deep breath. 'Later,' I said. 'I'm going to find you later.'

He laughed then. He let go of my hair and pushed me over on to my stomach, held me down with a fist between the shoulder blades.

And then he jammed the electrodes into the palm of my left hand.

The hand, and the rest of me, was ripped suddenly apart.

When everything cleared again, I could hear him saying '. . . C'mon now, boy, you don't want to get yourself hurt serious.'

I was having a hard time getting oxygen into my lungs.

The redhead was whispering. '. . . Use it on a guy's privates enough times, he just ain't no good no more. I figure—'

I heard the door slam open, crash against the doorstop. Jimmy?

A new voice, deep and growly and clipped. 'Farrell.'

I felt the big red-haired cop stand away from the bed, heard him say, 'Right, Sarge, just checkin' him for weapons. I got—'

'Hand it over.'

'Sergeant—'

'I'm not gonna say it again.'

A pause.

The redhead's voice. 'Shit. Didn' hurt him none. You can see he's the guy done it.'

The deep voice: 'Get him off there.'

Hands gripped my upper arms, pulled me away from the bed. Light-headed, breathless, I was swung around until I faced a fat man in a shiny blue suit. He wore a white shirt tight against his round belly, and a black bolo tie clasped with a chunk of polished malachite. He was bald and he needed a shave, and the pug nose and the bags beneath his brown eyes made him look like a world-weary pig. He was beautiful. My second *deus ex machina* in twenty-four hours.

'Uncuff him,' he said to the redhead.

The redhead moved behind me and freed my wrists. I brought them around and tried to rub the circulation back. Difficult with bandaged palms.

'Who died?' I asked the fat man.

'Alice Wright.'

My body sagged. 'Jesus.'

The fat man said to Farrell, 'Out. You and Jimenez take off.'

His pale grey eyes narrowed, the redhead glanced at me, looked me over, memorizing everything, then turned and left, walking past the fat man and out the door. He left it open. The fat man pushed it shut and turned to me. 'I'm Mendez.'

I nodded. 'Okay with you if I get a glass of water?'

He nodded.

I walked, still woozy, across a thousand miles of carpet to the bathroom. Found the water glass, ran the faucet, filled it. My hands were shaking again. I was turning into Barney Fife. I drank the water and looked in the mirror.

The gouge on my cheek was bleeding. With the back of my hand, I wiped the blood away.

Alice Wright dead. A regal woman.

Deal with it later. Right now deal with the fat man.

I went back into the bedroom.

Mendez had pulled the chair out from the flimsy writing desk, turned it around and straddled it, belly pressed against its slats, arms folded atop its back. He nodded to the bed. 'Take a pew.'

I sat down, shoulders slumped.

'I talked to the girl,' he said. 'Lisa Wright. She told me about the fight last night. You didn't report it.'

'She all right? Lisa?'

'I'm asking the questions now.'

'Right,' I said. I stood up. 'Let's do the whole number. You bring me in, I get a lawyer, and then you ask your questions. And then maybe I answer.'

'Sit down,' he said, quietly, calmly.

'Listen. I've had it. Three goons last night, and this morning I get your boy Farrell. He's a freak, Sergeant. Someday, and probably soon, he's going to blow up on you. I don't need this shit. Come on. Let's do it.'

'She's all right,' he said with the same quiet calm. 'She found the body, she's still a little shaken up, but she's all right. Now sit down. Let's make this easy on both of us.'

I sat down.

He looked at me, frowned slightly, looked down at the carpet for a long moment. He looked up at me again. He said, 'I've been a cop in this town for twenty years. My father was a cop here for longer. You have any idea the kind of maggots we get coming through here? Last week, a drug deal went bad. Guy killed a whole family with a pump shotgun. Mother, father, two little kids. Girls. Ten and eight. Farrell's the one found the bodies. He was crying when I got there. He's got an eight-year-old girl himself.'

'Yeah. He's probably nice to dogs, too.'

Something flickered across his face and he looked down again. He looked up. 'You're a private detective. You don't like a case, you don't take it. You take it and it gets messy, you call us in. Farrell doesn't have that option. No cop does.' His eyes narrowed very slightly. 'So until you scoop up some little girl and stuff her in a plastic bag, you keep your mouth shut about Farrell. Or about any other cop in my city. I'll handle Farrell. Right now, you tell me why you didn't report that assault last night.'

I took a deep breath. I'd been doing that a lot lately. 'They were wearing masks,' I said. 'No way I could identify them.'

He just looked at me.

'I should've reported it,' I admitted. 'All right? I just wanted to get to bed.'

His face remained expressionless. 'You changed your rooms last night. Why?'

'In case the Welcome Wagon came back.'

'Did you go to Alice Wright's home after midnight last night?'

'No,' I said. 'When was she killed?' I didn't want to ask the question. The answer would advance the process of making her death real.

'Twelve-thirty. One o'clock. Show me your hands.'

I stood up, awkwardly fished the Swiss Army knife out of my pocket, clicked out the scissors, sat back down and cut the gauze bandage on my left hand. I showed him my palm, the wounds looking now almost as bad as they felt.

He nodded. 'Other hand.'

I cut off the bandage, showed him my other palm.

He nodded.

I asked him, 'How was she killed?'

'Beaten to death. Some kind of Buddha statue.'

I winced. 'When did Lisa find her?'

'Eight o'clock this morning.'

Which meant Lisa had gone somewhere else after she'd left me. I didn't ask him where. It wasn't any of my business.

'Tell me about this dead Indian,' he said.

I gave him the abridged version.

He nodded when I finished.

I asked him, 'Was anything taken from Alice's house?'

'Jewels,' he said. 'Some cash. Could've been a burglary.'

'You think it was?'

'I don't think anything yet.' He reached into his suit-coat pocket, pulled out a thin plastic Ziploc envelope. He held it out to me. 'Mean anything to you?'

Inside the envelope was a small yellow square of memo paper. Written on it in a neat precise script were the words, 'Croft—Ardmore.'

'Ardmore's the name of a trading post in Arizona.' I told him about Peter Yazzie, Alice's childhood friend, then asked, 'Is that Alice's handwriting?'

He nodded. 'We found it next to the phone.' He slipped the envelope back into his suit-coat and stood up.

'I don't think you did it,' he said. 'Not with your hands like that. But you hanging around here, it's going to muddy up the water. I want you back in Sante Fe.'

'Wait a minute,' I said. 'You're telling me to get out of town?'

'Yeah. I'm telling you to get out of town. If I need you, I'll call you.'

'I've still got things to do. How much time do I have, Marshal? Till sundown?'

He nodded, unsmiling. 'Sundown'd be good.'

CHAPTER 13

After Mendez left, I tried calling Lisa. A man, probably a cop, answered and told me she couldn't come to the phone. He asked for my name, and I gave it. I asked him to tell her I'd call again. He said he would.

I hung up and looked around the room. I could stay there and brood or I could get out and do something. And try to do it before sundown.

*

'Jeez,' Grober said. He sat back away from his desk and folded his hands together beneath his belly. 'Murdered? Whatta you got going here, Josh?'

We were in his office. He shared the brick building with a bail bondsman and a 'painless dentist' downstairs and with a chiropractor across the hallway. This probably wouldn't be considered the choicest piece of downtown real estate in El Paso, located as it was south-west of the railroad tracks, near the warehouses and junkyards along the river. But the office itself was neat and clean, and the furniture was heavy and solid and dark, comfortable if not exactly new. The wooden ceiling fan overhead gave the place a raffish 1940s feel. You half expected Lauren Bacall to sidle in, plunk herself down on the big walnut desk, and cross two long legs while she lit the Fatima angling from the corner of her smile.

'I don't know,' I said. 'But things are happening.' I told him about the slashed tyres and the three men in stocking masks.

'How come you weren't carrying?' he asked me.

'No carry licence for Texas.'

'I got a little Raven I could let you have. A throwaway, be impossible to trace. Only a .25, but you get a troglodyte comin' at you and you put three or four of those little pellets right up his nose and I guarantee it'll give him pause for thought.'

'A troglodyte, Phil?'

'*Reader's Digest*,' he said. 'It pays to increase your word power. You want the gun? Give you a good deal on it.'

I shook my head. 'I'm in enough trouble with the cops as it is. Mendez wants me out of town.'

He nodded. 'He's a tough cop, Mendez. Honest too. And that's always a pain in the ass. So you're gonna split?'

'For now. Back to Santa Fe, and then off to the Navajo Reservation, maybe. You think you could run a few errands for me?'

'Depends on what it'll cost me. Nothing personal, Josh, but I figure all that time over at the library, messing around with dead guys, we're even now. I got expenses to worry about. And there's this new parabolic mike I want to get hold of.' Grober had always been fond of gadgets—fountain pens that were actually FM transmitters, tiny tape recorders that could nestle inside a paperback copy of Harold Robbins. 'I mean, friendship is one thing and business is something else, am I right?'

'You can bill us, Phil. Just so long as you don't get carried away. This is for me, not for a client.'

''Kay,' he nodded. 'What you need?'

'Do you have any contacts in the police department?'

'Sure.'

I said, 'I want the report on Alice Wright's death.'

'Which one? Crime Scene? Autopsy?'

'All of them.'

'You want actual copies or like summaries? Copies gonna cost you more.'

'Summaries'll be fine for now. And see if you can find out from the phone company whether she had a measured line.'

'You're looking for a record of local calls?'

'Long-distance, too.'

'Long-distance is no problem. Take a few days for their computer to bring up the numbers, is all. But almost no one's got a measured line any more.'

'Whatever you can get,' I said. 'Any calls she made recently. Especially last night.'

''Kay. That it?'

'Yeah.'

'You coming back here?'

'Maybe.'

'Well, lookit, next time you come by, let me know up front. I'll make reservations over at this place I know in Juarez. They got a girl there does things with parakeets you wouldn't believe. She goes through two or three of 'em a night.'

'Pretty hard on the parakeets, sounds like.'

'Hey,' he grinned. 'They all die happy.'

*

Back at the motel, I checked at the front desk to see if anyone had left me a message. No one had. From the room, I dialled Lisa's number. No one answered.

Since the phone was already in my hand, I got out my notebook and found the Michigan number Grober had given me yesterday, for Lamont Brewster, the last of Lessing's field-trip students. I dialled the number. No one was answering the phone in Michigan either.

I slammed down the receiver. A brilliant move that sent pain flashing up my arm.

I needed to keep moving. As soon as I stood still, the last twenty-four hours would catch up with me. Faces would start materializing at the back of my mind. The grinning face of the red-haired cop, Farrell. The three distorted faces beneath the stocking masks. The lined aristocratic face of Alice Wright.

I went to the desk, opened the folder that Martin Halbert had given me yesterday, and glanced through it, turning the fragile yellow pages carefully. Maybe, buried somewhere in all that technical language, there was a reason why an apparently harmless professor of oil geology had been battered to death sixty years ago. Maybe there was a reason why his daughter had been battered to death last night.

But I doubted it. And even if there were, I knew I'd never find it.

I put the folder under my arm and went out to the Subaru to carry it back to Martin Halbert.

Martin Halbert wasn't at home, the Asian manservant told me. I handed him the folder and asked him to thank Mr Halbert for me. He nodded and then waited, polite and unblinking, for me to turn and leave. I did.

I drove back down the mountain to the motel. This time there was a message. From Lisa. With a phone number for me to call. I went to my room and called it.

She answered on the second ring. 'Hello,' she said tonelessly.

'Lisa, this is Joshua.'

'Hello, Joshua. I'm glad you called.' She sounded neither glad nor sad nor anything at all. Her voice was as flat as the line on a heart monitor after the patient has died.

'I heard about Alice,' I said. 'I'm sorry.' The phrase, no matter how well-meant, no matter what the circumstances, is always inadequate. It can't rearrange the past.

I heard her take a deep breath against the mouthpiece. She said nothing.

'Are you all right?' I asked her. Brilliant question.

'No,' she said. Then, 'Yes. Yes, I guess so. I'm all right. The doctor gave me something. It was hard, before. When I . . . when I found her. But right now I just feel numb. Like I'm wrapped in cotton.' The words she spoke sounded as though they too were wrapped in cotton, each battened away from the others.

'Is there anything I can do?'

'No,' she said, and then a moment later, like a small child remembering her manners, 'Thank you. I'm all right. I called a friend of mine and she brought me here. I couldn't stay at the house.'

'Where is here?'

'A kind of clinic, I guess. It's very nice, like a resort hotel. The walls are two-toned. Cream and blue. There's a courtyard with Russian olives.'

So she'd called a friend, and the friend had taken her to someplace where she'd be looked after. I ought to be glad for her and grateful to the friend. Why should it bother me that she hadn't called me for help when she needed it?

'Lisa,' I said, 'I've got to leave town today.'

'Oh,' she said, her voice still affectless. 'Will you be coming back?' No real curiosity in the question; only a vague dreamy politeness.

'I don't know. Maybe. Is there anything I can do before I leave? Should I come over there?'

'Hmmm?' She was drifting of into the escape of sleep. 'No, that's all right, Joshua. Thank you. Will you call me later? In a couple of days? I guess I'm sort of fogged-in right now.'

'I'll call,' I said.

'At ease with the dead,' she said.

'What?'

'That's what she told me once. Alice. I asked her if she were afraid of dying. She said she was at ease with the dead. It's from a poem. A Norse poem, I think. Joshua?'

'Yeah?'

'I'm going to go to sleep now.'

'Take care, Lisa.'

'Uh-huh. Bye.'

She hung up. After a moment the connection was broken and the dial tone was droning in my ear. After another moment I hung up the phone and stood there. Remembering her the way she'd been last night, the tease in her smile, the sheen of her hair, those eyes of cornflower blue staring into my own with the unguarded seriousness that only youth can own.

Later. Deal with everything later. Right now, keep moving.

The main branch of the public library was on Montana Avenue, downtown. There were men outside it, on the bright green grass and along the broad concrete steps. Shabby in their hand-me-down clothes, battered and looking resigned to being battered forever, they sat there in the thin sunshine, some of them beside stuffed plastic bags that served as luggage, and with empty rheumy eyes they watched the traffic rumble by. None of the cars would be stopping for them. Not today, not tomorrow, not ever.

For a moment I was tempted to sit down and join them. Forget about the job, the life back in Santa Fe, forget about everything. Just sit there until the sun warmed my bones, and then just sit there some more.

Why not? What was the point? You asked some questions, scribbled some answers down in your notebook, and then suddenly a remarkable old woman was dead.

What was it she'd said?

I could hear her strong precise voice saying it now: 'The

acquisition of knowledge is invariably a destructive process. The question is, finally, what value do we assign to the knowledge acquired, and what value to the thing destroyed . . .'

Nothing. That was exactly the value I assigned to the knowledge acquired.

It was also the knowledge itself.

Later, I told myself. Deal with all of it later.

The microfilmed back issues of the local paper were downstairs. I filled out a request form and a young woman ambled off with it. She returned a few moments later carrying a small rectangular box. She handed it to me and I brought it over to one of the machines lined up against the wall. I took the spool out of the box, hooked it up to the reader, and started cranking the knob.

Some things were different in September of 1925. Harding was president. Barney Google was still alive. You could buy a used 1924 Ford for $429. A Chrysler Imperial, brand new, would set you back $1,995. At the Wright Kitchen Café, you could pick up a Sunday chicken dinner for twenty-five cents. In Jamestown, North Dakota, a woman could be fined, and one was, for smoking cigarettes in public.

Some things were the same. A flood struck the Rio Grande valley on the third of the month, killing off livestock, destroying homes, ruining the cotton crop.

The flood held the headlines until the ninth, when the murder of Professor Dennis Lessing took over.

I read through the account. Most of what was there I'd already heard from Alice Wright. The only new thing I learned, and for some reason it came as no surprise at all, was that the name of the detective who investigated the case had been Mendez.

Part Two

CHAPTER 14

La Jornada del Muerto. The Journey of the Dead. That's what the conquistadors called the long trek between El Paso and Albuquerque.

There hadn't been anything here then, and there wasn't much here now—a few small towns, Mesilla, Hatch, Socorro, and between them only sagebrush and flat baked trackless wasteland stretching to the rim of the world. After the sun disappeared, the wasteland stretched to the rim of the universe, out there where tiny isolated stars burned in the cold empty silence.

The car was hurtling down the tunnel of light drilled through the darkness by my headlights, but I had stopped moving myself. And, like the tail of a suddenly immobilized comet, my past had, all at once, caught up with its source.

I had liked the woman. I had admired her intelligence and humanity, her serenity, the swiftness and easiness of her laughter. All of it gone now.

If I'd never met her, never gone to El Paso, her death would've meant nothing, would've been just another one of those inevitable exits from the stage by an unknown extra. People were dying all the time, all around me lives were winking out; no matter how you felt about it, death was part of the scenery.

But I had met her, and liked her, and admired her.

On the other hand, if I hadn't gone to El Paso, she might still be alive.

Guilt is sometimes a secret sort of self-esteem. If I weren't such a bad little boy, Mommy and Daddy wouldn't be so unhappy, and gosh I sure do feel rotten about it. But at least I know, from the depths of my impotence—and finally all of us are impotent—that I have the power to cause pain.

I tried to be objective. I hadn't wished for Alice Wright's death. I hadn't had any way of knowing, before I went to El Paso, that my presence there might lead to it.

Somehow this was not a compelling argument.

Perhaps her death had nothing to do with my presence. Perhaps a burglar had caused it after all. She hears a noise in the living-room, gets up to investigate, and walks unwitting from this world into the next.

That was still less compelling.

Death can come by chance, at the intersection of our lives, with a hurricane's random path, a madman's random logic. I couldn't believe it had come that way to Alice Wright.

I knew that her death was connected in some way to her father's. And knew that by dragging that fifty-year-old murder up into the present, I had somehow triggered another.

But how? Who gained something by her death? Who lost something by her life?

Alice Wright had thought her mother killed her father. Her own death seemed to disprove that.

But maybe her mother was still the key. Maybe one of her lovers—about which Alice had known nothing—had tired of a bit part and tried to take over the lead.

But if so, where had he gone since? Her mother hadn't remarried, hadn't been involved, according to Alice, with anyone after her father's death.

But according to Alice, she hadn't been involved with anyone before it, either. And according to Brian DeFore, she'd been involved with him. I tended to believe Brian DeFore.

I couldn't see him, however, as a murderer. Even if he could slip away somehow from the old folks' home, he didn't have the strength for it, or the memory. His killing would be self-inflicted; and that, it seemed to me, he had done already, many years ago.

Sergeant Mendez's father? He'd been the detective investigating Dennis Lessing's death. Was it possible that he'd been having an affair with the dead man's wife? That he'd killed Lessing to get her?

I was spinning of into paranoia.

Or was I? Hadn't Mendez shipped me out of town? Afraid, perhaps, of what I might learn?

All right. Forget Alice Wright's mother for the time being. Anything I might've discovered about her would probably be buried with Alice. And even if someone else knew something, I was persona non grata in El Paso for the moment.

Focus on the part of the problem you can do something about. The other factor in the equation. The father. The father's afair with the woman on the Reservation.

And try to find out how any of this had anything to do with the disappearance of a hundred-year-old corpse.

Do the job you were hired to do. And maybe, just maybe, you'll be able to do something about the murder of Alice Wright.

When I reached Santa Fe at ten o'clock that Friday night, I was exhausted. Favouring both palms, which should have been impossible, and often was, I manhandled the suitcase into my house and dumped it beside the door. I shuffled into the kitchen, made myself a drink, carried it back out to the living-room, and flopped down on to the sofa. I was kicking off my boots when I decided to call Rita and let her know I was back.

Her phone rang long enough for me to start worrying. She never went to bed without turning on the answering machine. And she wouldn't have left her house—Rita didn't leave her house.

I sat there picturing all the things that could happen to a woman whose legs were paralysed. Finally, just as I was about to hang up and run out to the Subaru, the ringing stopped and I heard her voice.

'Hello.' She sounded as flat and lifeless as Lisa Wright had sounded earlier today.

'Rita?'

'Hello, Joshua.' Still without emotion.

'I'm back. I thought you should be the first to get the good news.'

She sniffled as though she had a cold. 'I'm glad. Could you call me in the morning, Joshua?'

No one wanted to talk to me today.

'What's wrong, Rita?'

'Nothing. Nothing.' She sniffled again, cleared her throat. 'I just don't feel very well.'

'Rita, what's the matter?'

'Nothing's the matter.' Another sniffle. 'Really. I'm all right. I'm fine.' There was a quaver now in her voice.

'I'll be right over,' I said.

'Joshua, no.' Sudden, insistent. '*Please*, I'm *fine*.'

'Fifteen minutes,' I said.

She wouldn't answer the door either, not until I leaned on the bell for a solid two minutes. At last the door swung open. I stepped in and pushed it shut behind me.

Her back was to me as she rolled the chair down the hallway and turned left into the living-room. I followed her.

Only one light was on, a small brass lamp on the table by the sofa. Without looking at me, she wheeled the chair around to face the sofa at that end, my usual seat. She wore a black silk robe and her black hair looked like she'd just brushed it. The skin around her eyes was puffy and the corners of her mouth were tight.

I sat down on the sofa and the tightness went from her mouth to her eyes and she said, 'Your face, Joshua. And your hands. What happened to you?'

I shook my head. 'Nothing. An accident. I'm fine.'

Now both eyes and mouth were tight. 'A fight.'

'I'm okay. Tell me what's wrong with you.'

'Joshua,' she said, 'there's nothing wrong with me. I think I may've picked up a flu. All I need is some rest.' Her mouth tightened again. 'And I asked you not to come over. You don't have any right to come barging in here when I want to be alone.'

'Rita,' I said. 'This is me, remember? The tall guy? I've known you for four years. That flu story isn't going to cut it.'

She looked at me for a moment and then put her head back. She closed her eyes and said, 'Please, Joshua.' Her voice was deliberate and strained, as though she were trying to keep it from cracking. 'Please go away. If I've ever meant anything to you, you'll leave me alone right now.'

I said, 'Rita, you know what you mean to me. It's the same thing you've meant to me for a long time now. But I've always thought that whatever else we might be to each other, or might not be, we were friends.'

She lowered her head and put her hand to her face, thumb against one temple, middle finger against the other. I couldn't see her eyes now.

'And I've always thought,' I said, 'that friends were supposed to—'

I stopped. Beneath her hand, tears were slowly rolling down her cheeks.

She sat motionless and silent.

'Ah, Rita,' I said. Her other hand rested on the arm of the wheelchair. I leaned forward and took it in mine. The rest of her remained still, but her thumb moved against my fingers.

Neither of us said anything for a while. I could hear the tears lightly tap, one by one, against her gown.

Finally she breathed in, deep and shuddery. She cleared her throat. 'There's some Kleenex in the bathroom,' she said. 'Could you bring me some?'

She never asked me to do anything for her; she wanted a moment alone.

I stood up, padded across the room and down the hallway to the bathroom, plucked three or four Kleenex from their box, and padded back. I handed them to her and sat down again on the sofa.

She wiped her eyes, blew her nose, put her hands in her

lap. For a few moments she didn't look at me. Then she did, and she was smiling. It was a sad, fragile smile. And once again, as often happened when I was around her, something turned, wrenching, within my chest. She said, 'I don't know what I'm going to do with you.'

I smiled. 'I've got an idea or two, if you'd care to hear them.'

She shook her head, sniffled, blew her nose again.

'So what happened?' I asked her.

'Your friend, Mr Begay. He happened.'

'He called here?'

She nodded, took another deep breath. 'He's in town. I asked him to come over. I wanted to meet him.'

'So what happened?'

'He came over. We talked. He told me about the woman on the Reservation. The woman having the dreams.'

'Yeah?'

'Then he was asking me about the shooting. About my back. I told him what the doctors said. That I wouldn't be walking again. I told him that I would. He asked if he could examine my spine.'

I was trying, not very successfully, to imagine Daniel Begay as a letch.

She saw my frown. She smiled that fragile smile again. 'No, Joshua, nothing like that. I just bent forward in the chair and he ran his hands down my back. No clothes were removed. It was all very clinical.'

'Right. And then what?'

'And then he sat down and he said, "I'm sorry to tell you this, Mrs Mondragon, but you're fooling yourself."'

CHAPTER 15

I stared at her for a moment. 'Jesus, Rita. So what? He's not a doctor. What right does he have to tell you you're not going to walk? What does *he* know?' As soon as I found out where Begay was staying, I was going to get over there and—quickly, neatly, as efficiently as possible—I was going to put out his lights.

Rita was shaking her head, smiling the fragile smile. 'No, Joshua, that's not what he meant.'

'So what did he mean?'

'That I'd stopped believing it was possible. And that until I believed it again, it wouldn't happen.'

'That's crap, Rita. You've been telling me for almost three years that you're going to walk again.'

Her fingers moved lightly around the balled-up Kleenex. She nodded. 'I said the same thing. He just sat there smiling at me. A nice smile, fond and affectionate, like he was my uncle, and he knew better than I did what I thought.' She pressed her lips together. 'I treated him like a bitch. I told him he didn't know what he was talking about.'

'He doesn't.'

She blew her nose again. 'He ignored me. He told me that I had to put some time aside every day, and sit quietly and picture myself. Standing up. Walking. Running. He told me that everytime I stopped believing, I had to call up one of those pictures. Think about it. Breathe it in and out. Become it.'

'Swell,' I said. 'Does he do crystal healing on the side? Channelling? Does he talk to dead pharaohs?'

She shook her head again. 'Joshua, he's right. I *have* stopped believing. I've been telling you that I'll walk again. I've been telling everyone. Sometimes I even tell myself. But it's all been a sham, a front. At night, when I'm lying there alone in the bed, and I can see the silhouette of the chair against the light from the window, I know I'm going to climb back into it tomorrow morning, and the morning after that, and the morning after that. Forever. Until I die. And sometimes I think it might be a good idea to hurry along the process.'

'The dying process,' I said.

She nodded, her face empty.

I said, 'No, Rita.'

She frowned. 'Wasn't it Nietzsche who said that suicide is a wonderful thing—that the thought of it has gotten many a man through many a bad night?' She shrugged. 'Many a woman, too.'

'You could've said something,' I said. 'You could've talked to me. You know that all you have to do is call.'

A brief shake of her head. 'I didn't want you to know how bad it could get. I didn't want to put that weight on your shoulders.'

'They're pretty good shoulders,' I said. 'I get a lot of comments on the shoulders.'

Another faint smile. 'They're fine shoulders, Joshua. But even if you brought them over here every night, and loaded them up, you'd still have to leave, sooner or later. And then I'd be all alone again. Me and my despair.' The faint smile, ironic now. 'Me and my shadow.'

Until this moment, the two concepts, *Rita* and *despair,* would've been impossible for my mind to join together.

'Rita,' I began, and then realized I didn't have a finish. I didn't know what to say.

She smiled. She had never looked so painfully beautiful as she did at that moment. 'Joshua, I'm all right. Really. After Daniel Begay left, I was fuming. Almost sputtering with anger. Not because he was wrong, but because he'd seen through me. And then I had myself a good cry. Wallowed in self-pity for a while.' The smile again. 'Something I seem to've gotten good at. But I'm all right now. Talking to the man was probably the best thing that could've happened to me.'

'And what happens now?'

She took another long deep breath. 'Well,' she said, 'first you tell me what happened in El Paso. And then we proceed from there.'

'That's not what I meant. What do we do about this despair business?'

'I'm going to call Daniel Begay tomorrow, and apologize, and ask him if he and I can talk some more.'

'He's not a doctor, Rita.'

'No, but he knows things.' Another smile. 'He even knew I'd want to talk to him tomorrow. He left his phone number. Here in Santa Fe.'

'So what is he, some kind of Navajo guru?'

She looked at me, her head cocked slightly to the side. 'Joshua, don't resent him. He's a good man. You know that.'

I did know that, but it was difficult not to resent someone, a stranger to her, who could see things in Rita that I hadn't. From time to time we can be petty little dorks, we mountain men.

'Now,' she said. 'Tell me about El Paso.'

'I'm sorry about Alice Wright,' she said. 'You liked her.'

'Yeah,' I said. I studied the pattern in the Persian carpet.

'Stop blaming yourself. You didn't kill her.'

'No,' I said.

'Joshua.'

'What?'

'Look at me.'

I did. 'What?'

'Stop it.'

'Shit, Rita, I did a hell of a job down there. I managed to get one old woman killed. If it hadn't been for her granddaughter, those three guys in the stocking masks would've turned me into chopped meat. If it hadn't been for a fat cop, I'd still be getting worked over by a goon with red hair and a badge. And then, on top of everything else, I get thrown out of town. I did a great job.'

We had shifted roles again. I was the one providing the self-pity, she was the one providing the thoughtful ear.

She said, 'How much of this is wounded ego and how much is guilt over Alice Wright's death?'

'I don't know.'

'Who knew where you were staying when the tyres were slashed on the Subaru?'

'What?' She was tricky, Rita.

She repeated the question.

'Alice and Lisa Wright,' I said. 'But I can't see either one of them slashing my tyres.'

'What about the archaeologist? Emmett Lowery?'

I shook my head. 'I never told him where I was staying.'

'What was the name of the motel?'

'The Buena Vista.' I frowned. 'Okay. Yeah. If he assumed I was staying at a motel, he could've looked up motels in the yellow pages and called them until he found me. Wouldn't take him long to reach the *B*'s. But why go to the trouble? And why slash my tyres?'

'We don't know that he did. It's possible that Alice or Lisa Wright told someone.'

'Lisa says they didn't.'

She nodded. 'And we believe Lisa, do we?'

'Sure,' I said. 'Why not?'

She smiled. 'Lisa's pretty?'

'She's pretty.' I shrugged. 'I didn't hold it against her.'

Another smile. 'Of course not.'

'As a matter of fact, I didn't hold anything against her.' I smiled back, comfortable now with self-righteousness. 'Including me, if that's what you're implying.'

'Joshua, your social life is none of my business.'

'It could be, though,' I said. 'If you'd let it.'

'Are you planning to go off to the Navajo Reservation?'

Tricky. 'That's a non sequitur, Rita.'

'Are you?'

'Yes.'

'What if Daniel Begay decides to give this up?'

'I'm still going.'

'Because Alice Wright was killed.'

'Right.'

'Do you think that you'll be able to learn anything about some woman Dennis Lessing knew sixty years ago?'

I shrugged. 'Won't know until I try. Did you ask Daniel Begay about Peter Yazzie?'

'Yes. He doesn't know him personally, but he knows his

family. He lives in Hollister.' Hollister was past Gallup, in
Arizona, and not too far from the Ardmore Trading Post.
'I've got the phone number,' she said. 'It was listed.'

'You call it?' I asked her.

'Yes. No one answered.'

'Been a lot of that going around.' I shrugged. 'Okay. So
I'll stop at the Ardmore Trading Post and then I'll drive on
to Hollister.'

Rita nodded. 'When do you plan to leave?'

'Tomorrow. After I talk to Daniel Begay.'

Another nod. 'When you go,' she said, 'bring the gun
along.'

I smiled. 'You figure the Navajos are restless?'

'Someone killed Alice Wright. Unless you're willing to
believe that her death was coincidental, it seems likely that
someone is very unhappy with this investigation.'

I nodded. 'I'll bring the gun.'

Early the next morning, after I showered and dressed and
ate a breakfast of scrambled eggs and scrapple, I made some
telephone calls. I dialled the first number Rita had given
me and reached a very young girl. When I asked her for
Daniel Begay, she dropped the phone on to what sounded
like concrete. A few moments later Daniel Begay was on the
line. I asked him if he could meet me in the office at noon.
He said he could.

I dialled the second number, Peter Yazzie's, in Hollister.
No one answered.

I dialled Arizona information and got the number for the
Ardmore Trading Post. Probably I should've called the
place earlier. Maybe if I had, I would've gotten through. I
didn't get through this morning. A busy signal droned at
me.

I found my notebook, flipped through it, located the
Michigan number Grober had given me. Dialled it. The
phone was picked up on the third ring.

'Hello?' A young woman's voice. Daughter? Granddaughter?

'Hello,' I said. 'May I speak to Lamont Brewster, please?'

'Just a sec. I'll get him.'

I waited. Lamont. A great name. The Shadow's first name. Who knows what evil lurks within the heart of man?

Me. I do.

'Hello?' An old man's voice, raspy with age.

'Mr Brewster?'

'Hold on a minute now. Ears aren't what they used to be. Gotta adjust this thing. Picked it up at Radio Shack, greatest little gadget ever made. Hello? You still there?'

'Mr Brewster?'

'Yes, sir. Speaking.'

'You can hear me all right?'

'Clear as a bell. What can I do for you?'

'Mr Brewster, my name is Joshua Croft.' This was long-distance—I might as well be impressive. 'I'm an investigator licensed by the State of New Mexico, and I'm trying to obtain information about the death of Dennis Lessing in Nineteen twenty-five. I understand that when you were a student, you went on one of Professor Lessing's field trips to the Navajo Reservation?'

'Uh-huh.' The voice neutral, giving away nothing.

'Mr Brewster, I have information that while Lessing was on these trips, he was seeing a young woman who lived somewhere on the Reservation. Did you know anything about that?'

'Okay now,' said the voice, 'let's just backtrack a little here. You're calling from New Mexico?'

'That's right.'

'Licensed by the state, you said. That doesn't mean you actually work *for* the state, now does it?'

As Chief Dan George once said, sometimes the magic works, sometimes it doesn't. 'No,' I admitted. 'It doesn't actually mean that. I'm a private investigator.'

A smoky chuckle came over the line. 'Oughtta be ashamed of yourself, trying to fool an old man.'

'I am, Mr Brewster.'

Another chuckle. 'Now tell me this—why would anyone

want to know what happened to Dennis Lessing sixty years ago?'

'It's a long story.'

'Time is one thing I've got plenty of, my friend. And we're talking on your nickel.'

'A client of mine is trying to locate the remains of a Navajo Indian that Lessing disinterred in Nineteen twenty-five, in Canyon de Chelly. Those remains vanished the night Lessing was killed. His murder was never solved. Early yesterday morning, Lessing's daughter was murdered. I think the two deaths are connected, and that both of them may be connected to the woman Lessing was seeing on the Reservation back in Nineteen twenty-five.'

'Alice Wright?' said the voice. 'The anthropologist? She's dead?'

'Yes.'

'Damn. Read her books. Smart lady. Murdered, huh? That's a damn shame. What's the world coming to, you wonder.'

An end, if Alice Wright was right. 'Mr Brewster—'

'This client. Why's he want those remains?'

'For religious reasons.'

'He'll be a Navajo then.'

'Yes. Mr Brewster, did you know about the woman Lessing was seeing?'

'I never did feel right about taking those bones back to El Paso.'

'You were there? On the last field trip?'

'Sure was. I was with Lessing when he found the body. Laid out in a kind of hollow there, in the rocks. Wrapped in cotton, but that was mostly rotted away by then, naturally. There was still some skin on the bones, all dried out, like parchment. And some hair on the scalp. Made my own hair stand up, I don't mind telling you. Didn't bother Lessing any, though. Wanted it for his daughter. Alice. Crazy, huh? The archaeologist working the dig, David Bedford, he screamed bloody murder, but Lessing just scooped everything up and stuck it in a big cardboard box. Carried it all the way back to El Paso in the back seat of the Ford. Sat next to it myself, half the time. Heard it rattling around in there, all the way to the Rio Grande.

'Like I say, I never felt right about it. Stealing a body that way. I remember thinking, nothing good's going to come of this. And nothing did, either. A week later Lessing was dead.'

'Did you give any thought, at the time, to who might've killed him?'

'Burglars, they said.'

'You don't know of anyone who might've had a reason to kill him?'

'Nope. And if I did, no offence, but I wouldn't say so to a stranger on the telephone.'

'Mr Brewster, what about this woman on the Reservation? Do you know who she was?'

'What makes you think she's got anything to do with this?'

'I don't know that she does. I'm trying to learn as much about Lessing and what went on back then as I can. If she's still alive, I just want to talk to her. If she's not, I'd like to talk to someone who knew her.'

'I can tell you straight off she didn't have anything to do with him dying. She was crazy about him.'

'I understand that she was a married woman.'

'Be an awfully short life if we had to live it without making any mistakes, don't you think?'

'All I need is a name, Mr Brewster. I know her first name was Elena. What was her last name?'

I could hear him breathing at the other end of the line.

'Mr Brewster?'

'Hold on, hold on. I'm trying to remember. Damn. Well, look, shouldn't be all that hard for you to find out. Her husband owned a trading post out there, and it had the same name he did.'

'Ardmore?' I said. 'Was it Ardmore?'

'That's the one.'

CHAPTER 16

She was petite and blonde and with her white skin and her red lips she had looked, Lamont Brewster told me, like a china doll. From his defensiveness when he spoke of her marriage, and from the hush in his voice when he described her, he had probably been more than a little in love with her himself.

The students and Lessing were camped near Piñon, and Lessing had asked Brewster to come along with him for supplies. In one of the field trip's two Fords they had rattled over dusty roads for forty miles to the Ardmore Trading Post. She had been behind the counter, a trim tiny figure in a blue gingham dress. A young woman, early twenties. When she looked up and saw Lessing, Brewster told me, 'I've just never seen so much happiness on a human face in my whole life. Almost hurt you to look at it, a happiness like that. Didn't seem possible that a human being could be that happy and stay alive.'

She had rushed around the counter and greeted Lessing with an embrace, and then, blushing, stammering, acknowledged the introduction to Brewster. Afterward, she had run to get her husband from the back room.

According to Brewster, Carl Ardmore had been a big, bluff, blond man who walked with a limp. He had greeted Lessing enthusiastically, shaking his hand, clapping his back.

I asked Brewster, 'Do you think he suspected the relationship between Lessing and his wife?'

Brewster's smoky chuckle came down the line. 'Suspected? He's the one introduced them. The whole thing was his idea.'

'He *knew* they were having an affair?'

'Sure he did. He couldn't have kids, see, and he wanted them. Physical problem—wounded during the war. That's the First World War, in France. Anyway, he liked Lessing. And he could tell, straight off, that his wife did too. He told her he understood. Told her he approved. Made her promise two things, though—that she wouldn't leave him and that if she had a child, they'd raise it together. He told Lessing the same thing, asked him to honour the promise.'

'How do you know all this, Mr Brewster?'

'Professor Lessing told me. About a week later. The day after she came to our camp. Came on horseback. Rode forty miles to see him.'

She had shown up at sunset, fifty yards away, a small figure atop a large dapple grey mare standing against a background of pink mountain. Without a word Lessing had left his students and walked off towards her. The two of them had disappeared, Lessing not returning till just before dawn.

'I was awake by then,' Brewster said, 'tending the fire. The rest were still asleep. Professor Lessing comes up to the fire, squats down, warms his hands for a minute. Then he turns to me and he smiles, this sad little smile, never forget it, and he says to me, "I love her, Brew." That's what they used to call me. Brew for Brewster.' The chuckle again. 'Also I had what you might call a fondness for beer back in those days.'

'And he told you about the arrangement?'

'Shoot. Arrangement? You make it sound like a real-estate deal. Those two folks loved each other. And love's got all kinds of ways to work itself, my friend. Not just the ways the preachers and the politicians say is right.'

'What did the other students think about this?'

'Don't know. Didn't ask, and they never said, not to me.'

'Why didn't Lessing leave his wife? Why didn't Mrs Ardmore leave her husband?'

'They gave their word to Ardmore, didn't they. Both of them. And back then, people put stock in their word.'

'Did Lessing see her again before he left the Reservation?'

'Expect so. I never asked. Wasn't my business. But there

were a few times he was gone all day. Then, of course, we all saw her when we were leaving, after Lessing found the body in the Canyon. We stopped by the trading post for him to say goodbye. I remember she was standing on the porch as we drove off. She had on the blue gingham dress again, and she was waving a white handkerchief.'

He cleared his throat. 'Pretty as a picture,' he said, his voice farther away than Michigan. 'I watched her till I couldn't see her through the dust. Waving that handkerchief back and forth.'

'Mr Brewster, do you think it's possible that Carl Ardmore killed Dennis Lessing?'

Irritably: 'Now, why in hell would he do a thing like that? I told you, he knew what was going on. He encouraged it. He liked Lessing, he respected him.'

'All right. Another question. What about Mrs Lessing, Dennis's wife?'

'What about her?' Grumpy still.

'Do you think she knew about the relationship?'

'Don't know. Wouldn't think she cared if she did. Don't mean to speak ill of the dead, but she was a cold woman.'

He hadn't been a member, evidently, of the group of students who felt otherwise. 'All right, Mr Brewster. Thank you for the help. I'm grateful.'

'You're welcome. Listen—what's your name again?'

'Croft. Joshua Croft.'

'Well, Joshua Croft, you're going to try to find her, that right?'

'If she's alive, I'll find her.'

'Well, if she is, you say hello for me, all right? You tell her Brew says hello.'

'I'll do that.'

He was silent for a moment.

I thought I knew what he was thinking—that probably she was dead. I said, 'I'll let you know what I find out, Mr Brewster.'

'Appreciate it,' he said. 'Appreciate it.'

*

It was eleven—over an hour on the phone—when I ended the call to Brewster.

I dialled Peter Yazzie's number. Still no answer.

I dialled the Ardmore number. Still busy. I rang the operator, asked for a verification check. She got back to me after a few moments and told me that there was trouble on the line. Out in the desert, where the trading post sat, this could mean almost anything, from a phone left off the hook to a pole left across the road. I didn't really think twice about it.

I should have. Things might've turned out differently, might have turned out better, with less pain, if I had thought twice about it.

I called Rita. She said that Daniel Begay had been there and gone, and that he expected to see me at noon. I asked her if she'd told him what had happened in El Paso. She said the subject hadn't come up. I didn't ask her which subjects had. Not right away.

I told her what I'd learned from Lamont Brewster.

When I finished, she said, 'I like the idea of her riding forty miles on horseback just to see him.'

'Probably not a lot else to do out there, that time of year. Punch cattle. Yodel.'

'Joshua.' Mildly reproving. 'I like this Elena Ardmore. I think it's a nice, romantic story.'

'Yeah,' I said. 'Terrific.'

'It couldn't possibly affect a realist like yourself, of course.'

'Nah. We mountain men got hearts of stone.'

'Brains, too.'

I smiled. 'Sounds like you're feeling better today.'

'I am.'

'So what did you and Daniel Begay talk about?' Casual, chatty, just shooting the breeze.

'This and that. Do you think Brewster was telling the truth?'

Still tricky. 'Well, he hasn't been answering the phone for a couple of days. I suppose he could've been down in El

Paso killing Alice Wright for reasons we don't know anything about.'

Patiently: 'Do you think he was telling the truth?'

'Far as he knew it,' I said.

'Lessing could've been lying to him, you mean. He could've invented that arrangement with Carl Ardmore.'

'Yeah. I'd like to know where Elena and Carl Ardmore were on the night Lessing was killed.'

'I think you're stretching, Joshua. And what about Alice Wright? If the Ardmores are still alive, they're both in their eighties. Like everyone else involved in this. You don't really think they dashed down to El Paso to deal with her?'

'*Someone* dealt with her. And the cops, remember, found a piece of paper with the name *Ardmore* on it.'

'From what you told me, she had to write that note sometime between the time you left her house and the time she was killed. You said she was killed around one in the morning. When did you leave?'

'Around nine.'

'Suppose, for whatever reason, she got in touch with someone at the trading post after you left. There's no way anyone could've gotten from the trading post to El Paso in time to kill her.'

'They could've called someone who was already in El Paso. Had him do it.'

'Who? Why?'

'Beats me. But it's a possibility.'

'Before we leap to any conclusions, let's wait until Grober gets the record of outgoing calls from her phone. Let's see if she did call the trading post.'

'Maybe she recognized the killer, and wrote down *Ardmore* to point us in the right direction.'

'Like in the Charlie Chan movies? Very good, Joshua. When did she write it down? While he was beating her to death?'

'Well,' I began.

'And if she recognized him, why didn't she write down his *name*?'

'He might've seen it, and then taken the note with him.' Warner Oland would've delivered this with a lot more conviction. Hasty man drink soup with fork.

She said, 'And if there were a connection between him and the Ardmores, he wouldn't take a note with *Ardmore* on it?'

Infuriating woman. 'You just don't like the idea,' I said, 'that Elena Ardmore could be involved.'

'And you're just grumpy because I won't tell you what Daniel and I talked about.'

'I? Grumpy? Surely you jest.'

'I promise you that I'll tell you about it sometime, Joshua. All right?'

'Come on, Rita. You really don't think that I'm silly enough to get grumpy just because—'

'Yes. Do you have your gun?'

'I have my gun. Would you like me to shoot myself?'

'I'd like you to be careful when you're out there on the Reservation asking questions.'

'Yes, dear.'

'I'm serious, Joshua.'

'I said okay. You can't take *yes* for an answer?'

'Call me when you get there.'

'Right. Rita?'

'Yes?'

'Are you really okay?'

Her voice softened. 'I'm fine, Joshua. Really. You take care, all right?'

'You too.'

After I hung up, I swivelled the chair around, hooked my feet on the windowsill, and stared up at the snow in the mountains, blue-white against the clear blue sky. I sat there thinking about Carl Ardmore. Wondering just exactly how you went about telling someone it was okay to sleep with your wife.

Daniel Begay showed up at quarter after twelve, his cane silently swinging, silently tapping along the office carpet.

No suit today; he was back in jeans and the grey wool coat. We shook hands and he placed his black Navajo hat carefully in one chair and sat down carefully in the other. He held the cane upright between his legs, hands resting atop its knob.

I didn't ask him anything about Rita. That impenetrable calm of his made personal questions seem like simple nosiness. Which of course they were.

I told him what I'd learned, and he listened without any expression on his face.

Finishing up, I said, 'Carl and Elena Ardmore. At the trading post. Do you know them?'

'Used to,' he said. 'Good people. They died.'

'When?'

'Carl Ardmore, he died in the fifties. His wife died 'sixty-three or 'sixty-four.'

So much for their rushing down to El Paso to dispatch Alice Wright.

I asked him, 'Did you ever hear any stories about Elena Ardmore having a relationship with Dennis Lessing?'

He frowned slightly, shook his head. 'I don't listen to stories like that.'

And so much for stories like that.

'Who owns the trading post now?' I asked.

'John Ardmore.'

'Who's he?'

'Their nephew, I heard. Carl and Elena, they couldn't have kids. John's parents died when he was a baby, and Carl and Elena adopted him.'

'Anyone else there?'

'He's got a son. The son helps him out at the store. John's getting to be an old man now.'

I nodded. Had Alice Wright called John Ardmore on Thursday night? And, if so, why?

Daniel Begay asked me, 'You think the body of Ganado is gone? For good?'

'Finding it doesn't seem very likely. I'm sorry, Daniel.'

He nodded. 'The woman down in El Paso. Mrs Wright.

You think maybe she got killed because you asked those questions?'

I shrugged. 'It could've been a coincidence. Could've been a burglar.'

'But you don't think so, right?'

'I honestly don't know.'

He smiled his small, barely perceptible smile. 'You don't know, maybe, but you think.'

I shrugged again. 'What I think doesn't really count.'

'Okay,' he said, and nodded once. 'What I think, myself, is that maybe we should quit this now. It's not good what's happening. People getting killed.'

'Fair enough, Daniel. No problem. We've got your address, we'll mail you a statement at the end of the month.'

He was watching me, faintly smiling again. 'Your friend, Mrs Mondragon, she says you're a real stubborn person.'

The pot calling the kettle black. 'She's a great little kidder,' I told him.

He nodded. 'You're not going to quit on this, right?'

I shrugged once more. 'Why not?' I said. 'No client, no case.'

He nodded again. 'So when are you going to the Reservation?'

CHAPTER 17

I frowned. It was a pretty good frown, I thought. 'Why would I go to the Reservation?'

'The Ardmore Trading Post is there. And yesterday, Mrs Mondragon asked me about Peter Yazzie.'

I grinned. 'Well, Daniel, you know, I thought I might take a drive out there today.'

He looked down at his hands, looked back up at me. 'It's a good idea, you think? What if someone else gets hurt?'

Good question. 'I'm going to do my best to make sure that doesn't happen.'

Another nod. 'Okay,' he said. 'You got a client.'

'Uh-uh,' I said.

'You're gonna keep doing this, you got to get paid.'

I shook my head. 'I'm going to do it anyway.'

'So I'll pay you anyway.'

'Nope. You hired me to go down to El Paso and ask some questions about the remains of Ganado. I did that. Mrs Wright's death may have nothing to do with the remains. Right now, I'm more interested in Mrs Wright's death. I'm sorry, Daniel.'

He nodded. 'Okay. Can you give me a ride?'

Talk about non sequiturs. 'Where to?'

'Gallup.'

'Gallup?'

'Truck's not running right. I got something I need to do in Gallup later today.'

I wondered if this were true; he'd given up, I thought, fairly suddenly on the idea of paying me.

But Gallup lay directly along on the route I'd be taking. 'Sure,' I said. 'How soon can you be ready?'

'An hour.'

Fine. That left me time enough to pack what few clean clothes I had left. 'Where should I meet you?'

'My nephew's house.' He gave me an address on the west side of Santa Fe.

Before I left the office, I called up Lamont Brewster in Michigan.

'Mr Brewster,' I told him, 'I'm sorry, but I just learned that Carl and Elena Ardmore died some time ago.' I was apologizing quite a bit lately.

He said nothing for a moment. Then: 'When did she die?'

'Over twenty years ago.'

Another moment of silence.

'Mr Brewster?'

'Yeah.' Distracted.

'I tried to reach you for a few days. Were you out of town?'

'I was over in Chicago, visiting with my nephew's family. Why?'

'No reason. Just tying up some loose ends.'

'Loose ends,' he said sadly. 'Sometimes it seems that's all there is, doesn't it?'

'Sometimes it does, yeah.'

I heard him take a deep breath. 'Well, Mr Croft, I appreciate it, your letting me know.'

'You're welcome.'

'Did she—hell, guess it doesn't matter. Appreciate your calling.'

'Goodbye, Mr Brewster.'

He hung up.

I called Rita next and told her. She was kind enough not to point out that, once again, I'd been wrong.

At one-thirty that afternoon I was on the porch of Daniel Begay's nephew's house, shaking hands with his nephew's wife, a short, plump, attractive woman. Then I was shaking hands with nephew's daughter, a slender, slyly smiling ten-year-old who looked like she might, given a chance, drop telephones on to concrete. (Nephew himself, a lawyer, was at work in the Capitol building.) Then I was helping Daniel load his duffel into the back of the Subaru, next to my suitcase. Then we were in the wagon and I was heading down Cerillos to pick up the interstate.

I was beginning to feel like a country-western singer, living out of his car and hustling from one dreary gig to the next.

Travel didn't seem to bother Daniel Begay. His coat off, his hands in his lap, he sat silently and silently watched the scenery roll by. If Pascal was right, if man is unhappy because he's unable to sit quietly in his room, Daniel Begay was probably a pretty happy guy. I got the feeling he could sit quietly, perfectly contented, inside an empty refrigerator crate.

It was a fine day. The temperature had climbed up into the fifties and the sky was clear, only a few clouds draped like bits of woolly white blanket along the grey slopes of the Jemez range, off to the right.

At Albuquerque I picked up I-40 West. Daniel Begay had nothing to say until we hit the boundaries of the Isleta Indian Reservation, about twenty-five miles outside the city. And even then he didn't say much: He only asked if it would be okay to open a window and smoke. It was as though he'd been postponing lighting up until we reached Indian land. I told him sure.

As the rich smell of burley drifted through the car, I turned to him. 'Daniel, what kind of a guy is this John Ardmore?'

He took the pipe from his mouth. 'Oh, he's okay.'

'And his son?'

He frowned. 'A drinker. Not a happy man. He was in Vietnam.'

He put his pipe back in his mouth and that, I gathered, was that.

We sailed along through the Acoma Reservation, past the towering white mesa and the village of Acoma. People have been living up there in the sky, pretty much uninterrupted, since the eleventh century.

There was a Stuckey's at Acomita, the next town, and I decided to try calling the trading post again.

I wasn't worried, not yet. But it was almost three o'clock now, and we wouldn't reach Ardmore's until at least six or seven at night. And it was a good thirty miles off the interstate. If I could reach this John Ardmore by phone, learn what I wanted to learn, I could skip a visit to the place and continue on to Hollister. Save myself some time.

Daniel Begay went inside for a Coke while I used the phone. The line was still busy, and the verification operator told me it was still troubled.

Driving back on to the interstate with Daniel sipping his Coke beside me, I glanced in the rearview mirror and saw a grey Chevy Malibu leaving the Stuckey's lot and sliding into the same entrance I was taking.

Something else I didn't think twice about.

*

We were driving through the Malpais, miles and miles of ragged black lava flow, when I turned to Daniel Begay and asked him, 'This Ganado. He was an important person? A chief?'

He turned to me, smiling that small faint smile. 'We didn't really have chiefs, like the kind you mean. He was a leader.'

'What's the difference?'

'A leader, he only made suggestions. To do a thing. If everyone agreed, then they did it.'

'What if everyone didn't agree?'

'They argued.'

'They argued?'

He gave a small nod. 'Until they agreed. Sometimes the leader won, sometimes he didn't.'

'So what made Ganado a leader?'

He shrugged. 'He was a healer. And he was very smart, and very brave. Once some soldiers, they took some Navajo women. They took Ganado's wife too, Tazbah. He tracked them down by himself. It took him two weeks. He killed them all, six of them, and took their horses. He brought all the women back.'

More south-west romance. *Love Among the Tumbleweed*.

'The woman on the Reservation,' I said. 'With the dreams. She's the descendant of Ganado and Tazbah?'

He shook his head. 'Ganado died without children. His brother, Mariano, he married Tazbah later, and they had children. The woman comes from these.'

'How did Ganado die?'

'From drink.'

'Drink?'

'One night they had some bad whisky. Everyone got drunk and then very sick. Ganado, he fell from the opening of the cave.'

Not the most illustrious of deaths. A slapstick departure. But I'd seen some of the caves in Canyon de Chelly, and you wouldn't need to be drunk or sick to fall from one.

'Where'd they get the whisky?'

'From a trader.'

'A white guy.'

He nodded. 'Sure.'

Another small way station along the Road of Progress.

I left the interstate at the tiny hamlet of Milan. From the Thriftway on Main Street, I dialled the Ardmore Trading Post.

Trouble on the line.

At this stage I was still more irritated than concerned.

Shooting back on to the interstate again, I glanced in the rearview mirror and noticed, behind me, a grey Chevy Malibu doing the same thing.

It could've been a different grey Chevy Malibu. But I didn't think so.

Coincidence? Maybe. Maybe the guy just had a touchy bladder.

Why would anyone be following us?

If he *were* following us, he must've picked us up in Santa Fe. I didn't remember seeing any grey Malibu back in Santa Fe.

Then again, I hadn't been looking for one.

The Malibu fell back to a position about a quarter of a mile behind me, letting other cars pass by.

Okay. Let's see what we have here.

Gradually, over a couple of miles, I put a bit more pressure on the gas pedal. Watched the speedometer needle slowly climb from sixty-five to seventy-five. Watched the Malibu in the rearview mirror.

Hard to tell at a quarter mile, but it seemed to me that the Malibu was matching my speed, maintaining the same distance between us.

I let the car gradually slow back to sixty-five. In the rearview mirror, the Malibu seemed to remain exactly the same size.

If I'd done it right, and if he were actually a tail, he might not've noticed the speed change. If he had noticed, he might not've thought it was anything special.

Depended, really, on whether he was a professional or an amateur. A professional, most likely, would've noticed, and known what it meant.

'What's wrong?' Daniel Begay asked me.

'Not sure,' I told him. 'Do you know anyone who owns a grey Chevrolet Malibu?'

He thought for a moment, finally shook his head. 'I don't think so. Why?'

'Because there's one on the road back there, and I think it's following us.'

'Why would anyone follow us?'

'I don't know.'

'You could stop the car and see what he does.'

If the Malibu were a tail, I didn't really want to see what the driver might do when we stopped in the middle of nowhere. Paranoia, probably; but I've always suspected that paranoids, despite their muttering, lived a long and happy life.

'What's the next town?' I asked him.

'Prewitt. About ten miles.'

'Anything there?'

'A gas station. A grocery store.'

'I think we'll stop in Prewitt.'

At Prewitt, when we pulled off the highway, the Malibu came with us.

I drove into the gas-station lot, parked the Subaru. The Malibu drove past, down the main street. Only the driver inside, a figure too dim to make out. Texas tags on the back of the car.

Daniel stayed in the car. I went into the station and used the telephone. The Ardmore's line was still troubled.

So was I.

The line should've been fixed by now. A store out in the boondocks—they needed that phone.

And by now I was fairly certain that the Malibu was a tail.

I got back into the car, put the key in the ignition.

'The car's down there,' Daniel Begay told me, nodding down the street.

'Where?' I saw nothing but the mountains unfolding off into the distance.

'Behind those trees.'

'I can't see it.'

'It's there,' he said simply.

I was convinced.

'Okay,' I said. 'We've got two choices, Daniel. We can confront him, find out what he's up to. Or we can lose him.'

He turned to me. 'How are we going to lose him on the interstate?'

I smiled. 'Well, if it's all right with you, we're not.'

He shrugged. 'It's okay with me.'

'I'll need your help.'

He nodded. 'Sure.'

I leaned over, popped open the glove compartment, took out the .38.

Daniel Begay smiled faintly. 'Magnum PI,' he said.

'Let's hope not, Daniel. Magnum got cancelled.'

CHAPTER 18

The cocked Smith and Wesson in my hand, I stood with my back flat against the big rock.

Fifty feet farther along, the Subaru was parked at an angle across the track, blocking it. The road had been bulldozed from the flank of the hill, leaving a rocky slope climbing up from one side and a steep cliff falling of to the other; anyone driving from either direction would have to stop. Hidden behind the rock, I was positioned at the spot where the driver of the Malibu would first see the wagon, just as he rounded the curve.

When he stopped, even for only a moment, I could reach him. If he figured it out, threw the car into reverse before I could get there, I could hit one of his tyres with a shot from the .38. With five shots, at six or seven feet, I figured I could handle a tyre.

This ought to work.

Daniel Begay was off in the rocks up ahead, beyond the Subaru. I'd asked him to stay there. In case this didn't work.

He had calmly assured me that if things went sour, if something happened to me, he'd be able to walk cross-country to the house of a Navajo he knew.

'Not far away,' he had said.

'How far away?'

'Oh, fifteen miles, maybe. That way.' Indicating the barren landscape towards the south with a quick upward tilt of his chin.

'Fifteen miles across that?'

He shrugged. 'It's only ground.'

'You're sure you want to do this?'

And he had smiled faintly and said, 'Sure.'

And now, my back pressed against the rock, I could hear the Malibu coming, the rumble of its engine growing louder as the car rattled over the road.

Any moment now it would wind around the curve.

Out here in the sunlight, the air was warm and it still carried the chalky taste of dust kicked up by the passage of the Subaru. In the blue sky overhead a hawk soared slowly up a thermal.

And then the Malibu was there.

The driver made it easy for me. He stopped.

He wasn't very bright. He was halfway out of the car, left foot on the ground, left hand along the open window, head poking over the door, when I swung around the rock and brought up the .38 in a Weaver stance, both hands around the butt. He turned to me.

'Don't move a muscle,' I told him.

He thought about it. He considered it carefully. The barrel of a .38 can look like the Holland Tunnel when it's pointed at your lungs. He decided not to move a muscle.

'Very slowly,' I told him. 'Put your right hand on the door. Make sure it's empty.'

Frowning, he put his right hand on the door. It was empty.

I took a step forward. 'Out of the car,' I told him. 'Slowly. Keep your hands on the door.'

He hesitated. 'I got to shut it off.' A Spanish accent.

'I'll pay for the gas. Out. Slowly.'

He pulled himself, slowly, out of the car.

He frowned again. 'So what's going on, mister?' As though he couldn't imagine why on earth I'd stopped him.

He wore jeans and workboots, a black T-shirt under an opened grey windbreaker. He was a few inches shorter than I was, but he looked at least a foot wider. Thick sloping shoulders, meaty chest, body-builder bulk beginning to blur with fat. Black hair swept back in an artful pompadour from a broad forehead. Deeply set brown eyes, wide Indio cheekbones, broad mouth, strong square jaw. A handsome face, but slack and brutal, the face of a man who wouldn't think very far beyond the pleasures, or the resentments, of the moment. They would be simple pleasures, complicated resentments.

On the right side of his face, just below the arc of cheekbone, was a two-inch square of flesh-coloured bandage.

'What happened to your face?' I asked him.

'An accident. Listen, mister, if you want money, you can have everything I got. All of it. I don't want no trouble.' Still playing the baffled tourist.

Holding the gun pointed at his chest, I took another step forward.

'The bandage. Take it off.'

He frowned at me.

'Take it off.'

He raised his right hand and in a single motion ripped away the bandage. He tossed it to the ground and held up his head, as though daring me to say something about the wound on his face.

A jagged tear in the flesh, neatly sutured together. The

sort of wound that might be made by a motel-room key used like a dagger.

'Good to see you again,' I said.

'Fuck you,' he said. But he blinked and his glance skittered away for a moment.

He'd been one of the three men in stocking masks, back in El Paso; and he knew that I knew it.

'Hands in the air,' I told him. 'Step away from the car.'

His hands up, he stepped away from the car.

I gestured to my right with the gun barrel.

He moved in that direction.

'Turn around,' I said. 'Hands against the top of the car. Feet back. Spread your legs.'

He did all this as though by rote. Presumably he'd done it before.

Walking towards him, I said, 'Get your feet back farther.'

Awkwardly, he shuffled his feet away from the car.

I frisked him. No gun. I tugged his wallet from his back pocket, stepped back, flipped it open. The Texas driver's licence behind the scuffed plastic shield said that he was Luis Salamanca from El Paso.

'Who sent you here, Luis?'

His head twisted towards me. 'Fuck you.'

He wasn't bright, maybe. But he knew for certain that he was one very tough dude. Probably as a kid, when the toughness was only a mask, he had needed it to survive. By now, with twenty or thirty years of brute force behind him, the toughness was real. It was, in a fundamental sense, his identity. And the only way to get him to talk was to shatter it.

And the only way to do that was to become like him, but worse.

It had happened to me for a few moments back at Lake Asayi, with those other three idiots. It had happened to Farrell, the red-haired cop in El Paso. It was an occupational hazard. The more often it happens, the harder it is to convince yourself that the violence is only a tool, a means, a mask. You have to choose your masks carefully, because they become, finally, your face.

'Listen, Luis,' I said. 'Very slowly now. You straighten out and you step back from the car. Good. Now you walk down the road, back the way you came.'

Following behind, I let him walk six or seven paces, then told him, 'Stop. Good. Down on the ground by the side of the road. Face down. Arms out in front of you. Good.'

Even with him horizontal, nose to the dirt, his elaborate pompadour stayed rigidly in place. A testament to his excellent grooming skills.

Holding the gun on him, I turned and called out, 'Daniel?'

An answering shout: '*Yes.*'

'Can you bring the station wagon down here?'

There was just enough room along the road for Daniel Begay to back the Subaru past the Malibu. He parked it ten yards beyond me and Luis, then stepped out and walked slowly, deliberately back to us, his cane lightly tapping in the dust. I was pretty sure that if he'd walked to his friend's house, fifteen miles away, he would have taken all day to reach it. I was also pretty sure that he would have reached it.

He looked down at Luis, looked up at me, and smiled. 'What do we do with him?'

He certainly had a flair for the apposite question.

'We'll see,' I said. 'Could you turn off the ignition on the Malibu? And look around inside? There's probably a gun.' Luis had been reluctant to leave the car. 'Look under the seat. And check the trunk.'

I watched Luis. Neither one of us spoke.

After a few minutes, Daniel Begay came back and showed me the gun. A Charter Arms .38. 'Under the seat,' he said. 'Nothing in the trunk.'

'Keep it,' I told him.

He shoved the pistol into his pocket. He smiled. 'I keep travelling with you, pretty soon I can open up a gun store.'

He looked down at Luis, looked back at me. 'So?'

'Luis here doesn't want to talk.'

He shrugged. He looked off at the mountains, looked back to me again. 'We could set him on fire.'

His voice was level; for a moment, before I saw the small slight smile, I thought he was serious.

On the ground, Luis moved his head slightly.

Daniel Begay said, 'We could siphon some gas out of his car.'

'Someone might see the smoke,' I said. 'You have a knife?'

'Nope,' he said.

'I've got a tyre iron in the Subaru.'

'There's an easy way, you know.'

'What's that?' I asked.

'You shoot him in the leg.'

I waited, watching Luis. He was breathing slowly, shallowly, as he listened. I said, 'I don't know, Daniel.'

'There's no one around to hear it,' he said. 'We can kick him over the cliff afterwards.'

'He's a pretty tough hombre,' I said. 'It might not work.'

'The first time, maybe. But he's got another leg.'

I watched Luis. 'I could hit an artery,' I said to Daniel Begay. 'He could bleed to death before he talked.'

'You got to aim for the knee.'

Luis's left leg moved slightly. I asked him, 'What about you, Luis? You have any input on this?'

Luis raised his head slightly. 'Fuck you,' he said, but his voice was tight. 'This is bullshit.'

'Okay,' I said to Daniel Begay. 'We'll do the leg thing. I'd better use the other gun. The police can trace this one.'

He pulled out the Charter Arms, offered it to me. I was still holding Luis's wallet in my left hand. I gave him the wallet, took the Charter Arms, stuck the Smith and Wesson into my pocket, aimed the new pistol, and pulled the trigger.

It went bang, like it was supposed to. Two feet from Luis's leg, dirt popped off the ground and spattered his jeans. He jerked galvanically and his pompadour suddenly unfolded into shiny black spikes. '*Jesus!*'

Daniel Begay said sadly, 'That's not very good. He's only four feet away. You want me to do it?'

'*It was Pablo*,' Luis said in a sudden wheeze. I think he was trying to shout, but you can't shout very well when you're lying on your belly.

'Pablo who?' I asked him.

He said nothing. His body was stiff and still. He was probably wondering what had happened to his toughness, probably trying to gather it back together.

I fired again, and this time the dirt kicked up between his legs.

He arched his head back, his eyes squeezed together. '*Jesus Christ, man!*'

'Pablo who?'

Holding himself immobile, his head still raised, he said, 'Pablo Arguelles, in El Paso. He gave me two hundred to come up here and watch you. Until Monday, he said. Let him know where you went.'

'Where'd you pick me up? Office or house?'

'Your house.'

I had given no one in El Paso my home address. But it was listed with my phone number.

'Why Monday?'

He shook his head and the black spikes of hair wobbled. 'How the hell do I know? Pablo's crazy. He tells me to do something, I do it.'

I fired the gun again. This time I missed by only a couple of inches. I was getting the unfamiliar pistol sighted in.

Under the windbreaker, the muscles of his shoulders were bunched together. 'It's the *truth*, man, I swear it on my *mother*!'

'Tell me about Alice Wright.'

He cocked his head. 'Who?'

'Alice Wright. In El Paso.'

'Never heard of her, man. I swear it.'

'Why did the three of you come after me in El Paso?'

'That was only business, man. Fifty bucks apiece, me and Ramon, if we helped Pablo bust you some. That was all, man, just bust you, not kill you or nothin'. Not really hurt you, you know?'

'Why bust me?'

'I dunno. Pablo says let's do it, so we do it.'

Pablo, like Ganado, was evidently a Leader of Men.

'What about the tyres on my car?'

'What tyres, man? Whatta you mean?'

Maybe someone else had done the tyres. 'What'd you do Thursday night? After you rousted me at the motel?'

'Went over to Juarez. To a whorehouse there.'

'All three of you?'

'Yeah.'

'What's Ramon's last name?'

'Gonzalez. Ramon Gonzalez.'

'What time did you go over to Juarez?'

'Eleven, eleven-thirty.'

'What time did you get back?'

'Not till Friday morning. Ten o'clock.'

'You know, Luis, it wouldn't be nice for you to lie to me.'

'It's the truth, man. I swear to you.'

'When did Pablo send you up to follow me?'

'Last night.'

'Pablo's in El Paso now?'

He lowered his head, shook it. 'No, no, man, up in Arizona somewhere—I don't know where, honest to God. He just told me Arizona, that's all he said.'

'He's there alone?'

He shook his head. 'With Ramon.'

'What're they doing in Arizona?'

'I dunno. I swear it, I dunno.'

'What kind of car is he driving?'

'I dunno, man. The Chevy, the one I'm driving, that's Pablo's. He was gonna rent a car.'

I said, 'If you don't know where Pablo is, how do you keep in touch with him?'

'I call his number, man, in El Paso, and I leave a message on his tape machine. Like I leave a phone number where

I'm at. He can call up from anywhere and find out what's on the machine.'

'He uses a beeper or a regular phone to get the messages?'

'Regular phone.'

'Did you ever see this tape machine? Do you know what brand it is?'

Some of the cheaper beeperless answering machines require only a single tone as a code to retrieve the messages. If you want to break into one of these machines over the phone line, and pilfer the messages, it doesn't take you long to run through the digits, zero to nine.

Luis shook his head. 'No, man, I never been to Pablo's house.'

'What's his address?'

'I dunno, man. I dunno. Somewhere on the west side of El Paso.'

'What's the phone number?'

He told me.

I turned to Daniel Begay. 'Is there a CB radio in the Malibu?'

He shook his head.

I asked him, 'How far is the nearest telephone?'

Daniel Begay said, 'About twenty miles. At Crownpoint.'

This dirt track was a side road off the paved highway between Thoreau and Crownpoint. We'd led Luis and the Malibu from the interstate at Thoreau.

I nodded. I turned to the Malibu. Because of the bend in the road, the car was broadside to me. I fired twice and hit each time, blowing both tyres.

Mighty fine shooting, pilgrim.

Given ten years I could do it again.

The Charter Arms was empty, but Luis hadn't moved. Maybe he hadn't been counting. Maybe he realized that he couldn't get to me before I had the Smith and Wesson out. I handed the empty pistol to Daniel and took out the Smith.

I said to Daniel, 'Could you go to the Subaru and start it for me? I'll be right there.'

He gave me Luis's wallet, nodded, and turned and walked slowly off.

I said to Luis, 'I'll leave your wallet a hundred yards down the road. When I honk the horn, you come get it. Not before. Crownpoint's to the right when you hit the paved highway. Shouldn't take you more than five or six hours to reach it. Be a nice refreshing walk, this time of day. When you get back here, and get the tyres fixed, you know what you do?'

'What?' His voice had changed: a wary hope had strengthened it.

'You drive back to El Paso.'

'Right, man, right. I'll do it, man. I will. I swear it.'

'Because I don't like you, Luis. Are we clear on that?'

'Right, sure, man. Absolutely.'

CHAPTER 19

A hundred yards down the road, I stopped the Subaru, put it into park, and opened Luis's wallet. I didn't know what I was looking for—a scorecard, maybe, so I could learn who the players were—but whatever it was, it wasn't there.

A hundred and fifty dollars in tens and twenties, a gas station credit card, a folded red cocktail napkin with a woman's name and phone number written on it in smudged ballpoint, a battered foil-wrapped Ramses condom. Luis obviously led a rich and rewarding life.

I tossed the wallet to the side of the road, put the Subaru back into gear, honked the horn once, and drove off.

'Thanks for the help,' I said to Daniel Begay. 'You sounded pretty bloodthirsty back there.'

He smiled his small smile. 'I got some Apache blood, maybe. What did you tell him back there?'

'I told him to go back to El Paso.'

He bounced once as the car hit a bump in the road. 'You think he will?'

'I doubt it. Right now he's convincing himself that I'm gutless.'

He nodded. 'Because you didn't kill him.'

'Yeah.'

I was moving the Subaru as quickly as I could over the washboard road, up and down the hills, and the car was fighting me, steering wheel spasmodic as we slammed into ruts and gullies.

Daniel Begay bounced once, twice, three times. He turned to me. 'We're in a hurry?'

'I'm not very happy,' I said, 'with the idea of Luis's two friends prowling around Arizona. And I'm beginning to worry about the trading post's phone not working. Those two could be there. Or they could be at Peter Yazzie's. I think we should get back to the interstate as soon as we can.'

He nodded. 'I got a nephew on the Navajo police. I could call him from Thoreau and ask him to have someone go over to the trading post.'

It was a good idea, and I said so, but as things turned out, we didn't have to wait until Thoreau to find the Navajo police. They found us. While we were roaring down the Crownpoint-Thoreau road at ninety miles an hour.

I heard the siren, looked in the rearview mirror, and saw the patrol car. I pulled the Subaru off the road and put it in park.

The cop took his time getting out of the cruiser. Waiting, probably, for the radio report on the Subaru's tag. Finally he opened the door, stepped out, and began to walk towards us with that slow, rolling gait they learn at police academies everywhere. Swagger 101.

Daniel Begay was twisted round in his seat to look out the rear window. 'It's okay,' he said. 'I know him.'

Unsmiling, big for a Navajo, the cop came to the window and looked down at me through a pair of mirrored sunglasses. They learn how to wear those at the academy, too. 'Licence and registration,' he said.

'Boyd?' said Daniel Begay.

The cop lowered his head, took off the sunglasses, and peered into the interior. I leaned back against the seat. The cop said, 'Mr Begay?' And then said somethig guttural in Navajo.

Daniel Begay returned the greeting, if that's what it was, and then said in English, 'Boyd, we're in kind of a hurry. This is an emergency.'

Boyd glanced at me, his face expressionless.

'This is my friend Joshua,' said Daniel Begay. 'He's helping me out.'

Asking him to clarify this didn't seem like a good idea just then.

Boyd nodded, tapped the brim of his hat with his index finger. I nodded back. He turned to Daniel Begay, put his large brown hand on the door of the Subaru. 'What's the trouble, Mr Begay?'

'We can't get through to the Ardmore Trading Post. Something's wrong with the phone out there.'

Boyd shook his head. 'Not the phone. The lines. Someone used a chainsaw on the poles. Three of them.' He shrugged his square shoulders. 'Kids, I guess.'

I said, 'When did it happen?'

He glanced at Daniel Begay, then back at me. He said, 'This morning sometime.'

'Is everything all right at the trading post?'

'Far as I know.' He started to say something, then frowned. Remembering that he was talking cop business with a civilian.

Daniel Begay had seen the hesitation. He said, 'It's pretty important, Boyd.'

Boyd shrugged again. Ignoring me, he told Daniel, 'Yesterday they sent somebody out there from Window Rock.' The headquarters of the Navajo Tribal Police was in Window Rock.

'Why?' Daniel Begay asked.

'Some homicide investigation down in Texas. El Paso cops wanted to know if the victim made a phone call to the trading post on Thursday night.'

'Did she?' I asked.

He glanced at me and frowned again. He was clearly not enjoying this. 'Yeah,' he told Daniel. 'She was trying to locate some old guy here on the Reservation.'

'Peter Yazzie,' I said.

Boyd looked at me again and blinked. He turned to Daniel Begay. Sadly he said, 'Mr Begay, I hope sometime you're gonna tell me what's going on here.'

'I promise, Boyd. Who answered the call at the trading post?'

'The son.' I thought I heard something in his voice—disapproval, maybe, or distaste.

Daniel Begay said, 'He tell the woman where Peter Yazzie lives?'

'Yes, sir. He did.'

Daniel Begay nodded. He turned to me. 'We should go straight through to Hollister. To Peter Yazzie's house.'

I frowned. 'I thought you had to be in Gallup.'

He shook his head. 'Not important now. Boyd? Could you ask Window Rock to send someone over to the trading post again? To make sure everyone's okay?'

Boyd nodded. 'When do I find out what's happening here, Mr Begay?'

'Soon, I think. I'll call you on the phone. And whoever goes over there, could they find out if anyone else been asking about Peter Yazzie?

'Could be two men,' I said. 'Hispanic. Pablo Arguelles and Ramon Gonzalez. Arguelles is a big guy with a moustache.' The moustache, barely visible under the stocking mask back at my motel, was the only distinguishing feature I could give him.

Boyd was frowning, balancing his loyalty to the Navajo police against whatever loyalty he owed Daniel Begay.

Daniel Begay said, 'And could someone check on Peter Yazzie in Hollister?'

Boyd shook his head. 'Hollister is state cops. Or the Duke County Sheriff.'

'You could call someone at the state cops and ask 'em to check.'

'What do I tell them for a reason?'

'Tell 'em the murder in Texas. Peter Yazzie could be a witness, maybe. And he could maybe be in big trouble.'

Boyd nodded sadly. 'Okay, Mr Begay. You're gonna get back to me, right?'

'I will. We got to go now, Boyd. The road clear up ahead?'

Boyd nodded. 'No more Navajo patrols. State cops on the interstate.'

'Thanks, Boyd.' He turned to me. 'Let's go.'

Boyd frowned again and stepped away from the car. I shifted into drive and put the Subaru back on the highway. As the wagon picked up speed, I turned to Daniel Begay and asked him, 'Daniel, do you have a secret identity? Are you really Batman?'

He smiled his small smile, and he shrugged. 'Boyd just likes me, I guess.'

Hollister, Arizona, and Peter Yazzie were at least a hundred and thirty miles away. If that was where they were going, Pablo and Ramon had a big head start on us.

I was worried now, and the worry made me feel that the Subaru was only loafing along, despite the ninety I could read on the speedometer. The barren, unrelenting sameness of the landscape only increased the sense of sluggish, and probably futile, progress. It was as though we were driving in slow endless circles around the same empty arroyos, the same ragged hills.

I tried bringing the car up to ninety-five, but the tyres needed aligning and the station wagon began to shiver as though it had malaria. If I kept that up, we'd fall apart before we hit the interstate. I eased back to ninety.

Daniel Begay turned and asked me, 'You think it was the two Mexicans who cut down the telephone poles?'

'Could be,' I said. 'They're in Arizona somewhere. They may be trying to stop everyone from finding out about Peter

Yazzie. They didn't realize that the El Paso cops have already gotten through to the trading post.'

'They must've brought those chainsaws with 'em. From Texas.'

I nodded. 'If they bought them around here, or rented them, they would've drawn attention to themselves.' I smiled at him. 'You want a job as a private detective?'

'Don't they know we got cars up here? Cutting off the phone, that's not gonna stop people from knowing things.'

'No, but it'll slow the process down. That may be all they want—to get to Peter Yazzie before anyone else does.'

'How do they know about Peter Yazzie?'

'Alice Wright knew something, something about Yazzie, and I think that was what got her killed. She must've talked to Yazzie on Thursday night, after she called the trading post. And maybe she made the mistake of telling the killer what she knew.'

'But the other Mexican, the one in the Chevy, he said they weren't in El Paso when she was killed.'

'Maybe they weren't. Those three are hired meat. They're following orders. Whoever's giving the orders is the one who killed Alice Wright.'

'And now he wants them to kill Peter Yazzie.'

I nodded. 'Maybe,' I said. 'I hope not, but maybe.'

He sat there quietly for a moment. Then he said, 'Maybe the state cops, maybe they'll get to Peter Yazzie in time.'

'Maybe,' I said. But I knew that if Pablo and Ramon had cut the Ardmore phone lines early this morning, they could have been in Winslow before noon.

Daniel Begay said, 'This could be all wrong, too. Maybe it was only kids who cut down the poles.'

I nodded. 'Could've been.'

But I don't think either of us believed that.

I didn't want to stop at Thoreau, but the Subaru needed fuel. I whipped into the gas station, handed a twenty to Daniel Begay, asked him to get the tank filled, then trotted over to the pay phone with my notebook. I dialled the

Ardmore Trading Post. Busy. Dialled Peter Yazzie. No answer. I flipped through the notebook, found Grober's home number in El Paso, and dialled that.

When he answered, his voice was jolly: 'Hello *hello*.' I heard a woman giggling in the background.

'Phil, this is Joshua, listen to me—'

'Hey, Josh, how ya doin', buddy? Connie's over here, we're having ourselves a Crisco party.'

'Phil—'

''Cept we're not usin' Crisco. Nasty stuff. Fattening, too. Connie brought some coconut oil. We both smell like macaroons.' I heard the woman giggle again, and then Grober say, *'Whoops.'* The phone clunked against something.

'Phil?'

Laughter in the background, Grober's and the woman's.

'Phil?'

'Hey, Josh.' A bit breathless. 'Phone got away from me there. Slippery little sucker. What's up? Whoa! Connie!'

'Phil, goddammit, listen to me. You have a pen there?'

'Sure, you betcha. No need to get your bowels in an uproar. Connie, hand me the pen, honey. Right. *Yeeoww!*' Laughter from Grober, wild feminine giggles off to the side. *'Hand* it to me, I said. Jeeze, no respect at all. Gimme that. 'Kay, Josh, whatta you got? I think this thing'll still write.' More giggles.

'Take this down.' I gave him Pablo Arguelles's number. 'I'm in Arizona. There's a guy up here using his answering machine in El Paso as a cut-out. The machine's at that number. The name is Pablo Arguelles.'

'Arguelles. 'Kay. You got an address?'

'Somewhere near Fort Bliss.'

''Kay, I'll find him. Hold *on*, honey. So whatta we talkin' here, Josh? You want a tap?'

Driving along the highway, I had in fact considered having him tap Pablo's phone. It might be useful to know who left Pablo his messages, and what was said. A tap would mean a break-and-enter for Grober, but he was good at those. And when he learned what kind of answering machine Pablo was using, he'd know what codes it required. He could erase any messages off the machine, from his own phone, before Pablo had a chance to retrieve them.

But getting into the house might take time—nearby neighbours, maybe a wife or a girlfriend living inside. And I didn't want Pablo and Ramon, in front of me, to link up with Luis, behind me.

'No,' I told him. 'Just cut the line.'

'Will do, Josh. Handle it first thing in the morning.'

'Phil, there's some serious hurry-up involved in this. You've got to do it now.'

'Holy *shit*, Connie, that's *cold*!' A delighted feminine squeal. 'C'mon now, honey, cut it out.' Laughter from both of them. 'Josh?'

'Phil, this is important.'

''Kay, okay. I'll do it now. But I got to charge you double-time. Nothing personal, Josh, but it's the weekend.'

'Fine, Phil, whatever. One other thing.'

'What? *Whoa!* '

'Two more names. Ramon Gonzalez, Luis Salamanca. See if you can find out anything about them.'

''Kay. Arguelles, Gonzalez, Salamanca. Sounds like the Dodger lineup. Listen, I got those police reports for you. Mailed 'em up yesterday. Express. You should of got 'em today.'

'Thanks, Phil. I've got to go. I'll be in touch.'

'Yeah,' he said, 'so will Connie.' He laughed.

I hung up and ran back to the Subaru. Daniel Begay was already in the car.

Back on the interstate, I glanced at my watch. Six o'clock. An hour and a half to Hollister, if I pushed it. And if I managed to avoid the state police.

We were heading into a spectacular Southwest sunset, one of those accidents of windblown dust and billowing cloud and brilliant angled light that sweep across the entire horizon and look like a film director's gaudy notion of the Dawn of Creation.

To me, just then, the streaks and smears of carmine and crimson made the clouds look as though they'd been stained with blood.

CHAPTER 20

By a quarter to eight, when we reached Hollister, the sun had long since set. The stars were out and the desert air was chill.

Daniel Begay knew the street where Peter Yazzie lived— he seemed to know every inch of land between here and Santa Fe—and he gave me directions as I drove. Probably I would've been able to find the house on my own. In a town the size of Hollister, there weren't a lot of wrong turns.

The house was a small square building, cinderblock plastered to masquerade as adobe. It was unlighted and it looked abandoned. There were no cars in the street in front, and none in the driveway. We left the Subaru, walked up the steps. Outside the car, the cold in the air reached all the way to the bone. Daniel was wearing his grey wool coat; I'd gotten a turtleneck out of the suitcase and put it on beneath my windbreaker.

Daniel Begay knocked on the door. No one answered. He knocked again. Same thing.

He turned to me. 'I know some people. Not far from here. Maybe they know where he is.'

'Is there a bar or a restaurant in town? A place where people hang out?'

'The Coyote Tavern.' He frowned slightly. 'Not a very good place.'

'Why don't you drop me off and I'll ask around in there. You can take the car and look up your friends. It'll save us some time.'

He nodded. He may have smiled. I wasn't sure.

*

I realized, as soon as I walked into the dim interior of the Coyote Tavern, that I was the odd man out. For one thing, I wasn't wearing a cowboy hat.

Like everyone else, I was wearing jeans and boots. But my jeans didn't look as though I'd been born wearing them, and my boots didn't look as though I'd be wearing them when I died. Unless I happened to die tonight. There were two or three men at the bar, turning to check me out, who looked like they wouldn't mind arranging that.

Except for the bartender, everyone in the place was an Indian.

Cigarette smoke lay in blue streamers beneath the low wooden ceiling. Willie Nelson's 'Whisky River' was pumping from the jukebox. There were five or six Formica-topped tables scattered around, all of them occupied. I saw only two women in the crowd, both young, both heavy-set, both with the gleaming round faces of Eskimo maidens. I walked across the room and felt glances probe along my back. Here and there, the soles of my boots met something sticky on the black linoleum floor.

At the low-slung bar there were two empty stools. To the left of these, five men sat hunched, ignoring me now—they had decided, apparently, that I represented no immediate threat. To the right, three more men. The drink of choice seemed to be the boilermaker. A shot of whisky, a bottle of Coors.

The bartender was an ageing biker. Big and bearded and brawny, his grizzled long brown hair tied behind his neck in a pony tail, he stood leaning against the back-bar below a lighted Coors sign with his thick arms crossed over his barrel chest. He wore a black leather vest over a black Harley Davidson T-shirt.

The black T-shirt reminded me of Luis, back on the Crownpoint road. I wondered how he was doing. If he'd managed to hitch a ride, he could be in Crownpoint already. He could already be making arrangements with Pablo.

Had Grober shut off Pablo's telephone?

The bartender's glance flicked to the bandages on my

hands, flicked to the bruises on my face, and his eyes showed nothing. He'd seen bruises and bandages before. He unfolded his arms and put his hands along the edge of the bar as he leaned towards me. He nodded. 'What'll it be?'

I was tempted to order a Brandy Alexander. With a maraschino cherry. And maybe one of those little paper parasols.

I told him Jack Daniels on the rocks and a glass of water.

He pushed himself away from the counter and went to make it.

I moved the stool aside and stepped up to the bar.

The place needed a good cleaning. The bar top was tacky, the air held the sour smell of stale beer. I was hopeful, at any rate, that the sour smell was only the smell of stale beer.

The bartender set the drink in front of me, set the glass of water to its side.

I gave him a five-dollar bill. He turned to the cash register behind him, tapped a key, and the drawer popped out. He scooped out some cash, pushed the drawer shut.

He hadn't rung up the sale. Either he was the owner and scamming the IRS or he was stealing.

He put my change on the bar. Two bills, two quarters. I took a sip of the bourbon, slid a bill towards him, and asked, 'You know a guy named Peter Yazzie?'

He shrugged. 'I know a lot of guys.'

It's the movies. They give us all a swell selection of snappy patter.

'This one's a Navajo,' I said. 'An older man. In his seventies.'

He put his hands along the edge of the bar again. He looked down at the bar, looked back up at me. 'What're you? Cop?'

I shook my head. 'Private investigator. Look. It's important. I need to get in touch with him.'

He shook his head. 'Sorrry, guy. Can't help any.'

I was fairly sure that if the bar were empty, if no one were there to hear him—and, naturally, if I'd slipped him some more paper—he would've told me.

I said, 'Anyone else been asking about Yazzie?'

He shook his head.

I took another sip of bourbon. The first one had gone off in my stomach like a claymore: I hadn't eaten anything since early this afternoon, before we left Santa Fe.

I asked him, 'What time did you come on?'

'Seven.'

'Is the day guy around?'

'Nope.'

I nodded. 'Thanks.'

He nodded, picked up the bill, and sauntered to the other end of the bar.

I turned to my right. The old man sitting there was looking up at me from beneath a straw cowboy hat with a curved brim. Clouded brown eyes, toothless gums.

'You know Peter Yazzie?' I said.

He shook his head. 'Don't know nobody,' he said. 'Don't want to.'

I was making fine progress.

'Hey,' someone said behind me. I turned.

It was a round red face he had, jowly, pockmarked, shiny with sweat, and almost level with my own. The cowboy hat was perched at the back of his broad head. His short black hair was matted in strands to his forehead. His narrow eyes were unfocused and rimmed with red. A wispy moustache shaded his overhanging upper lip. Over his denim shirt he wore a vest of stained, battered sheepskin. His hands were empty. He was large.

'Whaddy you want with Peter Yazzie?' he said. He was perhaps thirty years old, and from his breath he'd been drinking steadily for at least twenty-five of those.

'I want to talk to him,' I said.

'Yeah?' He was weaving very slightly, forward and back. He narrowed his eyes, cocked his head, and said, 'I think you should get the fuck outta here.'

I glanced at the bartender. He was still down at the other end of the bar. He appeared to like it down there.

I looked at my new best friend.

White men had plundered his land and raped and robbed and killed his ancestors. White multinational industry was still pillaging the land as we spoke and churning carcinogens into the air above it. A white government agency supervised his life from cradle to grave, treating him and his people at best like wayward children and at worst like animals.

But it had been a rough week. I was in a bad mood. And the booze I'd taken on an empty stomach was already providing its lift, its sham sense of competence and power.

'I don't think so,' I said.

He looked me up and down. His eyes narrowed again as his glance found mine. 'I'm drunk,' he announced.

'Yeah,' I said.

'Right now, you could take me.'

'Yeah,' I said.

'Me maybe, but what about them?' He waved his arm loosely towards the rest of the crowd.

Most of them were busy talking, either ignoring us or pretending to; and few of them could hear us over the honky-tonk. But at one nearby table, four old men regarded us with mild detached interest, like Nobel Prize winners watching the opening round of *Jeopardy*.

'What about *them*,' he said again.

I turned back to him. 'I'll put my wagons in a circle.'

It took a while—almost anything would have taken him a while—but then suddenly he was laughing. 'Wagons,' he said, and laughed some more. 'Good one. Wagons.' He shook his head. 'Good one.' He clapped me on the shoulder. 'Wagons. You're okay, you know?'

He turned to the left, nodding, and addressed the rest of the bar: 'Hey, he's okay.'

No one was thrilled. No one offered to adopt me into the tribe.

His arm still over my shoulder, he said, 'Hey, Wagons, lemme buy you a drink.' That breath could've melted chrome.

'No, thanks,' I said. I showed him the Jack Daniels. 'I've got one.'

'Well, lemme buy *me* a drink.' He turned to the bartender. 'Hey! Jerry! Shot of Seagram's!' He turned back to me. 'You're the second guy today been askin' about Peter Yazzie.'

His name was John. He didn't tell me his last name. Possibly he'd forgotten what it was. He did tell me that he'd been in the bar all day, which came as no surprise, and that the man asking about Peter Yazzie had arrived at around two o'clock. 'Big Mexican guy, a mean-lookin' dude with a moustache.'

Pablo. He *had* come here, and he had beaten us by a full five hours.

Where the hell was Peter Yazzie? And what had he said to Alice Wright?

The day bartender, John said, told Pablo that he didn't know where Peter was, but that Peter's cousin, William, might be able to help. John wasn't sure, but he thought Pablo slipped the bartender some cash and got William's address.

Apparently, the day man had less scruples than Jerry, the biker. Or maybe just less witnesses.

'Where does William live?' I asked John.

He waved a hand vaguely. 'North.'

I didn't push it.

John said, 'But if old Peter don' wanna get found, he ain' gonna get found.' He nodded with a drunk's slow, deliberate certitude. 'No way, Wagons. No way. If he's up in them mountains up there, ain' no way nobody gonna find him. Not any damn Mexican, that's for sure.'

'Why would he go up into the mountains?'

He frowned into his empty shot glass. 'Didn' say he did. Didn' say he didn'.' He looked at me, his head a bit unsteady on his neck, and suddenly he scowled. 'You ask an awful lot of questions.'

Maybe we wouldn't be blood brothers after all.

Just then, off to my left, a quiet voice said, 'John.'

We both turned, John a little more slowly than I

Daniel Begay stood there, hands on the knob of his cane.

John's face lit up. 'Hey! *Hosteen* Begay!'

Braced against his cane, expressionless, Daniel Begay leaned towards him, looking up into the round face, and said something in Navajo. His voice was low and very soft. I was probably the only other person in the bar who could hear it.

John's face fell. His shoulders sank. 'Well,' he began, but didn't finish.

Daniel Begay was still speaking, softly, firmly.

John nodded. He looked at Daniel Begay. He nodded again, abashed, like a guilty child who's been told to go stand in the corner.

Daniel Begay stepped back. Without another word, head lowered, John walked away from the bar, across the room, and out the front door. It seemed to me that the people in the bar devoted a lot of energy to ignoring this.

Daniel Begay moved into the space John had left at the bar. The big bartender, Jerry, was already there, leaning forward deferentially. 'Get you something, Mr Begay?'

'A Coca-Cola,' Daniel said.

Jerry shuffled off to get it. Daniel Begay watched him, and for the first time since I'd known him I thought I saw displeasure on his face. Nothing much: just a faint contraction around the eyes and mouth.

I told him, 'Pablo was here.'

He nodded. 'He was at Peter Yazzie's house today. Someone saw him and the other man.'

Ramon.

I asked him, 'Did anyone see what kind of car were they driving?'

'A Ford. Blue.'

Jerry returned with the glass of Coke and set it before Daniel Begay. 'On the house, Mr Begay.'

Daniel Begay nodded. 'Thank you.'

As Jerry left, Daniel Begay watched him once more.

'You don't like him?' I said, and nodded to Jerry.

He shrugged lightly. 'It's not him. He's okay, I guess. It's his job. He sells alcohol. It's a poison.'

I'd been about to take another sip of my bourbon. I decided it could wait.

I asked him, 'What else did your friends have to say?'

He took a sip of his Coke. 'A sheriff's car went to Peter Yazzie's house on Friday night.'

'Asking questions, probably, for the El Paso police,' I said.

Daniel Begay nodded. 'After they went, he packed his stuff into his truck and he left.'

'The sheriff must've told him about Alice Wright's death. Maybe Yazzie thought that the information he gave her was what got her killed. Maybe he thought he was next.'

Daniel Begay nodded. 'Maybe.'

I said, 'Do your friends know where he went?'

'He's got a cabin in the mountains. Up north of here. Probably there.'

'How far is it?'

'Fifty miles, about.'

'You find out where it is?'

He nodded.

'Where?'

'I got to show you.'

I said, 'Daniel, I think it's probably a better idea if you stay here.'

He said, 'It's hard to find. Impossible.'

No small smile now. He planned to come.

I didn't like it, but there are a lot of things I don't like, and I can't do much about any of them. I said, 'John told me that Peter Yazzie has a cousin. William.'

Daniel Begay nodded. 'I know.'

'You know where he lives?'

He nodded. 'I found out.'

'The other bartender, the day guy, told Pablo about him. I'd guess that Pablo went there. I think we should check him out. See what Pablo had to say.'

He nodded.

*

We stopped at the local Thriftway and I bought some sandwiches and two containers of coffee. Daniel Begay wanted to pay for it. I reminded him that I owed him a meal. He nodded. We drank the coffee as I drove.

A bit north of town, I followed Daniel's directions and left the highway for a dirt side road.

William Yazzie's house was the last one on the road, perhaps a hunded yards beyond the nearest neighbour's. It was a small, one-storey frame building, ramshackle, sagging slightly to the right, like a wall-mounted picture that had been brushed by a negligent shoulder. No lights were on, inside or out. Weeds tufted the plot of rocky ground in front. I pulled into the driveway, behind an old Dodge pickup.

We left the Subaru and crossed the yard. Daniel Begay knocked on the door. The same thing happened here that had happened at Peter Yazzie's house. Nothing.

Daniel Begay cocked his head and frowned. 'I smell something,' he said. He opened his mouth slightly, as though tasting the air. He closed his mouth, sniffed lightly, once, twice. He turned to me. 'Gas.'

I squatted down by the door, put my hand near its base, fanned the hand, and swept air up towards my face.

Gas.

CHAPTER 21

I stood up. 'Come on, Daniel,' I said, and took a backward step. 'Away from the house.'

He looked at me. 'He's in there.'

'I know. We'll get to him. But we've got to do it right. Come on.'

He walked beside me to the station wagon, turning once to look back over his shoulder at the house.

'In the car,' I told him.

We both got in and I started the engine. I backed out of

the driveway and drove in reverse about thirty feet up the road, until I thought it was safe.

It was a guess. I had no idea how far the debris might be thrown if the house went up.

I leaned in front of Daniel Begay, popped the glove compartment, fumbled around inside until I found the Tekna flashlight and my leather gloves. I twisted the top of the flashlight. Still working. I put on the gloves.

I said to Daniel, 'It's probably better if you're outside the car. On the side opposite the house.'

Lips tightly pressed together, he nodded.

We both got out. Daniel Begay circled the Subaru.

'I mean it,' I told him. 'Stay here.'

He said, 'Joshua.'

I think this was the first time he'd actually called me by name.

'Yeah?'

'You know what you're doing?'

'I hope so.'

I went back to the house.

There were two double-hung windows facing the street. I chose the one to the right of the front door, turned on the flashlight, swung the bright white beam around the room. Saw an old armchair with padding swelling from its seams. An old swayback love seat. A cheap fibreboard coffee table.

Nothing that looked like a person.

I examined the latch on the inside of the window. It wasn't set. All I had to do was push up on the sash. And pray it didn't create a spark.

It shouldn't.

I pressed upward. Nothing. I tried pulling down on the upper window. Nothing. Both had been painted shut.

Hell with this.

I smashed the butt of the flashlight against the glass, jerked my hand away. The window shattered and a sickening reek came tumbling from the innards of the house. The gas was piled up to the ceiling. No one inside could possibly be alive.

I crossed over to the other window. The curtain was drawn, and I couldn't see inside. I smashed the glass. Again, the stench of gas billowed out.

I turned to Daniel Begay. He was standing beside the Subaru's front bumper. 'Daniel,' I called out. 'For God's sake, stay there. I'm going around back.'

He said nothing.

I circled the house. The door at the rear had a window. I played the beam of the flashlight around inside. A sink. Some cupboards. A small, narrow counter. And something on the floor, a large bundle in front of the oven. The bundle had legs, and they were folded up beneath it.

I smashed the window, stood back as the glass scattered. I ripped away a big shard still hanging from the frame, tossed it behind me. I pulled the glove from my left hand, took a deep breath, poked myself in. Using the flashlight, I looked for locks along the door. Only a pushbutton on the knob. I reached in, slowly turned the knob. The door opened.

Wanting very badly to hurry now but knowing that I couldn't, I eased the door open. Still holding my breath, I stepped cautiously, flat-footed and very slow, along the linoleum floor. I reached down to the bundle, found the neck, searched for a pulse with my fingertips. There was none.

Gas was still sighing from the oven. I shifted the glove and the flashlight to my left hand, turned the knob off with my right. I stepped back across the linoleum and outside, leaving the door open behind me.

I let out my breath, sucked in a lungful of air. It was tainted with the stink of gas.

My left hand was sticky. I shone the flashlight on it. Something black and shiny. Blood. I thought for a moment that I'd cut myself at the window. Then realized, with a small involuntary shiver, that it belonged to the man on the floor.

I wiped it off on some weeds.

I walked around to the front of the house. Daniel Begay was on the front yard, walking towards me.

'He's dead,' I told him.

He nodded, and started to walk past me.

'Give it a minute,' I said. 'There's still gas in there.'

He stopped. Looked at me. 'They killed him.'

'Yeah.'

He nodded again. His face had no expression.

For five minutes neither of us spoke. I don't know what Daniel Begay was thinking, but I know that I was blaming myself. I should've called the local cops this morning, should've given them everything I had. They might've known that Peter Yazzie had a cousin. Might've warned him.

Finally, silently, Daniel Begay walked of towards the rear of the house. I followed him.

Inside the kitchen door, he stood there for a moment. The room still smelled of gas, but most of the stuff had dissipated. Safe now to turn on the overhead light. I flicked the switch.

Daniel Begay stepped forward to the body.

The police don't like things moved at a murder scene, especially the body. When Daniel gently began to lower the old man from his kneeling position to the floor, I almost said something.

But no one should have to spend his death huddled like that.

When Daniel Begay set the old man's bare shoulders on the linoleum, we both saw what Pablo and Ramon had done to him.

They had taken time with their work. The man was shirtless, and the cigarette burns covered his arms, his sunken chest, his face. Some of the burns were crusted over now, small round eyes open wide in horror. Some were still weeping serum and blood. They'd cut him, too, sliced him along the cheeks and along the stomach. When the cigarettes and the knives hadn't worked, they'd simply held his right hand into the flame of the stove-top burner. The clawed fingers were scorched, the flesh seared away.

Someone had given him a heavy blow along his right

temple. Probably just before they arranged him at the oven door.

Daniel Begay reached into his back pocket, took out a folded white handkerchief. He unfolded it carefully and laid it gently, almost ceremoniously, over the man's face.

He stood up. 'We got to go now,' he said. 'We got to get to Peter Yazzie.'

He was right. Peter Yazzie was the key.

I told him, 'We've got to call the cops first.'

He shook his head. 'That's the sheriff. He'll keep us until the state police come. They'll keep us too. Too much time. The body is still warm. They only left a while ago. If we hurry, we can maybe stop them.'

'What about the Navajo police? Can we call them? Have them get to Yazzie before we do?'

'Maybe. If someone is close enough.'

'All right. If there's a phone here, don't use it. The cops'll check outgoing calls. There was a gas station back on the highway. We'll call from there.'

He nodded. 'We got to go now.'

'One minute, Daniel. I'll be right back.'

It was in the living-room and it wasn't hard to find. I knew what I was looking for.

No one who saw William Yazzie's body could believe that he attempted suicide. The setup with the oven didn't make sense unless Pablo and Ramon had some way of obliterating those wounds.

It was a simple appliance timer, the kind you use to start the coffee perking automatically in the morning. They'd hooked it up between the wall outlet and the cord of a standup lamp. Maybe, although I doubted it, the timer had belonged to William Yazzie. More likely, Pablo or Ramon had driven back into town and picked it up at a hardware store. They'd stripped three inches of insulation from the lamp's cord, leaving the two wires bare. When the timer went off and sent current down the cord, the wires would short out. The spark would set off the gas. Boom.

The subsequent fire would make it impossible to tell that

William Yazzie had been burned before it broke out. The blow to the side of his head would likely be attributed to the explosion. If he were alive when they put him by the stove, and I thought he had been, then his lungs would be filled with gas.

A suicide, followed by an accidental explosion.

The timer was set to nine o'clock.

I looked at my watch. Eight forty-five.

If Daniel Begay and I had arrived only a little bit later, we'd have been as dead as William Yazzie.

Even with no gas in the room, the short circuit might start a fire. I tugged the timer from the outlet—carefully, using the edges of my fingertips so I wouldn't leave prints. Or smudge any that Pablo and Ramon might've left.

I was fairly certain that they hadn't left any. So far, Pablo was showing himself to be a good deal smarter than I would've thought. And a good deal more ruthless.

When I turned around, Daniel Begay was standing there, watching me. I explained the timer.

He nodded. His face still expressionless, he said, 'Bastards.'

I agreed. I very much wanted to meet Pablo and Ramon again.

Daniel Begay made his phone call from the gas station on the highway. It took a while. At last he clambered back into the Subaru, pulled the door shut, and nodded towards the north. 'We go that way.'

I wheeled the station wagon back on to the highway. 'Who'd you talk to?' I asked him.

'My nephew in the Navajo police.'

'He's going to send some people to Peter Yazzie's?'

'He says it's not good to use the Navajo police. He says they're gonna want to know about Peter Yazzie's cousin, and we could get in trouble with the sheriff in Hollister. For leaving the brother's house without calling him. He says you're a stranger here.'

'But you're not.

'No,' he said. 'I'm an Indian.' His face was unreadable. The sheriff apparently didn't care for Indians.

'Daniel,' I said, 'half the people in town heard me asking about Peter Yazzie and his cousin.'

He shook his head. 'My nephew will make some phone calls. No one will remember we were there.'

Indian Magic. A few phone calls and our trip to Hollister never happened. 'What about the bartender?'

'Someone will talk to him.'

'And what about Peter Yazzie? We could use some help with this, Daniel.'

'My nephew will come in the morning, as soon as he can. And he's got some friends near the cabin. Twenty miles away, maybe. He's calling them, to tell them to go over there.'

I frowned. 'You're sure we couldn't call Window Rock and get some more troops up there?'

He shook his head. 'There are some Navajo police I can't trust. They'd be glad to see me in trouble.' He shrugged. 'It's politics.'

It didn't seem reasonable that politics should get in the way of saving a life. But it was something, I knew, that had happened before, all over the world. And no doubt Daniel Begay knew what he was talking about.

I said, 'Will your nephew tell his friends to be careful?'

He nodded. 'They'll be careful.'

As long as we stayed on paved road, I kept the Subaru up to ninety. At night, travelling that fast is a calculated risk; your headlights can't reach far enough ahead for the speed. A cow, a couple of sheep, anything wandering across the highway can create a disaster. We were lucky.

About thirty miles north of Hollister, Daniel told me to slow down. We were in the foothills now, scrub pines on either side of the road, juniper and mesquite. The road I wanted, Daniel told me, was just ahead.

It led off to the right, up into the mountains, and it wasn't much more than a rocky path.

The Subaru was tired. I'd been pushing it hard all day, in four-wheel and in two. It's a good, reliable car, but it's not a tank. Now, as it bucked over the track, things were rattling around somewhere under the floorboards.

Fortunately, there hadn't been any snow lately. Under the trees, here and there, were still some crescent shelves of white left unmelted from the last storm, whenever that had been, and, along the road, some flat clumps of sooty ice looking hard as rock. But nothing that would affect the car.

Other things affected the car. The path narrowed and began to fray. Gullies crisscrossed it. A few times, when I rounded a turn, the headlights showed nothing but empty space where the side of the mountain plunged away from the edge. The gravel beneath us became pebbles, the pebbles became rocks, the rocks became small boulders. Every three or four hundred yards, the station wagon bottomed out, and twice I was afraid I wouldn't be able to keep going.

I turned to Daniel Begay. 'Daniel. You said that Ramon and Pablo were driving a Ford?'

He nodded, watching the road ahead. Since he'd told me about the men going to Peter Yazzie's cabin, neither of us had spoken.

'Regular car, not a Bronco?' I asked him.

He nodded.

'You need a four-wheel here,' I said. 'There's no way they could get a Ford through this. Not at night, anyway.'

Still facing forward, he said, 'They don't know that.'

'I think they do, Daniel. I think they got all the information they needed from William Yazzie.'

His mouth tightened and he turned to me. 'Yes?'

'How long would you say that William Yazzie had been dead?'

He frowned. 'A couple hours, maybe. He was still warm, and there was no heat in the house.'

'They set that timer for nine o'clock. If they left him there at six-thirty, seven, they could've set it for any time they wanted. It'd only take a half-hour or so for the gas to reach the living-room?'

'Yes?' he said again, waiting.

I steered the Subaru around a large irregular rock. 'Let's assume that they learned from William Yazzie that they couldn't get up here at night in the Ford. Maybe they plan to come tomorrow morning. They're in no real hurry, right? They don't know we're behind them.' They didn't if Grober had managed to clip Pablo's phone wire.

'Meanwhile,' I said, 'they've got time to kill. Maybe they're using it to set up an alibi for themselves. At nine o'clock, when the house was supposed to blow, they could've been sitting in a bar somewhere?'

'Where?'

'I don't know. Could be anywhere.'

He turned, looked out the windshield. He nodded. 'Maybe,' he said.

Maybe was right.

It wasn't much, but it was still a hope; and hope, just then, was something that both of us needed.

CHAPTER 22

'Here,' Daniel Begay told me.

How he knew, I'll never understand. So far as I could tell, it was just one more scant rutted path leading off through the trees, as so many had before.

I drove past it. Fifty yards beyond, the main track widened enough for me to pull over and park the Subaru. When I turned off the headlights, the narrow world before us—the brown gullied track, the ragged tree trunks, the green fans of pine needles—suddenly winked out.

I couldn't even see Daniel Begay sitting beside me. I asked him, 'How far down that path is the cabin?'

'A hundred yards, they said.'

'I'm going on foot. You stay here with the car.'

'He doesn't know you. And he thinks people are after him.'

'He's right.'

'He could shoot you by mistake. You can't speak Navajo, you can't tell him you're a friend.'

'I can tell him in English.'

'He won't believe you in English.'

'Daniel, Pablo and Ramon might be there already. I don't want anyone else getting hurt.'

'Me neither,' he said flatly. 'I got to come.'

I considered it. After driving along the length of that winding road in the Subaru, I was more convinced than ever that Pablo and Ramon couldn't have covered it at night in a standard Ford.

There was always the possibility, of course, that I was wrong. I'd been wrong before.

But Daniel, for his part, was right: He spoke Navajo and I didn't. And this was his country and not mine.

'Okay,' I said. 'Come on.'

From the glove compartment I took the flashlight and the Smith and Wesson.

I had a feeling that sooner or later we'd need more firepower than we had. I found myself wishing, briefly, that I was one of those honchos who made a point of carrying plenty of spare ammunition. A couple of speedloaders, maybe a box of loose rounds in the trunk. Maybe a bandelier. If I had been, I could've loaded the other pistol, the Charter Arms we'd taken from Luis this afternoon. It was empty now; I'd wasted all the bullets demonstrating what a bruiser I was.

We opened the doors quietly and stepped out of the car. The air was bleak and bitter. In the spring, with the thaw, it would smell of pine and wildflowers. Now it smelled of frozen earth, like a grave.

I eased my door shut and turned on the flashlight.

'No,' said Daniel Begay softly as he came around the front of the station wagon. 'No light. Your eyes will get used to the dark.'

Once again, he was right. I turned off the flashlight, stuck it in the pocket of my windbreaker.

After a few minutes, the shapes of individual trees began to form themselves, leaning away from the murk. There was no moon, but the sky was splashed with hardwhite stars, and by their light I could just make out the road, a darker blur against the surrounding night.

'Okay?' said Daniel Begay.

'Okay.' The pistol was in my hand. 'Let's go.'

We set off down the road. The dirt was hard-packed, crusted here and there with thin brittle patches of ice that snapped under foot.

From time to time I stumbled and sent rocks rattling. Twice I turned my ankle on invisible ruts. Daniel Begay moved along, cane swinging silently, as though he were pacing down Fifth Avenue in broad daylight.

We reached the pathway leading to Peter Yazzie's cabin.

'Flashlight?' said Daniel Begay.

I slipped it from my pocket, handed it to him.

He turned it on, narrowed his eyes, and aimed the beam towards the path.

It didn't take an Indian to see from the tyre marks that someone had diven off the main road on to the path. 'Two cars,' he said, and turned off the flashlight. 'One big, a truck. The other smaller. The smaller one came later.'

'The Ford?' I felt the flashlight as he touched it gently to my arm. I took it, put it back in my pocket.

'Too small,' he said. 'A Jeep, maybe.'

'Your nephew's friends?'

'Maybe,' he said. 'Maybe the Mexicans rented one.' That was a possibility I'd been arguing with myself. It seemed to me that renting a four-wheel was something they'd avoid—they wouldn't want any record left of their visit to this area.

So it seemed to me. Maybe it seemed different to Pablo and Ramon.

'Come,' said Daniel Begay.

Off to the right, an owl hooted. My fingers tightened on the butt of the pistol.

It was darker in here, branches thicker overhead, trees

crowding us on either side as the path sloped gently down the flank of the mountain. A battalion could have been hidden on either side of us and we'd never have seen them.

We moved slowly. The only sound was the scuffle of my boots against the ground, the occasional crunch of ice.

And then, fifty or sixty yards into the forest, I heard something else. Off to my right, not more than two or three yards away. The unmistakable metallic click of a gun's hammer being cocked.

I froze. So did Daniel Begay. We couldn't see whoever was out there, but obviously he could see us.

Daniel said something in Navajo.

From out of the darkness came a quiet voice: '*Hosteen* Begay?'

'Chee?' Daniel said.

I heard a faint rustle of underbrush, and then a man stepped on to the path.

In the dimness I couldn't distinguish his features, but he was short, only a bit taller than Daniel Begay. He moved with a tight, alert springiness, like someone young, in his twenties or early thirties. The rifle he held—a Winchester lever action, it appeared to be—was pointed directly at my stomach.

'This is my friend,' Daniel said, indicating me with a small nod. 'Joshua Croft.'

The rifle barrel lowered and the man nodded. 'Gary Chee,' he said.

I nodded back and realized that my mouth was dry. A slug from a 30–30 Winchester can bring down a grizzly bear.

'Is he there?' Daniel Begay asked Chee.

'His truck, but not him. There are tracks.' He said something swift and guttural in Navajo.

Daniel Begay turned to me. 'There's a place near here. A few miles away, in the forest. A religious place, you understand? A shrine. The tracks go towards there. He went by himself.'

I asked Chee, 'No sign of anybody else?'

'No.'

I asked Daniel Begay, 'Do you think he'll be coming back to the cabin?'

'Maybe.'

Chee said, 'There's food in the cabin. I looked with my flashlight. He's coming back.'

Daniel Begay asked him, 'You're alone?'

'My brother drove over to the Wide Ruins road. In case they come that way.'

Daniel Begay nodded, turned to me. 'The road back there, it goes on to the road to Wide Ruins.'

He turned back to Gary Chee. 'Your car is still here.' It wasn't a question: he'd seen two sets of tracks coming in, none going out.

Chee nodded.

Daniel told him. 'Drive back to the Hollister road. When they come, you follow behind. Far behind. Don't let them see you, okay? When they get near here, honk your horn. Then leave the car and track them on foot. Be very careful.'

No one asked my opinion and I didn't offer it. Daniel Begay's ancestors had been doing this sort of thing when mine were grumbling about the lord of the manor.

Chee nodded. He said something in Navajo.

Daniel nodded, spoke some Navajo back to him.

Chee nodded again, turned to me, nodded goodbye, and turned and set off down the path, towards the cabin, a vague black form disappearing into a deeper blackness.

I asked Daniel Begay, 'What did he say?'

'He wanted to know if he should kill them.'

I couldn't make out his features, but I didn't think they'd tell me anything if I could.

He said, 'I told him, yes, if he had no choice.'

Before we reached the cabin, Gary Chee drove past us in an ancient canvas-topped Jeep, heading back the way we'd come. Only his parking lights were on.

The cabin was small, perhaps fifteen feet by fifteen, built of chinked pine logs and covered with a low roof sloping from front to back. It sat at a slight angle to the path, its wooden door and two small windows facing a clearing where an old long-bed pickup was parked. Around it, and behind, tall ponderosas loomed like gigantic cowled monks, mute and still, black against a star-filled sky.

When we got there, Daniel Begay and I had another argument. He wanted to go off into the woods, alone, to find Peter Yazzie. To talk to him. I thought this was unwise: dangerous at night, especially for an older man with a bad leg.

'At least let me come along,' I said.

He shook his head. 'It's a shrine,' he told me. 'A holy place. You're not allowed. You're not allowed, even, to know where it is. I'm sorry.'

And so, as usual, Daniel Begay won.

He went off into the woods. I stumbled back through the darkness to the Subaru. I was feeling better now—we'd arrived ahead of Pablo and Ramon—but I still held the gun and I still listened carefully for sounds I didn't want to hear.

I drove the station wagon on to the road again and then slowly forward sixty or seventy yards until I found another side trail. This one looked like nobody had used it in months—the entrance was fringed with summer brush, stripped bare now, spidery and black. I drove the wagon over it, winced as something rocky scraped at the undercarriage, then drove on another thirty feet or so, stopping where the track made a turn that concealed the car from the main road.

I always keep a few things on the floor behind the front seat. The result of a Boy Scout background. I took the sleeping bag and the canteen, and the bag of sandwiches. I carried the bag and the strap of the canteen in my left hand and the sleeping bag tucked under my left arm. Which left my gun hand free while I walked back to the cabin.

The front door was locked, dead-bolted, but I didn't want to wait inside there anyway. Pablo and Ramon might drive directly down the pathway, park their car, and knock on the door, just like Avon ladies. As I'd told Daniel, so far as we knew they didn't realize we were in the neighbourhood. But if Grober *had* snipped Pablo's wires, cutting him off from Luis, from everyone, Pablo might be getting edgy about now. And edginess might make him tricky.

I wanted a spot that gave me a good all-around view of the approaches to the cabin. A good field of fire.

I found it on a small rise below a ponderosa pine twenty yards south of the cabin. From here I could see the path, which ran east to west; could see the front of the building and its southern sides. Unless Pablo and Ramon knew exactly where I was, if they came anywhere near the cabin they'd have to show themselves.

They wouldn't know where I was. In the shade of the ponderosa, so long as I remained still, I'd be invisible.

I spread out the sleeping bag on the far side of the rise, unzipped it partway, and climbed in, boots and windbreaker and all. I tugged the canteen and the sandwiches in after me—I might be here for a while, and I didn't want them freezing.

The ground was hard and lumpy, the air was painfully cold. I wasn't comfortable. But the goose-down bag was rated at zero degrees, Everest stuff, and I knew I could make it through the night. I settled in and began my wait.

The waiting is the hardest part. Lying there immobile as time becomes elastic and the seconds yawn slowly past. Growing drowsy, inattentive, until suddenly you jump, startled, at the rustle of bush, the gasp of wood creaking in the cold.

I ate a sandwich. Turkey and cheese. Hard to tell which was which. I drank some water.

Overhead, between the branches, I could see a patch of black sky clotted with stars. More stars in those few square feet than in an entire city sky. Each a sun; most with planets whistling round. And possibly, on some of those, oxygen, carbon, plants, animals, possibly even people. Maybe up there they were managing things better than we were down here.

Plenty of time to think when you're lying out in the cold.

I thought about Alice Wright and wondered what it was she'd told her murderer. Wondered *why* she'd told him anything.

I thought about William Yazzie and remembered him huddled in that pathetic lifeless heap before the oven. Remembered the suppurating open wounds along his weathered flesh. The knife slashes, the black congealing blood.

I thought about Daniel Begay. On his say-so, a Navajo cop had let us race illegally across the Reservation. After a phone call from his nephew, made on his behalf, a roomful of people were prepared to swear they'd never seen us. At his direction, with no hesitation, a young Navajo had set off to follow two very dangerous men. Asking only of Daniel whether it was okay to kill them.

Some people on the Navajo police, he'd told me, wouldn't mind seeing him in trouble. Why?

Who *was* he anyway?

From time to time, too, I thought about Rita. Remembered her crying, something I'd never seen her do before. Not even when she was shot. Not even when she learned her husband had died.

I wondered if she were all right. Wondered if she were awake right now, staring in the darkened room at the stiff angular silhouette of the wheelchair.

And I thought, quite a lot, about Pablo and Ramon.

Who had turned their key? Who had sent them up here?

If they arrived here before we left, or before Daniel Begay's Navajo-cop-nephew showed, I knew I'd probably have to kill them. Or try to. They likely wouldn't leave me any choice.

I don't care for the idea of taking a life. No one's ever mistaken me for God.

I hoped it wouldn't come to that. I told myself they wouldn't start up the dirt road until dawn. Told myself they'd be coming from the west, the same way Daniel and I had come. Told myself that in the Ford they'd take at least two or three hours to get here. Told myself that Daniel Begay would be back soon with Peter Yazzie, and that all of us could take off to the east, towards the Wide Ruins road, before Pablo and Ramon turned up. Told myself that if they *did* turn up sooner, Gary Chee's horn would warn us.

I was wrong about almost all of this.

CHAPTER 23

Rita said, 'What's the matter, Joshua?'

I said, 'I'm getting too old for this shit, Rita.'

We were walking near Diablo Canyon along the bank of the Rio Grande. Wild grasses whispered at our ankles; the river giggled and chortled. To the north-east, beyond the brown expanse of water, beyond the tawny sandbars and the shimmering eddies where sunlight flashed, beyond the green blur of cottonwoods, a single flat white cloud lay impaled on the grey peaks of Bandelier.

My shoulders were hunched, my hands were in my pockets. Rita held on to my arm. She wore a blue silk blouse, a long black skirt.

She smiled. 'Too old?'

'You know you're too old,' I said, 'when everyone you meet reminds you of someone else. When everything you do, you've done before.'

She laughed lightly, head against my shoulder, sunlight flickering down her hair. 'No, Joshua,' she said, and squeezed my arm. She looked up at me. 'That's not what it is. You're just starting to recognize some of the themes.'

I turned to her, frowning. 'Themes?'

'Themes. Like in a piece of classical music. Don't you see? The movements repeat themselves, sometimes the same and sometimes as a variation, an elaboration. It's the repetition of the parts, and their connection, that helps create the beauty of the whole. Unless you can recognize the themes, you can't understand the music. You can't learn.'

'Learn what?'

'Learn—'

She stumbled then, a rock, a hole, something snatching at her foot. Her mouth opened in surprise and she began to go down, body slumping away from me. I reached for her, frightened, and then I was falling too, and the ground was a long way off and a long time passed before I hit it, and by then Rita was gone.

I opened my eyes with a start. Grey light seeped down through the twisted, crowded arms of the ponderosa. Colour had returned to the universe, but reluctantly: drab pale browns and dingy greens. The world seemed washed-out and exhausted, as though the effort of surviving the night had left it drained. The squat log cabin under the huddle of pines looked abandoned, derelict.

I was still lying on my stomach. The pistol was still in my hand; I'd fallen asleep holding it. I scowled: angry with myself.

An instant later I was asking myself what it was that had awakened me.

The quiet was absolute. Nothing moved anywhere. And then I sensed, rather than heard, something behind me.

Flipping away the sleeping bag, I wheeled around, brought up the gun.

Ten feet off, Daniel Begay stood leaning on his cane, watching me.

I let out my breath in a rush. '*Jesus Christ*, Daniel.' I lowered the pistol. I wasn't nervous. My heart always started slamming against my ribs about this time every morning.

He made his small faint smile. 'He's in the house. Peter Yazzie.' The words made little puffs of vapour in the cold.

I sat up more slowly than I would've liked; the muscles of my back had locked together. 'The two of you came back,' I said, 'and he went inside, without me hearing it?'

He shrugged. 'We didn't want to wake you up.'

'You knew where I was?'

Another shrug. 'It was the only good place to be.'

Given enough time, I might possibly learn to resent Daniel Begay.

I slipped the pistol into my windbreaker pocket. Grainy-jointed and stiff, I pulled myself to my feet. I looked at my watch. Six-thirty. 'You've talked to him?' I said.

'Some.'

'I think we should get out of here, all of us, before we talk some more.'

He nodded.

As I rolled up the sleeping bag, Daniel collected the canteen and the bag of sandwiches. We walked to the cabin and Daniel knocked on the door.

Peter Yazzie opened it. He was an old man, thin, tall but stooped now, moving slowly, cautiously, as though his spine had fused and any suddenness might shatter it. He wore scuffed boots, faded jeans, a black shirt spotted with pale blue polka dots, and a threadbare navy-blue peacoat, opened. His white hair was drawn back in a bun and circled by a plain black headband. His face was lined and slack, the leathery brown skin hanging loose from the bone. His eyes were rimmed with red and completely desolate. I don't think I've ever seen anyone who looked so stricken, so defeated.

Perhaps it was his cousin's death; perhaps Daniel Begay had told him. But I sensed that this was something more, something that penetrated to the core, a grief so total and final that it could never be expunged.

He nodded to me as Daniel introduced us, and then, looking down, stood back to let us in. He shut the door behind us.

I looked around. Everything neat and functional, no clutter anywhere along the wooden floor. Two more windows flanking the stone chimney. A small fireplace, swept clean. In one corner, a swaybacked army cot, an olive drab blanket pulled taut over the mattress, and a red wooden dresser. An upturned wooden box serving as a nightstand, and atop it a kerosene lamp. In the opposite corner, a kitchen area: sink, cupboards, a card table. Cans of food, a loaf of bread on the table. To my right, crowded like an afterthought into the north-west corner, a boxy partition with a door; the bathroom, probably.

I turned to Peter Yazzie. His glance danced away. 'You want coffee?' he asked me, the gruffness making his voice sound as though he hadn't used it lately, or had perhaps used it too much.

'We should leave,' I said. 'We can get coffee later.'

He nodded, still not looking at me. Beside the door stood an unpainted wooden table, slightly lopsided, that held an old blue canvas carry-all. Without another word he picked up the bag, wrapped his left arm around it, and opened the door.

The rifle bullet hit him in his left side and tore a ragged red hole in the back of his coat. The sound of the shot, a flat brutal *crack*, came only an instant later, even before the carry-all began to tumble to the floor.

Daniel Begay was faster than I would've thought possible. He dropped the canteen and the sandwiches, scuttled to the entrance, slammed his cane at the door. The door banged shut. A second later, another bullet ploughed through it, popping splinters off the wood.

Daniel bent over and grabbed Yazzie's arm and pulled. I darted to his side and grabbed the other arm, and together we towed the man away from the door, out of the line of fire.

Peter Yazzie was still alive. His eyes were open wide, moving slowly back and forth, and he was breathing. With every breath, a thin whistling noise trilled from his chest. The lung was punctured.

We had to close off that wound, and soon.

Daniel Begay had the same thought, and acted on it before I could. He glanced around, then quickly limped over to the canteen and the plastic bag of sandwiches, grabbed the bag, dumped the sandwiches to the floor. He hurried back to Yazzie and unbuttoned the man's wet shirt.

The entry wound was half an inch wide, circled by a ridge of meat pushed up from beneath the frayed skin. Blood was sputtering, pink and frothy, from the hole. I didn't want to think what the exit wound would look like.

Daniel Begay folded the plastic bag and pressed it against the wound.

'The blanket,' he snapped.

In a crouch, I dashed across the room, yanked the blanket from the cot, and dashed back. The man with the rifle must've seen the movement, because the nearest front window exploded, bits of glass scattering through the cabin, rattling against the floor.

'Hold this,' Daniel Begay said to me, and nodded to the patch of plastic.

I handed him the blanket, put my gloved right hand against the bag. Through the plastic, through the leather of my glove, I could feel the heart moving down below the ribs like an anxious bird.

Daniel reached into his pocket, plucked out the switchblade, snapped it open. He slashed the blade through the blanket, tore a strip away, folded it, and slipped it under Yazzie's peacoat, searching for the wound in his back. Daniel Begay's eyes and mouth showed nothing as he worked.

'Okay,' he said, and took over the plastic bag. His right hand was red now, as though he'd dipped it in paint. He used his left to arrange the blanket over Yazzie's shoulder and down his front. Without looking at me, he said, 'The other one will be coming to the back, in a circle. Through the trees.'

If he wasn't there already.

'Mr Yazzie,' I said.

He looked at me, his face pale and damp. Shock.

'Mr Yazzie, do you have a gun here? A rifle, anything?'

He looked at Daniel Begay. His eyes were loose in their sockets, confused and dazed.

Daniel Begay spoke Navajo to him, spoke it again, and after a moment Yazzie whispered something.

'The dresser,' Daniel Begay said, and nodded to the far corner. 'His nephew's gun, he says.'

I duckwalked over to the dresser, checked that it couldn't be seen from the window, and then stood and jerked open the top drawer. Empty.

The second drawer. Clothes: shirts, jeans, underwear. Nothing else.

I found it in the third drawer, wrapped in an oily cotton rag. It was a US Army Walker Colt, one of the heaviest handguns ever made. This was an original, not a replica, and it was well over a hundred years old.

An antique. A relic.

But the gun was in good shape. I could see the gleam of oil at the base of the hammer. And everything I needed to get it working was lying there beside it: a small can of powder, a powder measure, a buckskin pouch filled with lead balls, a tin of caps, a can of Crisco, a small funnel.

It wasn't a rifle, but it was a weapon, and right now we needed all the weapons we could get.

I'd played with an Italian copy of a similar gun once. A friend in Santa Fe owned it, a black powder fan, and he'd dragged me out into the country one Saturday to put it through its paces. It was noisy when it went off, and it produced as much smoke as a locomotive, but its heavy eight-inch barrel, despite the smooth bore, made it more accurate than my stubby thirty-eight.

The other front window exploded, glass spinning through the air. The bullet slammed against the fireplace, whined off the stone and into the floor.

No one inside here had moved; the man with the rifle was only giving us something to think about.

I scooped up everything and brought it with me to the floor. I ripped off my gloves. I opened the can of powder first, smelled it. It smelled fine to me, but I had no idea how it was supposed to smell.

'Daniel.'

He looked at me.

'Matches.'

He frowned but said nothing. With his left hand he reached into his coat pocket, found the matches, tossed them over.

I pinched out a few grains of powder, put them on the floor, struck a match, held it to the powder. *Foosh*: a flare of flame, a puff of white smoke.

Okay.

I used the funnel to fill the brass measuring tube. The knurled knob at the tube's bottom was drawn down, exposing the calibrations on the inset tube. It was set to forty grains. Forty grains was what Jorge had used, back in the arroyo north of Santa Fe.

I upended the pistol, poured powder from the tube into the first chamber in the cylinder. I opened the buckskin pouch, shook out a ball, seated it atop the powder. I clicked the cylinder forward until the chamber was beneath the loading lever, and pushed the lever down against the ball.

'Two things you must be careful with,' Jorge had said. 'You must leave no air space between the ball and the powder. If you do, the charge may explode back on you, and perhaps take off your hand. And you must make certain that the top of the ball is flush with the top of the chamber. If it protrudes too far, it will jam the cylinder.'

I clicked the cylinder forward. The top of the ball was where it was supposed to be. There was a fine shaving of lead around the lip of the chamber. I flicked this off, opened the Crisco, scooped out a dollop with my finger, slopped it over the ball. Waterproofing.

I glanced at Daniel Begay. He had taken off his coat and used it to prop up Peter Yazzie's feet. Yazzie was muttering softly in Navajo now. Daniel said something, put his hand on the man's forehead.

Time was skipping away. By the time I finished with Peter Yazzie's blunderbuss, an army of overweight idiots could've circled around the cabin.

Just do it, I told myself.

I loaded all six chambers and fitted caps to all six nipples behind them. Normally, with a gun like this, you'd load only five chambers, keep an empty below the hammer. Especially if you were planning to lug it around. It had no transfer bar like a Ruger, no hammer safety like a Smith. The only safety on the gun was a pin at the rear of the cylinder that slipped into a notch on the hammer, holding the hammer between chambers so that, theoretically, the hammer wouldn't accidentally smack down on a cap.

But I wanted six shots. I needed as much armament as I could carry.

I tugged on my gloves. Time to go.

Ducking, I scurried over to Daniel Begay. His hand was still beneath the blanket, still holding that square of plastic to the mouth of the tunnel that led to Peter Yazzie's lung. I reached into my pocket, plucked out the Smith and Wesson, held it towards him.

'You know how to use this?' I asked him.

He nodded and took it in his left hand.

'You're going to have to cover the front window,' I said. 'Don't show yourself, but take a shot at him now and then. Keep him busy. All right?'

He looked down at Peter Yazzie. In the pallid damp face, the eyes were closed now, the mouth was open. His breath came ragged, catching in his throat. He didn't have much time. Daniel looked back up at me. He nodded again.

Crouching, I grabbed Peter Yazzie's carry-all, dagged it across the floor to the nearest rear window, and slowly raised it up against the glass.

Nothing happened.

Keeping clear of the window, I stood up, slipped its latch, pushed it open.

The other man, Ramon or Pablo, could be out there, waiting for something more interesting than a carry-all. Waiting for me to do exactly what I was doing.

I hefted the Colt. It was heavy, five or six pounds of metal and wood. If I missed when I shot at someone, I could always throw it at him.

I turned the cylinder until its pin clicked into the hammer's notch. The loaded gun was as safe now as it was ever going to be. I unzipped my windbreaker, stuck the weapon inside, zipped up the windbreaker.

Go.

I swung away from the wall, caught the sill with my left foot, kicked myself out.

I landed on my right foot, stumbled, went down, caught the ground with the palm of my left hand, righted myself and then scrambled towards the nearest tree.

The shot came at me from off to the left.

CHAPTER 24

That stumble probably saved my life. The shot whistled through the air my head would've occupied if I'd been upright. By the time he got off his second shot, I was behind the tree.

He was about fifty yards away, using the trees for cover himself. The pistol sounded like a nine-millimetre, which meant he might have thirteen or fourteen rounds left in the clip.

He had more ammunition than I did, but at the moment we did have a few important things in common. Each of us wanted to dispose of the other, and each of us wanted to get close enough for a clear shot without, in the process, getting disposed of.

I wondered briefly what had happened to Gary Chee. Where was he and his Winchester? Why hadn't he honked his horn to warn us?

Then, off to the left, I saw a movement at the cabin. I looked back and saw Daniel Begay at the window. I waved him away. He nodded, as expressionless as always, and disappeared. A moment later, a muffled shot came from inside. Daniel, keeping the rifleman busy.

The ground sloped more steeply here. Two or three yards down to my right, a small ragged ravine ran roughly perpendicular to the contour of the hill, then veered off to follow the slope westward. If I could reach it, I should be able to get close to the shooter, come up on his left without being seen.

Keeping behind the ponderosa, I lowered myself to a crouch. I cocked the hammer of the big Colt and took a quick glance around the tree trunk.

His gun cracked and a bullet thudded into the tree. He had moved closer.

I pulled the trigger, not aiming at anything, just trying to get his head down. The big pistol boomed and flame shot from the barrel through a billow of white smoke. An impressive performance—but I was busy taking advantage of the smoke, hiding behind it as I rolled along my length down the hill towards the ravine. I heard another shot, and then I was tumbling over the edge.

Four feet down, I landed heavily on my hands and knees, banging the knuckles of the hand that held the Colt.

Okay. He couldn't see me now. But I couldn't see him, either.

Move.

Still on my hands and knees, I scuttled forward between the rocks. Despite the cold that turned my breath to vapour, sweat was prickling down my side.

After three or four awkward yards, I cocked the Colt's hammer again and poked my head and the gun barrel over the lip of the ravine.

A good thing I did. He was thirty feet away and he was running directly towards me through the trees. He was a big man, and getting bigger, and he wore a shiny black leather jacket and carried a fat black automatic pistol in his right hand. I don't know why he didn't go for the ground when he saw me, or swerve for cover behind a tree. Maybe he couldn't check the momentum of his run. Maybe he'd seen the white smoke and realized that I was outgunned. Maybe he just wanted to get this over with.

But he did see me and, still at a run, he raised the pistol and the barrel spouted fire as he started shooting. Chips of rock raked my cheek.

I aimed the Colt at his middle—no time to line up the sights—and pulled the trigger. The gun jumped in my hand and instantly the cloud of smoke obscured him. I fired through it twice more, blasting away at the spot where I thought he'd be.

When the smoke cleared, I saw that he was down.

I climbed up from the ravine and approached him, the Walker cocked in my hand. Two rounds left.

He was on his back, both arms outstretched. His pistol, a Beretta, lay on the brown pine needles a few feet from his right hand.

There was no moustache above his lip, so presumably this was Ramon. I'd hit him twice, once in the stomach and once—a fluke shot, one of the two I'd sent into the smoke—directly through the heart. He was dead. He looked very surprised about that.

I was surprised too, and something like molten lead lay at the pit of my stomach.

I took a deep breath, told myself that later I could be as sick as I wanted to be. Right now there was work to do.

I picked up the Beretta, tucked the Colt under my left arm. I thumbed the automatic's magazine release and the clip popped into my hand. Eight rounds left, and one in the chamber. I snapped the magazine back into the butt, bent over, and checked Ramon for an extra clip. Found it in the left pocket of his jacket. Shoved it in my windbreaker pocket. I put the big Colt down on the ground beside Ramon. I wouldn't need it now.

I looked back at the cabin. Daniel Begay stood at the far window watching me. I nodded to him and he nodded back. Then I set off through the trees, uphill, towards the rifle. Overhead, beyond the tangle of branches, the sky had gone from grey to pale opalescent blue.

Twenty yards from the cabin, taking cover behind a tree, I waited and watched until Pablo fired again.

There.

He and his rifle were up the mountainside about a hundred and twenty yards away, hidden behind a jumble of grey boulders at the far end of a small scraggly clearing in the pines.

To reach him, I made a wide swing around to the right, coming at him slowly and cautiously through the trees. The big ponderosas were widely spaced, their trunks as thick and straight as Doric columns. There was very little underbrush here—the branches overhead had choked off the sunlight, leaving only a slippery brown blanket of pine needles along the uneven slope. And there were no animals, no flittering birds, no capering squirrels. Except for the intermittent crack of rifle fire and, twice, a dull distant pop as Daniel Begay used the Smith and Wesson, the shadowy forest was as hushed as an empty cathedral.

I was perhaps a hundred feet away when I first saw him, a figure in a red windbreaker hunkered over the rifle.

I began to move even more slowly then, Natty Bumpo in the tall timber, listening to my own movements around the whisper of my own breath. Watching out for loose twigs and branches among the brown needles. Placing the ball of each foot against the ground first, and then, gently and firmly, the heel. By now, Pablo would be wondering what had happened to Ramon. If he were smart, he'd be worried. So far, I had every reason to believe that he was smart.

But I got to within thirty feet of him. Close enough, I decided. And then, as I watched him, I saw the thick shoulders suddenly tense beneath the windbreaker, tautening the red fabric, and I knew that he realized he was no longer alone. I knew he was getting ready, preparing himself for the swing to the left. A simple matter: bringing up the rifle, firing as he turned. The rifle was a scoped Mini-14, semi-automatic, no bolt, no lever, all he had to do was keep pulling the trigger . . .

Holding the pistol in both hands, sighting down along the barrel, I stepped away from the tree. 'I hope so,' I said. 'I really do hope you try it.'

He didn't move. He might have been carved from wood.

'Right hand in the air,' I said. 'Put the rifle down with your left. Very slowly.'

He did this, leaning the rifle carefully against the rock, barrel skyward.

'Both hands in the air now. Stand up.'

Arms raised, he stood back away from the boulder.

'Turn around.'

He was about my height, six two, and a bit bulkier, outweighing me by fifteen or twenty pounds. Without the stocking mask, he was actually quite a dreamboat. Strong, handsome features: a square jaw, an aquiline nose, the innocent brown eyes of a doe. A Hispanic Tom Selleck.

He wasn't very pleased to see me. The first thing he said was, 'I should've cut your balls off when I had a chance.'

'The snows of yesteryear, Pablo. Put your hands back behind your neck. Fingers locked. Now here's what's going to happen. We're going to walk down to the cabin. You're going to stay six feet ahead of me. If you make a move to the left or right, if you do anything even a little bit tricky, I'm going to shoot you in the leg. And then I'm going to kick your ass all the way down the mountain. Understand me?'

He was looking at the pistol, his eyes narrowed. 'That's Ramon's gun,' he said.

'We traded toys,' I said. 'Let's go. And Pablo? I saw what you did to Peter Yazzie's cousin. I'd be happy to blow your leg off.'

'Fuck you,' he sneered.

I had him properly terrorized, no doubt about it.

I nodded towards the clearing. A faint trail loped down between the scrub brush and the rocks. 'Go.'

He went.

'Who sent you up here, Pablo?' I asked the back of his head. 'Whose idea was it to kill Peter Yazzie?'

He turned his head slightly and said over his shoulder, 'Fuck you.'

It seemed that Pablo, like his friend Luis, didn't possess much in the way of small talk.

I should've been ready for him to make a move. I should've seen it coming. I wasn't, and I didn't. Foolishly, I was looking down towards the cabin, where Daniel Begay was stepping out the front door. I was wondering if Peter Yazzie were still alive.

The trail wound past a small ponderosa at the edge of the clearing. At chest height, a branch of the pine hung over the path. As he reached it, Pablo notched the branch below his elbow, walked a few more paces with it braced against his chest, and then, in a single swift sidestep, slipped neatly away. The branch snapped up and back like a catapult and whipped across my face.

Instinctively, moving too late to protect my eyes, I raised the barrel of the Beretta. In the next instant, Pablo was on me, going for the gun.

The branch had slashed at my eyes—I couldn't see through the blur of tears. But I could feel. He had one powerful hand clamped around my right wrist, the other clamped at my throat. I sensed him shifting his weight, knew he was about to use his knee, and I swivelled to the right. His knee thumped into my hip and I brought up my left foot and knifed it down on to the spot where his instep should be.

He grunted and his leg buckled, but he didn't let go. Suddenly we were both heading for the dirt, me on top of him, my wind knocked away, and then him on top of me as we tumbled ragtag down the slope. Somewhere in the acrobatics, the gun got lost.

And then we were free of each other and I was scrambling to my feet, still blinking away tears. I didn't know where the gun was, but Pablo might, so it seemed fairly imperative to get to him before he got to it. He must've had the same idea, because the next thing I knew he threw himself at me and I went hurtling down the hill.

I hit the ground on my back and slid along the pine needles, and then Pablo was there again and his foot was coming at my ribs.

The foot smashed into my side and air whooshed from

my lungs as I felt something crack, but I caught his leg in both arms and wrenched it to the side, against the knee joint, and he came down, grunting again.

I hadn't felt any real pain yet—too much adrenaline flooding the system—but just then, as I pulled myself up, a sharp precise flame went ripping along my left side. Something broken in there.

Irrelevant now. We were both on our knees and Pablo was turning to me and I put everything I had into a roundhouse left to his face. His head snapped to the side, but he kept enough presence of mind to wrap his hand around a jugged hunk of rock and then turn to me, slashing it towards my skull.

I dodged back and he followed through by hurling the rock. It whacked into my right shoulder, numbing my entire arm, and then he came to me, head lowered, and grabbed my arms and he butted me, his head snapping up and ramming my jaw. My teeth clacked together and my eyes lost focus, and then he was atop me again, arms around my throat, and what little air I had was going.

He said, through clenched teeth, the corners of his mouth spotted with foam, 'You're as dead as that fuckin' Indian, asshole.'

Wrong thing to say. I remembered William Yazzie heaped in front of the oven door, remembered the slowly weeping burns along his body, and I went crazy.

It was a cold, deliberate kind of madness, but it was madness nonetheless. Even with my head pounding, my eyes beginning to swell, I didn't black out. My vision didn't mist over. Throughout all of it I saw him with an almost surreal clarity: the narrowed dark brown eyes, the lips curled back from the gritted teeth, the clownish streaks of sweat running though the grey dust that powdered his face.

I brought up my hands and whapped them, as hard as I could, palms flat, against his ears.

For an instant his grip on my throat loosened. He shook his head and the grip tightened again. I banged his ears once more and he growled and pulled away his right fist, he was going to pound at me until I stopped, and I drew back my right hand and I suddenly straightened the arm, all the power of my shoulder behind it, and I drove the base of my palm up against the base of his nose.

It was a killing stroke, driving splinters of cartilage and bone into his brain, and it was one I thought I'd never use.

Pablo's eyes rolled and he made a sudden sad little sound, almost a sigh of regret, and then he shuddered once and toppled over.

I pushed his leg away. After a long moment, I sat up. After another moment, I rolled over on to my hands and knees and I retched, pain searing along my ribcage. It seemed for a while that I wouldn't ever stop retching.

That was how Daniel Begay found me, crouched like a wounded animal, head hanging limp over a spill of vomit.

I pushed myself off my knees and sat down again, gasping at the pain. I looked up at him and wiped my mouth against the sleeve of my windbreaker.

'You okay?' he said.

I nodded. 'Peter Yazzie?' I already knew the answer; Daniel Begay wouldn't be here if Peter Yazzie were still alive.

'Dead,' he said, and then he limped over to Pablo, put his fingers along the man's neck.

I lowered my head. So it had all been futile. The race to Hollister, the drive over the mountains. The deaths of Ramon and Pablo. Five deaths, including Alice Wright and William Yazzie and now his cousin. All for nothing.

'I talked with him,' Daniel Begay said. 'Last night, at the shrine.'

I looked up at him. 'He told you why all this was happening?'

He nodded.

He told me about it back in the cabin while he took tape from his duffel and wrapped it around my ribs. Peter Yazzie lay silent and still beneath the olive drab blanket.

Afterward, outside, we went over our options. Daniel

Begay told me that he and his nephew could handle everything here. I told him to call Rita, let her know how I could reach him.

By my watch, it was only eight-thirty. I felt as though I'd been up and awake and wretched all my life. The adrenaline was gone now and I was listless and creaky and sore, and the taste of ashes in my mouth told me that I'd carry for a long time the knowledge that three men had died here this morning.

I went back to the Subaru, took a codeine tablet from the first-aid kit and washed it down with water from the canteen. Only one tablet; I had another long drive ahead of me.

I reached the Flagstaff airport at eleven-thirty, just in time to catch the twelve o'clock America West flight to Phoenix. In Phoenix, I killed some of the two-hour layover by making a few phone calls. I didn't call Rita: I didn't think she'd approve of what I had in mind. I killed some more time by wincing and hissing whenever I moved too suddenly. A little after three, I climbed on to another airplane, and by five-fifteen I was back in El Paso.

I rented a Chevy, then found myself a bottle of Jack Daniels and a motel room, this one in a new motel. I knew I shouldn't be drinking—I had to be awake early in the morning—but I drank anyway. I drank until I stopped seeing dead people, until they left me in peace, and that took a while.

CHAPTER 25

McKelligan Canyon was a former rock quarry that had become part of a big municipal park. It still looked like a rock quarry. Three or four miles long, grey and grim in the muddy light of dawn, it was a huge winding trench scooped from the side of the mountain. The bleak rock walls, two or three hundred feet tall, leaned over the small rented Chevy as I wheeled it down the narrow blacktop at the bottom.

I approached a sign that gave directions to McKelligan Park Amphitheatre off to my left. I kept driving. The rock walls grew higher, pushing back the cloudy grey sky.

It was hard to believe that I was still within the limits of a city. Of any city. I could have been cruising along the depths of a lunar crater, blasted and bare. And yet this was the same mountain whose western slope the Subaru and I had climbed only three days ago, when I went to see Martin Halbert.

The road looped back upon itself where the canyon ended. The cliffs towered in a steep semi-circle around a narrow picnic area. Between the arroyos that gullied the canyon floor, four or five translucent fibreglass canopies shielded metal tables and benches from sunlight that hadn't reached them yet, and, from the look of that sky, might never reach them. Parked beside the first of the tables was a red Trans-Am, pretty much the sort of car I expected. And sitting at the table, his elbow against its surface, his chin resting in his palm, was Emmett Lowery.

I parked the Chevy behind the Pontiac and got awkwardly out of the car—I'd been up for a couple of hours already, but I was still moving like a robot. I walked stiffly over to the table and sat down opposite Lowery.

He looked as fit and vibrant as he had last Wednesday. His dark black bangs were neat and shiny. He was wearing jeans and another grey UTEP sweatshirt. This one had sleeves. He probably owned a whole closetful of the things, with sleeves and without. An outfit for every occasion.

He sat back and grinned the same toothy boyish grin he'd grinned in his office. 'Hey,' he said, and nodded to the bruise on my face. 'That's quite a shiner. What's the other guy look like?'

'Like he's dead.'

He frowned—genuinely surprised, I think. 'Dead,' he repeated. He tried for the grin again, but it didn't quite come off. 'Come on. You're kidding me.'

I shook my head. 'Getting shot at affects my sense of humour. So does shooting people.'

He held up a hand, a gesture he probably used in the classroom. 'Wait wait wait. Shooting people?'

'It's a long story. Begins over sixty years ago. But why don't we start a little more recently. Why don't we start with your slashing the tyre on my car.'

Another frown. This one was less convincing. 'What?'

'You're the only one who could've done it. Wouldn't have taken you long to find me. A few phone calls to the nearby motels.' As Rita had pointed out.

He smiled then. 'Now look, Croft. You asked me to meet you at what, let's face it, is a ridiculous hour on a Monday morning. You wanted someplace private and open. All very mysterious. But intriguing, I'll admit. So you got what you wanted.' The smile again. I liked his grin better. The smile was a professor's smile, long-suffering and superior. It told me I was an idiot, annoying but perhaps, from time to time, mildly entertaining. 'And naturally,' he said, 'I'm flattered that you'd want to incorporate me into your paranoid fantasies. But why on earth would I want to slash your tyres?' Smile. 'As opposed, I mean, to someone else's?'

'To slow me down. It was fairly stupid. But you were in a bit of a panic, weren't you, Emmett?'

His mouth tightened for an instant when I spoke his name, but he managed another smile. 'The last time I was in a panic was, let's see,' he looked off, looked back at me, 'the sixth grade. A history test.' He shrugged, still smiling. 'As it happened, I aced it.'

'Forget it, Emmett. I know you. I know who you are. You've been in a panic most of your life. Working out in the gym, hanging out in the singles bars. What've you got to show for it? How many women can you bench press, Emmett?'

His face flushed. 'Now just a minute—'

'How does it feel to be a hollow middle-aged stud with some nice biceps and capped teeth and hair colour that came out of a bottle?'

He was leaning forward, his face folded shut. 'Where the hell do you get off, talking to me like that? You want trouble?

I'll give you trouble, ace. I'm a goddamn black belt, you dumb shit. I could rip your fucking head off.'

'It might be fun to watch you try, Emmett, but I haven't got time. Where's Halbert?'

His eyes blinked and his glance shifted quickly away, quickly back. 'What? Halbert?'

'Your pal. Your partner. Emmett, why do you think I asked you to meet me someplace in the open? Someplace like this? So you could tell your asshole buddy about it. So he could come along and listen in and find out what I knew. And you call me a dumb shit? God, Emmett, you are one pathetic dildo.'

He swung himself off the bench and leaped into a fairly professional karate stance. He chopped at the air a few times. He looked deadly and efficient and very short. For a moment I was tempted to get up and step on him.

He snarled, 'Come on, motherfucker. *Come on!* Right now, right here. I'll make you eat your fucking heart.'

'That'll be enough, Emmett,' said Martin Halbert, stepping lightly up from the arroyo where he'd been hiding. 'Can't you see what he's doing? He's trying to get you angry. And he seems to be succeeding admirably.'

He wore cordovan loafers, dark brown socks, beige twill slacks, and a beautifully tailored light brown suede sportcoat over a blue oxford button-down shirt that contrasted nicely with his snow-white hair and his deep mahogany tan. He was still carrying his age very well. He was holding a gun, a revolver, and he carried that very well too.

'Shoot the fucker,' said Emmett Lowery, and a few flecks of spittle flew from his lips. 'Blow his fucking brains out.'

'Calm down, Emmett,' said Martin Halbert, who hadn't taken his eyes off me since he emerged from the arroyo. 'Mr Croft obviously has something to tell us. I think we should hear him out, don't you?'

'I think we should pound his fucking face in.'

His gun still aimed unwaveringly at my chest, Halbert turned to him and the brown skin crinkled at the corners of his blue eyes as he smiled. 'Sit down, Emmett. Don't try my patience.'

Lowery frowned. He took a breath, as though about to say something, and then abruptly he sat down at the far end of the bench. He glowered at me to convey the notion that if he'd had his way, I'd be porridge by now. Maybe he even believed it.

Halbert sat down on the bench, opposite me, his body moving with the easy grace of someone twenty years younger. The gun barrel continued to point at my chest.

'Now,' he said. 'Mr Croft. I gather that you think you know something important. Perhaps you'll be good enough to share with us what it might be.'

'I know that Emmett's father killed Dennis Lessing. I know that he stole the remains of a Navajo named Ganado from Wright's study.'

'That's *bullsit*!' said Lowery. 'Pure unadulterated *bullshit*. Who the fuck do you think you are?'

'Quiet, Emmett,' said Halbert. He smiled at me. 'And why would Emmett's father do something like that?'

'Because your father asked him to. Your father wanted leases on the land where Lessing had found oil. Navajo land. The head of the Navajo Tribal Council, a man named Leo Chee, refused to sign them. Ganado was one of Chee's ancestors. Once your father had the body, he had the leverage he needed with Chee. All he had to do was threaten to scatter the body somewhere in the desert. Throw it in a river somewhere. A traditional Navajo would do almost anything to avoid that. And Chee was a traditional Navajo, at least partly. And your father sweetened the pot a bit. Gave him a small kickback in cash, for the part that wasn't traditional. And so Chee signed the leases. It turned out, though, that he couldn't live with himself after what he'd done. A few months later, he killed himself.'

Daniel Begay had told me that the grandfather of the woman on the Reservation, the woman whose dreams started all this, had been head of the Tribal Council, and that he'd committed suicide. Not surprisingly, it hadn't meant anything to me then.

'This is bullshit, Croft,' said Lowery. 'You can't prove a single word of this.'

Smiling, watching me, Martin Halbert lightly raised his left hand to signal for silence. 'Why kill Dennis Lessing?'

'It was Lessing's guide, Raymond Yazzie, who told Lessing about Ganado. That he was Chee's ancestor. Lessing told your father, and your father knew what the body would mean to Chee. He told Lessing to go to Chee and blackmail him into signing the leases. Lessing refused—wouldn't have anything to do with it. Probably, although there's no way to prove it now, he planned to blow the whistle on the deal.'

Halbert was still smiling pleasantly and the gun was still pointing at my chest.

'But Emmett's father,' I said, 'didn't have the same compunctions. He was ambitious. With Lessing gone, Jordan Lowery would be the king of the department. Especially if he had a rich patron like your father waiting in the wings. Ready to fund the oil-geology field trips, ready to offer scholarships to the school. And I'm sure your father gave Lowery a nice cash payment for delivery of the remains.'

'He never delivered the remains,' said Halbert, smiling. He turned to Lowery. 'Did he, Emmett?'

'Jesus Christ, Martin!' said Lowery. 'Don't talk to him, for godsakes. Shoot him!'

'He kept the body,' Halbert told me. 'And with it, a detailed description of what he and my father had done. A sort of insurance policy, he told my father. And, courtesy of my father's generosity, it provided him an annuity for the rest of his life. An annuity that Emmett inherited. Courtesy of my own generosity.' He smiled at Lowery. 'Isn't that right, Emmett?'

Lowery was affronted. 'Dammit, Marty, I never asked for much. You know that. A tiny fraction of what you've made of those leases. Admit it.'

Halbert smiled once more. 'Oh, I admit it, Emmett. You've been most reasonable. You've taken only insignificant little bites, like a mosquito. Annoying, certainly, but nothing I couldn't live with.'

He turned back to me, smiling still. A man amused by the twists and turns of life. 'It was Emmett who told me what my father had done. He sent me a copy of Jordan's confession and suggested that he and I work out an arrangement. Emmett had taken over the blackmail from Jordan when Jordan died. And he thought it only fair that I take over the responsibility for payment from mine.' He turned back to Lowery. 'About a month after my father's death, wasn't it, Emmett?'

Lowery scowled. 'Why should you be the only one to benefit?'

'Why indeed?' said Halbert, smiling. He turned to me. 'You learned all this from the Indian, I suppose. The son of Lessing's guide.'

'Peter Yazzie,' I said. 'After Lessing's death, his father helped Jordan Lowery arrange things with Chee.'

Halbert nodded. Brow slightly furrowed as though he were puzzled, he said, 'Why do you suppose he kept silent all this time?'

'He was protecting his father. Just like you were. just like Emmett was.'

'But why tell Alice? If he'd only kept his mouth shut, none of this would've happened.'

'Guilt,' I said He had been, Daniel Begay told me, a man with a heavy burden of guilt. For his father, for what his father had helped do to the tribal lands. It had come as a relief to tell Alice Wright the truth. And then, when he learned of Alice's death, the guilt had returned. He had wanted, Daniel Begay told me, to die. It was for that, to find death, that he had gone up into the mountains. He had found it.

Martin Halbert shook his head, as though guilt were something he didn't entirely comprehend. Probably it was.

He looked at me. "Tell me. How did you know that Emmett and I were connected?"

'I knew your fathers were. I knew Emmett had probably

been the one who slashed my tyres. But I wasn't sure, not really, until you stepped up out of that arroyo.'

He smiled again. 'You were attacking poor Emmett to get him flustered. What if you'd been wrong?'

'I would've apologized to poor Emmett. But I didn't think I was wrong. It made sense that if Alice Wright had learned the truth from Peter Yazzie, you'd be the one she'd call. You were the one, unforunately, that she respected. I think that after Alice called you, you probably tried to get in touch with your friend Pablo. But he was in Juarez by then, and you had to go over to Alice's on your own. Where'd you find Pablo anyway? On one of the oil rigs?'

He ignored the question. 'Mr Croft, I want you to understand something. My father, as I told you, could be a ruthless man. But I believe to this day that he was also a great man. Do you know what those leases have done for the Navajos? They've provided income. They've provided jobs, food, clothing, medicine, a chance for a better life. Additionally, and entirely of his own volition, my father channelled some of his own profits back to the tribe in the form of a scholarship fund. Hundreds of Indian childen, childen who might otherwise be raising sheep, have gone on to get a college degree. Today they're doctors, lawyers, artists.'

I shrugged. 'Nothing wrong, necessarily, with raising sheep.'

Halbert smiled. 'I haven't noticed you carrying a shepherd's crook, Mr Croft. And don't you understand? That was all in the past. Think of what we can do now.' He leaned forward, his eyes shining with the brightness of a true believer. 'When we begin to develop the Reservation's geothermal resources, to harness that tremendous untapped energy, we can bring the benefits of civilization to thousands more of those people. Consider it, Mr Croft. An unlimited source of clean, nonpolluting power.'

'You don't know that it's unlimited. You don't know that it's nonpolluting. You don't know what'll happen to the rest of the land when you bleed away the energy. And besides, once the Navajos hear about all this, you won't be getting your geothermal leases.'

He smiled. 'Mr Croft, even in these times, difficult for all of us in the oil business, I'm a very wealthy person. You're clearly an intelligent man. If I can't appeal to your idealism, then surely I can appeal to your wallet? Surely we can come to an accommodation?'

'Did you try appealing to Alice Wright's idealism before you killed her? Did you try appealing to her wallet?'

He lowered his glance for a moment! Not in shame; no, I think this was supposed to be his homage to the dead woman! 'That was regrettable,' he said, looking up! 'She simply wouldn't listen! She called me that night and told me what Yazzie had told her. I went over there and I did everything I could, believe me, to reason with her.'

'Yeah. Spare me from reasonable men.'

'I sincerely regret her death. I've said that.' He frowned slightly, as though irritated that he'd have to repeat himself. 'But no single individual, not even a woman like Alice, has the right to stand in the way of the things we can accomplish. One life, Mr Croft, balanced against improvements in the lives of thousands.'

'Especially yours,' I said. 'And what about Dennis Lessing's life? Peter Yazzie's? Leo Chee's?'

He leaned forward intently! 'Mr Croft—'

'Forget it,' I said. 'It's all over. You've got money, and this is Texas, so the odds are you won't burn. Maybe you won't even do time! But no matter what happens, everyone in the state will know what your father did. And they'll know what you did.'

He cocked his head slightly and looked at me! 'The most you could possibly have, Mr Croft, is the testimony of an elderly, and probably senile, Indian. I don't think anyone will pay too much attention to that.'

'You're forgetting the three men you sent after Peter Yazzie! Two of them are dead, but the third one's still alive. He'll testify.'

He smiled. 'About what, exactly? How much does he

know? Very little, I should think. And even if he were to know something, which I very much doubt, we both realize that he can be reached. One way or another, given enough time, anyone can be reached.' He smiled again. 'So tell me, Mr Croft, why shouldn't I simply shoot you now and remove another obstacle?'

I said, 'Phil. Not too close.'

The rifle bullet kicked up dirt about four feet away, and an instant later the sound of the shot rolled down the cliffside from the cave where Grober was hiding, and then echoed hollowly back and forth across the canyon.

'Friend of mine,' I told Halbert. 'Grober. He likes gadgets. His rifle, for example. That's a Belgian .308 FN/FAL. It'll send a slug through a telephone pole. And this, for example.' I turned the collar of my windbreaker, showed him the wireless transmitter pinned to the lining. 'Everything you've said is on tape. He's got video up there too. Telescopic lens.' In the dark, at four in the morning, it had taken us over an hour to lug everything up the winding path, Grober grumbling all the while. 'Should all be very impressive in court. You're finished, Halbert.'

For a moment his eyes narrowed, as though he were considering his options. He didn't really have many.

Thoughtfully, as though debating the merits of a Cabernet, he said, 'I could put a bullet in you before your friend could possibly fire his rifle.'

'Maybe,' I said. 'You ever been gut-shot by an assault rifle? And it wouldn't erase the tape.'

He frowned suddenly. 'Emmett,' he said. 'Get in your car. Start the engine. I'll drive.'

Lowery looked up nervously towards the cave, a round black hole in the grey rock, a hundred yards away. 'Marty, that guy's got a fucking *rifle*.'

'He's not going to shoot, so long as we don't harm Mr Croft here.' He asked me, 'Correct?'

'Probably,' I said. This was, in fact, exactly what I'd told Grober.

Halbert nodded. 'Get in the car, Emmett.'

With another glance up the mountain, Lowery stood. He walked towards the car slowly, carefully, as though he were walking through a mine field.

'Give it up,' I told Halbert. 'There's nowhere you can go. There's nothing you can do.'

'We shall see. I have resources of my own, Mr Croft. In the car, Emmett.'

Lowery opened the passenger side of the car, got in, pulled the door shut. He leaned over, started the engine, then leaned back and stared glumly out at me and Halbert.

Halbert swung his legs off the bench and stood up. He smiled down at me. He waved the gun barrel lightly, taking in the table, the canyon, the cave up the hill; everything connected to the moment. He smiled. 'This was all very clever. You're an enterprising man, Mr Croft. I'm sorry we didn't meet at some earlier time.'

'I'm not.'

He lifted his chin. 'What I did was right. For my father. For the company. And even, although I doubt you'll ever understand it, for those Indians on the Reservation.'

'You're right. I'll never understand it.'

'No,' he said. 'I suppose not.' For a moment he seemed genuinely saddened. And then he smiled again. '*Adios*, then.' He backed away from me, the gun still pointing at my chest. He circled around the Trans-Am and Lowery opened the driver's door. Halbert got in. With a sudden rattle and ping of gravel, the car shot forward, fishtailing off the dirt on to the pavement.

I said into the transmitter, 'I'm going after them, Phil. Don't lose that tape.'

It was foolish of me. I knew the rented Chevy would never catch Lowery's Pontiac.

But I couldn't let them drive away without doing something. Even if what I did was futile.

He had regretted Alice Wright's murder. *Regretted*. Somehow regret seemed a small price to pay for bludgeoning someone to death.

When I got the Chevy on to the road, the Trans-Am was

a hundred yards ahead of me. Halbert drove well and quickly, whipping smoothly through the turns. By the time he reached the stop sign at the end of the canyon road, he'd stretched his lead to a hundred and fifty yards.

He stopped at the intersection, showing a nice regard for the rules of traffic, and then squealed off to the right, up Scenic Drive. I didn't stop, and I barely slowed down, and the rented car skidded across the far lane before I got it pointed where I wanted it.

I couldn't see him now; the road twisted too much as it climbed up over the brown cities of El Paso and Juarez.

Even on the Reservation, careening over the mountain, I hadn't driven as recklessly as I drove now. I roared around switchbacks at fifty miles an hour, and metal screeched as the Chevy banged and ripped against the rock wall. I slapped the car into hairpins and careened back out into the wrong lane. Any oncoming traffic would've killed me.

And then I spotted the red Trans-Am, far up there to my right. It was on Rim Road, above me, and Halbert was heading for his house.

I saw what happened, and I still don't know how it happened. The cops never actually figured it out either. Maybe Lowery panicked and grabbed for the wheel. Maybe the brakes or the steering gave way. Or maybe Halbert simply realized that it *was* all over, that there really *was* nowhere to go, and that no matter what happened now, his father's secret was a secret no longer.

Racing up the high road, the Pontiac kept on going straight just as the road began a broad arc to the left. The car smashed through the remaining wall and still it climbed, sailing along the empty grey air for a moment as though, impossibly, it might succeed in soaring like a bird across the broad brown valley.

And then it began to drop. There was no fire when it hit the ground. There usually isn't, except in the movies.

CHAPTER 26

Canyon de Chelly makes McKelligan Canyon look like a scratch doodled in the dirt with a twig.

I was on the rim of the mesa. A few yards from where I stood, the ground fell straight down for nearly a thousand feet. Halfway across the spectacular chasm, and marking the juncture of de Chelly and Monument canyons, the tapering red sandstone monolith of Spider Rock rose eight hundred feet from the burnt-umber talus at the valley floor. Past Spider Rock and past the thin white far-off ribbon of Chinle Wash were the hogans and the winter-bare orchards of the Navajo, burned to ashes once and reduced now by distance to the size of toys.

This was the lower branch of the canyon system. It was in the upper branch, in Canyon del Muerte, that Dennis Lessing had discovered and appropriated the body of Ganado. And now, as I stood here, it was to Canyon del Muerte, somewhere in the rocks, that Ganado was being returned.

A few days had passed. After Halbert and Lowery had sailed off into oblivion, and before I called Sergeant Mendez, I had called Rita. She said that Daniel Begay had spoken to her, and asked her to tell me that nothing had happened on the Reservation.

'What?' I said.

'That's what he said. That nothing had happened there. That he'd taken care of everything. He was very insistent about my telling you. And so I've been sitting here since yesterday, waiting for you to call. I thought you might like to explain what's going on. I could be wrong, of course.'

'Not wrong. Just premature.'

'Are you all right, Joshua?'

'I'm fine. I'll call later today.'

An official investigation of the deaths at Peter Yazzie's cabin would've involved more than the Navajo police. The

Reservation is federal land, and a murder report automatically brings in the FBI. Daniel Begay had evidently decided to handle the situation on his own.

It's a big place, the Navajo Reservation, nearly the size of New England. You could lose a couple of bodies inside it as easily as losing splinters of bone in a gravel pit.

Sergeant Mendez had not been delighted to see me. He had not found my story either believable or particularly entertaining. He wanted to know where I'd gotten it, and he was displeased with my evasions, no matter how winningly I presented them.

Since both Lowery and Halbert were dead, I saw no point in producing Grober's tapes. They implicated me, after all, in two deaths—even if, according to Daniel Begay, the deaths had never occurred.

For a day or two Mendez considered providing me with municipal accommodations. They probably wouldn't have been any less stimulating than my motel room, where I spent my time recuperating. I called Rita and told her what had happened. She didn't find my story any more entertaining than Mendez had. I called Lisa Wright once. She was better, but still distant, and she said she was going away for a while, to visit a friend in California. I wished her a good trip. More time passed.

And then the cops found the remains of Ganado.

They were in a metal steamer trunk buried in Lowery's cellar. With them was the detailed statement that Martin Halbert had mentioned, signed by Emmett Lowery's father, Jordan.

According to Sergeant Mendez, the house in which the trunk was found had originally belonged to Jordan Lowery. There was evidence, Mendez said, that the trunk had been there at least since the late 'fifties. But no one could say, with any certainty, whether it had been there since the murder of Dennis Lessing.

If it had, I don't understand why. It seems to me that both the Lowerys would've wanted it someplace farther away, where neither of the Halberts could get to it. Maybe the Lowerys had simply claimed that it had been. Maybe one or the other of them had moved it. Maybe the Halberts had never seriously bothered to look.

I don't understand, either, the relationship between Emmett and his father. At some point Emmett had found out, or his father had told him, about the arrangement with Marin Halbert's father. Rita thinks his father told him. In any event, Emmett had, without a qualm, embraced murder and blackmail as his birthright.

Finally, I suppose, I don't really understand Emmett. But the piece of evidence that connected the trunk to the late 1950s was something I found suggestive. Lying amid the disarray of bones and beside the brittle folded confession of his father, the police found a single Calla lily. Tied to it with black ribbon was an announcement of the memorial service for Jordan Lowery. The service had been held in September of 1959. Emmett had been eighteen then.

Mendez showed me the lily. It was in a Ziploc evidence bag. Just a thin, bent, shrivelled stalk and some grey desiccated petal fragments turning to powder. The sergeant let me open up the bag.

It smelled exactly like dust. Only in a dream could anyone believe that it smelled like a flower.

I heard a distant car behind me. I turned and saw Daniel Begay's Ford pickup winding over the barren, gently rolling hills. I hadn't seen him since last night in Chinle, when I brought him the remains. Sergeant Mendez had given them to me in a cheap cardboard suitcase. I'd handed the suitcase in as baggage at the El Paso airport, flown to Flagstaff, then driven to the Reservation with the case on the back seat of the Subaru.

Last night, Daniel Begay had told me how Pablo and Ramon had reached Peter Yazzie's cabin without being detected. They had come from the east, from the Wide Ruins road. Gary Chee's brother, the man who was supposed to be watching that approach, had been asleep in his car.

Now, Daniel's truck pulled in behind my station wagon

and stopped. Daniel opened the door, got out, closed the door, and limped slowly over to me. He held out his hand and I took it. He said, very formally, 'I thank you again.'

'You should thank Sergeant Mendez, down in El Paso. He could've kept the body as evidence.'

He nodded. 'I'll call him.' He rested his hands on the top of his cane and looked out over the canyon.

Neither of us spoke for a while. The sky was clear, the day was bright but breezy. The wind made a faint low whistle as it gusted over the canyon rim.

Daniel Begay said, 'You did a good thing, Joshua.'

I frowned. 'A lot of people died.'

The flat black brim of his hat dipped as he nodded. 'But you did what you could.'

'Wasn't enough, was it?'

He shook his head. 'You got to make peace with it. You got to remember that things balance out.'

The wind tugged at my hair. Somewhere in the canyon, it moaned around the rocks. 'At ease with the dead,' I said.

He looked at me, eyebrows raised slightly.

'Something Alice Wright told her granddaughter,' I said. 'About herself. She said she was at ease with the dead.'

Daniel Begay's hat brim dipped again. 'That's what you got to do. Get to the place where you're at ease with the dead.'

'It's going to take a while, Daniel.'

'Sure,' he said. 'It always does.'

After I left Daniel Begay and Canyon de Chelly and the bones of Ganado, I drove to the Ardmore Trading Post. It was sixty miles in the wrong direction, but sixty miles, after what I'd already driven, didn't seem like much. And I wanted to see the place where Dennis Lessing and Elena Ardmore had known each other.

And maybe someone there—maybe Elena's nephew, John—would be able to answer the questions I still hadn't answered myself. Why had Dennis Lessing's wife been having self-destructive relationships with Lessing's students? Had she been involved with Jordan Lowery as well? Had Jordan been, as I suspected, the one who told her about Lessing's affair with Elena? And if so, how had he known?

I noticed the three new telephone poles as I drove up to the squat wooden building. The old poles, neatly sawed at the base, lay in the brown caliche beside the road.

Inside, the trading post looked like an extremely ambitious 7-Eleven that had fallen on hard times. There were candy racks and soda coolers and rows of canned goods, but there were also bags of flour and rice and corn on the shelves, and bolts of cloth, and yellow and red boxes of ammunition. Everything seemed dusty and disused.

A man sat behind the counter on a stool, reading *Soldier of Fortune* magazine. He was in his thirties, too young to be Elena and Carl Ardmore's nephew. I asked if John Ardmore was around.

He looked up. He was small and wiry and suspicious. The small veins of his cheeks and nose were bright red. 'You selling?'

I shook my head. 'A friend asked me to look him up.'

'What friend?'

'Vasco da Gama.'

'Never heard of him.'

'He'll be disappointed. You know where John is?'

He shrugged and looked down at the magazine. 'Out back. Working on the car.'

I thanked him and he ignored it and I ignored that and went out the front door and around the side of the building.

An old Jeep was parked behind the store, its hood up, and a man was bent over the engine, his back to me.

'Mr Ardmore?' I said.

Ducking out from under the hood, the man straightened up and turned around. He was in his sixties, slim and erect, wearing boots and jeans and a zippered denim jacket. His hair was swept back from his forehead in a thick white mane, and the face beneath it was a weathered version of the face I'd seen staring out from the UTEP yearbook in El

Paso. No elaborate handlebar moustache, but the same dark deep-set eyes, the same strong cheekbones, the same wide sensual mouth.

He frowned slightly and said, 'Help you?' and I realized that I hadn't spoken.

'Yeah,' I said. I smiled. 'Sorry. You reminded me of someone.'

His grin came quickly and easily. 'I hear tell everyone's got himself a double. Guess you seen mine someplace.' He plucked a stained handkerchief from his back pocket and wiped his knuckles, then offered the hand. 'John Ardmore.'

I shook the hand. 'Joshua Croft.'

'Pleasure. What can I do for ya?' He leaned back against the Jeep, hands along the fender.

'A man in El Paso asked me to stop by here if I was ever in the area. He used to know your aunt and uncle.'

Ardmore nodded. 'This fella got a name?'

'Dennis Lessing.'

He looked at me blankly for a moment, then shook his head. 'Know some folks in El Paso. Don't recollect no Lessing, though.' If he was lying, he deserved an Oscar.

'It was a long while ago,' I said. 'Before your time.'

He grinned again. 'Not much went on before my time. I been here since the Flood. Me and Noah used to shoot pool.'

'This was in the 'twenties. 'Twenty-four, 'twenty-five.'

He lifted his eyebrows. 'Well now, that does go back some. He knew Elena and Carl?'

'Yeah. He was pretty impressed by both of them.'

He nodded. 'Good people. The best. Raised me like their own. Better, maybe. Everybody liked 'em. I get folks come through ever' summer, lookin' to say hello to 'em, and they been gone now for years. Carl went in 'fifty-seven. Elena in 'sixty-three.'

I took a breath, let it out. 'Well, if I see him again, I'll tell him.'

'In the 'twenties, huh? He can't be no spring chicken himself, this frienda yours.'

'Nope.'

'You tell 'im, he's ever up in this neck of the woods, come on by and say hello. We'll get us some coffee and shoot the shit a while. Can't offer no beer. Not allowed on the Res.'

'I'll tell him,' I said.

'Which way you headed?'

'East. Santa Fe.'

'Got time for some coffee yourself?'

'Thanks, but I'm running late.'

'You come back through here, you make sure you stop in and spend some time.'

'I'll do that.'

We shook hands again and I left.

Some questions can't be answered, and some questions shouldn't be asked.

That was almost five months ago. It's spring again. The buds are sprouting on the trees, the tourists are sprouting on the Plaza.

Daniel Begay has been through town a couple of times. Rita told me she's seen him, but she's never said what they talked about and I've never asked. He and I had lunch once, and he insisted on paying. In June I'm meeting him at Asayi and we're going to do some serious fishing. I still don't really know who he is, what he is, but I've got an idea or two.

In February I bumped into Lisa Wright on San Francisco Street, downtown. She's showing her work in a gallery here now. She looks a little older, a little more wary around the eyes, but still very beautiful. She told me she was getting married in the summer. It was cold, and we were both in a hurry, and we exchanged numbers and promised to call, but neither of us ever did.

It seemed to me that she had become, at least partially, at ease with the dead in her life.

I haven't, not really. Now and then Alice Wright wanders through my unguarded moments. Now and then I see Peter Yazzie and his cousin. Now and then I wonder about

Emmett Lowery. And sometimes, less often now, I can hear that terrible small sad sigh of Pablo's.

But, as Daniel Begay said, things balance out. Rita called me at my house two nights ago. At first I thought she was crying. Soon I realized she was laughing so hard she couldn't talk.

'*Joshua*,' she said for the third time, and then she laughed some more.

I started laughing myself, laughing at her laughter, and feeling ridiculous for it, and laughing at that. 'What is it, Rita?'

She caught her breath. 'Listen. Listen to this.'

I listened and I heard nothing. 'Rita? Rita, you there?'

'Did you hear it?'

'Hear what? What am I supposed to hear?'

'My toes.' More laughter.

'What?'

'My stupid *toes*. My *toes*, Joshua. They're *moving*.' She laughed again.

'Rita—'

'I can move my *toes*, Joshua. Don't you understand?'

And then I did. 'I'll be right over,' I told her.

THE END

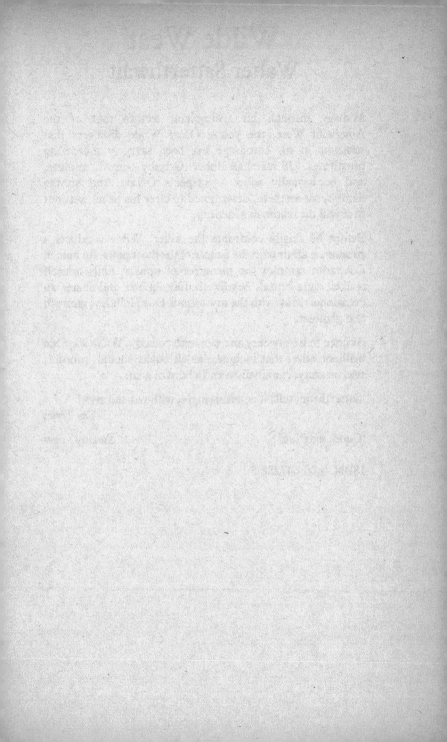

Wilde West
Walter Satterthwait

Midway through his triumphant lecture tour of the American West, the young Oscar Wilde discovers that someone in his entourage has been savagely murdering prostitutes. US marshall Robert Grigsby – gruff, resolute, and occasionally sober – suspects Oscar. And so the flamboyant aesthete, determined to clear his name, sets out to reveal the madman's identity.

Before he finally confronts the killer, Wilde conducts a passionate affair with the fiancée of the most powerful man in Colorado; samples the pleasures of opium; finds himself stalked by a brutal, bearlike buffalo hunter and shares an occasional drink with the mysterious Doc Holliday, gunman and gambler.

At once tense mystery and perverse comedy, *Wilde West* is a brilliant novel that includes, as all books should, murder, sex, insanity, cannibalism and a herd of goats.

'Satterthwait tells it entertainingly, with wit and style'
The Times

'Good, ugly fun'
Sunday Times

ISBN 0 00 647288 5